**She cursed under her breath as the candle flickered out just as she opened the bedroom door.**

It was almost completely dark inside. She decided to make the best of things and felt her way into the room, closing the door behind her. After a minute her eyes began to adjust. Piece by piece she peeled her sodden clothing from her skin.

Flipping back the corner of the bedcovers, she slipped in then rolled onto her side, barreling right into a warm body.

She would have screamed if she wasn't so shocked all the breath left her body in a silent puff. Her skin was touching someone warm and muscled and most definitely naked. She felt the stiffening of their body as they woke suddenly at the contact. Henrietta scrabbled backward so quickly she fell out of bed and onto the floor.

Even in her shocked state she was aware of how ungracefully she was moving and sent up a silent prayer of thanks that the room was so dark it hid her nakedness completely.

"What the devil are you doing?" a deep male voice asked from the darkness. It sounded vaguely familiar.

## Author Note

I'm never sure which season is my favorite. I love summer, with the long days and promise of sunshine, and there's something magical about spring, with the flowers blooming and the baby ducklings waddling through the village. That said, there's something rather romantic about the time of year when autumn slips into winter, the days get shorter and there is a cold bite to the air. It might be because it was late autumn when I first started dating my husband, so when I think of that first flush of romance, I always picture cold walks wrapped in warm scarves and returning home to a cozy house.

When I started writing *One Snowy Night with Lord Hauxton*, I wanted to evoke that romantic winter feel. I had in my mind snowy scenes and wintry walks and the all-important warming by the fire. I'd also always wanted to write a book where the hero and heroine were trapped together, cut off from everyone else by the snow. I've always fancied a few days of that sort of isolation myself—a few days of being with the one who matters the most with no distractions of the outside world. Henrietta and Thomas certainly have time with just the two of them trapped together in the snow. I hope you enjoy their story—perhaps by the fire with a warm drink while the snowflakes are falling outside.

# LAURA MARTIN

—

## One Snowy Night with Lord Hauxton

# HARLEQUIN®
## HISTORICAL™

Recycling programs
for this product may
not exist in your area.

ISBN-13: 978-1-335-50584-2

One Snowy Night with Lord Hauxton

Copyright © 2020 by Laura Martin

This edition published by arrangement with Harlequin Books S.A.

For questions and comments about the quality of this book,
please contact us at CustomerService@Harlequin.com.

Harlequin Enterprises ULC
22 Adelaide St. West, 40th Floor
Toronto, Ontario M5H 4E3, Canada
www.Harlequin.com

**Printed in U.S.A.**

**Laura Martin** writes historical romances with an adventurous undercurrent. When not writing, she spends her time working as a doctor in Cambridgeshire, UK, where she lives with her husband. In her spare moments Laura loves to lose herself in a book and has been known to read from cover to cover in a single day when the story is particularly gripping. She also loves to travel—especially to visit historical sites and far-flung shores.

## Books by Laura Martin

### Harlequin Historical

*The Pirate Hunter*
*Secrets Behind Locked Doors*
*Under a Desert Moon*
*A Ring for the Pregnant Debutante*
*An Unlikely Debutante*
*An Earl to Save Her Reputation*
*The Viscount's Runaway Wife*
*The Brooding Earl's Proposition*
*Her Best Friend, the Duke*
*One Snowy Night with Lord Hauxton*

### Scandalous Australian Bachelors

*Courting the Forbidden Debutante*
*Reunited with His Long-Lost Cinderella*
*Her Rags-to-Riches Christmas*

### The Eastway Cousins

*An Earl in Want of a Wife*
*Heiress on the Run*

Visit the Author Profile page
at Harlequin.com for more titles.

For Luke, Jack and George, there's no one else I would rather be stuck inside with.

# *Chapter One*

'Ten more minutes,' Thomas muttered to himself through gritted teeth as he forced his spine to straighten in the saddle. It was bitterly cold, with a thick blanket of snow on the ground and more beginning to fall in soft flurries from the clouds above. Even in the darkness he could see the weather was only going to get worse. There was a heavy quality to the sky and a relentless icy wind.

Through his thick coat he could feel the muscles of his back begin to tense again and his shoulders start to hunch. It would be a relief to reach Hailsham Hall and divest himself of his wet clothes and warm his body by a roaring fire. He doubted his hosts had waited up for him—the snow had disrupted many travel plans and they would forgive him for his lateness. He was looking forward to a few days spent in their company, but he wouldn't mind heading straight to bed tonight—it had been an arduous ride through the treacherous conditions and he was exhausted.

Careful to hold his horse steady, he picked a path

through the snow up the sweeping drive. It looked beautiful under the layer of pure white, the trees that lined the avenue glistening with frost and the gardens beyond seeming to stretch out for ever as the snow concealed hedges and walls.

Like all large country estates, its approach seemed to take for ever, the drive stretching on for half a mile before Thomas finally was able to dismount in front of the house. It was completely dark, with not a single candle flickering in a window. Quickly he ran up the steps and knocked on the door, listening carefully for any sound of movement beyond.

To his surprise the door was opened almost immediately by the elderly butler his friend Heydon had employed the whole time Thomas had known him. The man must be well into his seventh decade now, but didn't give any sign of slowing down.

'Good evening, my lord,' he said, making a proper little bow before peering out into the darkness beyond. 'Did you ride in this weather?'

'I did.'

'And your carriage? Your luggage?'

'I would imagine it will arrive in the morning.' He'd set off at the same time as the carriage with his valet and luggage before the snow had started coming down, but on the icy roads it had been much easier to make progress on horseback than in an unwieldy carriage. Emmerson, the capable man who drove the carriage and cared for the horses, was sensible and no doubt would have stopped somewhere along the way by now to await better conditions in the morning.

'Very good, my lord.' As the butler spoke he effi-

ciently helped Thomas divest himself of his sodden coat
and gloves. 'The forest suite is prepared and ready for
you. Lord and Lady Heydon unfortunately have been
detained by the weather in Hampshire, but they sent
word to expect you and apologise for the delay.'

'I've heard the snow has been worse in Hampshire
and to the west.'

'Indeed, my lord. I shall show you up to your room
in just a moment, if you would just excuse me first so
I can get someone to see to your horse.'

'Of course.'

The butler was only gone for a minute, barely enough
time for Thomas to start to feel the warmth of the house
seep through his clothes and start to permeate his skin.
He hoped there was a roaring fire in the grate in his
bedroom.

'Would you like me to arrange for some hot water
to be sent up? Or perhaps a change of clothes?' Perkins
enquired as they started upstairs.

'No need to wake the rest of the household,' Thomas
said. The house really was quiet, most likely the servants taking the opportunity for an early night while
their master and mistress were away. A hot bath would
be heavenly, but not if it meant waking up some poor
housemaid to run the water up and down the stairs when
it was well past eleven o'clock. A bath could wait until
the morning.

'Very good, my lord.'

Thomas had stayed at Hailsham Hall a number
of times over the last couple of years. Although he'd
known Heydon much longer, the Duke had only made
Hailsham Hall his main residence after marrying Car-

oline, his Duchess, three years earlier. It was a grand property, although certainly not the largest Heydon owned, but Thomas could see why they chose to make it their home. Despite its size it had a cosy, homely feel to it. It was solidly built without draughts or rattling windows and sat in a beautiful part of the Kentish countryside only twenty miles from the centre of London.

Perkins opened the door to the forest suite and allowed Thomas to step inside.

'Would you like me to help you undress, my lord?'

'No need.'

'Very good. If you will just allow me a moment to start a fire, the room will be warmed in no time.'

The butler might have been elderly and the most senior member of Heydon's household, but he didn't hesitate in kneeling down in front of the grate and expertly coaxing the kindling so within a minute a fire was roaring.

'Thank you.'

With a little bow the butler retreated, closing the door to the bedroom behind him.

The bed looked tempting, soft and luxurious with piles of blankets and enough pillows to envelop Thomas on every side. Quickly he began to peel off his wet clothing, hanging each layer over the back of a chair. He knew the clothes would be gone by the time he woke in the morning, replaced with a clean set he would borrow until his luggage turned up. Heydon's household was efficient and conscientious, always ensuring any guest was well looked after.

Every single layer of his clothing was soaked so he stripped naked, standing in front of the fire for a minute, allowing the heat to warm his skin. He wouldn't normally sleep with a fire burning in the grate, but to-night he would make an exception. Carefully he prod-ded it with the poker, rearranging the wood so it would soon die down to a warm glow, then he slipped under the blankets and felt his body sink into the mattress. It was heavenly.

Gripping hold of the reins, Henrietta slowed her horse even more and then with a grimace slid from the saddle. It was too unsafe to ride with the snow obscur-ing the driveway and already Meribel had slipped and almost lost her footing twice. A third time the horse might not be so lucky.

'Almost there,' Henrietta said soothingly, reaching up and taking Meribel's bridle to lead her along the drive.

As they walked Henrietta felt the fresh sting of tears in her eyes and tried to blink them away. She'd always been rash, always acted before thinking, but this was possibly the most foolish thing she'd done. It had been snowing when she'd left London this morning and al-though there had been a respite in the middle of the day it had begun to come down in earnest the past two hours.

'You couldn't stay at home,' she murmured to her-self. It was true—even if there had been a tornado or a hurricane raging outside her front door she still couldn't have stayed at home, not after...

She felt the coldness as her tears reached her cheeks and used the back of her gloved hand to swipe them away. Swallowing hard, she tried to force her mind away from the argument she'd had with her mother and the awful moment the painting Henrietta had been working on for the past year had been destroyed. All that work, all those hours, all that heartache as she'd poured her soul into the painting, destroyed in a moment. No, she couldn't stay at home, she might not be able to ever go home again. Her anger at her mother was all-consuming and she couldn't imagine ever wanting to see her again.

Looking up, she felt relief blossoming as she saw the darkened outline of Hailsham Hall a few hundred yards away. When she'd fled from the house with only the clothes she wore and a little money in her reticule, there had been no question in her mind where she would come. Her cousin Caroline would welcome her and shelter her and allow her to grieve over the loss of the painting that had become her life these past few months and also the loss of her relationship with her mother. It would be her sanctuary, her refuge.

She'd left a hurried note at home before she'd fled— even in her distress she wasn't so cruel as to disappear from home without telling her parents where she was— but even so she didn't think her mother would seek her out so far from London.

'Wait here, Meribel,' she whispered soothingly to the horse as she climbed the steps. The house was silent, even the grounds were silent, the snow muffling any rustles or scurries of wildlife. Softly Henrietta knocked on the door, listening for the sound of footsteps within.

Nothing. Not even the hint of someone stirring.

She knocked a little louder, not wanting to wake the

entire household, but hoping someone would hear her, otherwise it would be a night in the stables.

Still nothing. Henrietta knew from previous visits one of the footmen had his bedroom downstairs in the basement rather than upstairs with most of the other servants so he could be alerted if there were any late-night or early morning visitors, but the house was huge and she was not expected so it was unlikely she would wake even him.

One last time she raised her fist and this time hammered on the door, sending up a silent apology if she ended up waking the entire household. For a few moments she held her breath, listening intently, then almost gave out a cry of relief as she heard movement inside.

It took a minute for the door to be unlocked and the bolts to be drawn back, and Henrietta had to restrain herself from embracing the half-asleep footman who opened it.

'Miss Harvey,' he said, blinking with surprise. For a moment he just stood there and then hurriedly remembered himself and opened the door to usher her in.

'I'm so sorry for the late hour,' she said, feeling the warmth of the house envelop her. 'And the unexpected arrival.'

'Let me take your coat, miss. Do you have any luggage?'

Henrietta grimaced. 'No.' Caroline would lend her some clothes and everything else she could need would be easily found in the house.

'Lord and Lady Heydon...'

'Oh, please don't think about waking them. I'll explain everything in the morning.'

The footman blinked at her and then shook his head. 'They're not here, miss. They sent word they were detained by the snow in Hampshire.'

Henrietta chewed her lip. 'Never mind,' she said after a few seconds. 'I'm sure Caroline won't mind me staying here a few days in her absence.'

The footman brightened. 'Of course, miss. Lady Heydon even sent word to ready the forest suite.'

'To ready...?' Henrietta frowned as she trailed off. There was no way Caroline could know she was coming. Instead of arguing she smiled brightly. 'Then that is where I will rest tonight.' It wasn't the room she normally occupied when staying with Caroline and James, but any room with a soft bed and warm blankets would be welcome on a night like tonight.

'Shall I show you upstairs, miss?'

'No need. I know the way. If you would be so kind as to see my horse around to the stables?'

'Of course, miss.' The footman handed her his candle and peered out into the freezing night. 'Perhaps I'll fetch my coat first. Sleep well, miss.'

Henrietta felt the weight of her sodden skirts dragging as she climbed the stairs. In her haste to flee from the London town house she had left in the clothes she had been wearing, a rather unsuitable dress designed for entertaining indoors rather than riding twenty miles in the snow. Her cloak was thicker and warmer, but still not ideal for riding in any weather, let alone the blizzard that had slowed her for the last couple of miles. It would be a relief to slip out of her clothes and climb under the blankets.

Upstairs she made her way quickly to the forest suite,

cursing under her breath as the candle flickered out just as she opened the door. It was almost completely dark inside, but she was pleasantly surprised to see some glowing embers in the grate. It wasn't enough to see by, but gave the room a wonderful warmth.

Henrietta hesitated. She could go back downstairs and ask for another candle, but that would delay the moment she could collapse into bed and all of a sudden she felt overcome with weariness. Or she could try to light the candle with the glowing embers in the grate, but risked burning her fingers in the darkness. Instead she decided to make the best of things and felt her way into the room, closing the door behind her. After a minute her eyes began to adjust and she could see the outline of furniture.

Carefully she picked her way over to one of the high-backed chairs and steadied herself as she started to remove her boots. Piece by piece she peeled her sodden clothing from her skin, hesitating as she reached her shift and petticoats. Running her hands over the damp material, she pulled them up by the hem—it was silly to go uncomfortable for the sake of modesty. In a moment she would be beneath the covers and in the morning she could ask one of the maids to bring her clean clothes.

It felt strange to be standing completely naked in the darkness and quickly she felt her way over to the bed. Flipping back the corner of the covers, she slipped in and rolled on to her side, barrelling right into a warm body.

Henrietta almost screamed. In fact, she *would* have screamed if she wasn't so shocked that all the breath left her body in a silent puff. Her skin was touching someone warm and muscled and most definitely naked. She was so close she could feel the minuscule movements, the stiffening of his body as he woke suddenly at the contact. For a moment she was frozen to the spot, unable to move, unable to think of anything except skin against skin. Then she scrabbled backwards so quickly she fell out of bed and on to the floor.

Even in her shocked state she was aware of how ungracefully she was moving and sent up a silent prayer of thanks that the room was so dark it hid her nakedness completely.

'What the devil are you doing?' a deep male voice asked from the darkness. It sounded vaguely familiar, but Henrietta couldn't quite place it.

'You're in my bed.'

He let out a chuckle of astonishment. 'I think you'll find you're in *my* bed.'

She heard him fumbling around and then the unmistakable scrape and click of a tinderbox.

'No,' she shouted, gripping hold of the bedcovers above her and pulling furiously, trying to dislodge enough to cover her naked body.

There was silence and then to her relief the sound of the tinderbox being set back down on the bedside table.

'Miss Harvey,' the man said. 'It is Miss Harvey?'

'How…?' She paused, trying to still the racing of her heart so she could breathe slower and think clearer. 'Who are you?'

'Lord Hauxton.'

Henrietta felt the flush of embarrassment tinged with something else she didn't want to examine too closely.

Lord Hauxton was Heydon's closest friend, a man who she had socialised with on many occasions. And now she had climbed into bed with him completely naked and pressed her body against his. For an instant she was distracted by the memory of the feel of his skin against hers, the wonderful hardness of his muscles.

Struggling to her feet, she managed to dislodge all of the covers on the bed, pulling them into a huge pile to the side of the bed and only then was able to quickly wrap a sheet around her body.

'Perhaps you could throw one of those blankets my way,' Lord Hauxton said calmly. Even though it was completely dark she found herself straining her eyes in the direction of the bed. She should look away…

With one hand holding her own sheet she tossed a blanket in Lord Hauxton's direction and watched the shadows shift as he stood and wrapped it around himself.

For a long moment neither of them moved.

'Am I safe to light the candle now?'

Henrietta hesitated before answering. She knew they needed at least a little light to sort themselves out. One of them would have to find a new bedroom, ideally without alerting the entire household that they'd occupied the same room, even the same bed. Thank heavens they were in the countryside otherwise the scandal would be all around London by lunchtime.

'Yes.' As he struck the tinderbox a few times, Henrietta ensured she was covered adequately by the sheet she had pulled from the bed.

The candle flickered and lit, casting a soft light across the room.

'Good evening, Miss Harvey,' Lord Hauxton said with a bow as his eyes came to meet hers. She felt a delicious thrill as his gaze flickered over her body and couldn't stop her own perusal of his half-naked form. The blanket she had tossed him had been casually wrapped around his waist, but his entire torso was naked above and Henrietta was having a hard time *not* looking.

'Good evening, Lord Hauxton.' She heard the tremor in her voice and realised how nervous she felt and how calm he was in contrast. It was as if finding a naked woman slipping into bed beside him was a regular occurrence for Lord Hauxton.

'Now, what on earth are you doing in my bedroom, Miss Harvey?' he asked, adding, 'Not that I'm complaining.'

Her eyes snapped back to his and she saw the grin on his face and realised he was enjoying this, enjoying every awkward minute.

'It's not your bedroom.'

'True.'

Henrietta thought back to when she'd arrived, the sleepy footman and the comment about James and Caroline sending word to have the forest suite readied for their guest. For Lord Hauxton, the guest they presumably knew was arriving. Not her.

'I think I must have been shown to the wrong room.' She began backing away, trying to gather up her sodden clothes with one hand while holding the sheet in place with the other. 'I arrived rather late and the footman said something about the forest suite being ready for a guest and I suppose he thought that was me.' Henrietta spoke quickly, the words tumbling out over each other in her haste to try to explain. She didn't think Lord Hauxton would suspect this was a ploy to get into his bed and force a proximity between them, or worse, a marriage proposal, but she didn't know him *that* well.

'I will just find another bedroom to spend the night in,' she said, grasping her boots and almost dropping everything else.

'I couldn't let you do that. It wouldn't be gentlemanly.'

She blinked, for a moment thinking he was suggesting they both stay in the same room.

'You stay here, enjoy the warmth and I will find another room.'

Henrietta was almost at the door and shook her head vehemently.

'It's no problem, Lord Hauxton. I'll be out of your way immediately.' She reached for the door handle, the movement making the bundle of clothes begin to slip from her arms. Frantically she shifted, trying to grab hold of the clothing and in doing so lost her grip on the sheet that was covering her modesty. As it slipped from her body Henrietta knew there was nothing she could do to hide her nakedness and for one awful second she stood frozen, unable to even scrabble for the sheet on the floor.

Lord Hauxton stepped forward, bent down and picked up the sheet, but instead of passing it back to her whipped it out in the air and round her shoulders, ensuring she had hold of the ends before he stepped away.

'Thank you,' she whispered, her cheeks burning with

mortification. Then she turned and fled from the room, not caring that her wet clothes were left in a bundle on his bedroom floor.

## Chapter Two

Stretching, Thomas rolled on to his side, half expecting to see a naked Miss Harvey lying in the bed next to him. It was fully light outside now and must be well into the morning, but he had slept poorly. Every time he had closed his eyes he saw the image of pretty little Miss Harvey standing naked in the candlelight. It wasn't an image he was going to forget easily.

It had been a bizarre night, waking to find a casual acquaintance climbing into bed with him. If it had been anyone else he might have thought it were a ploy to force him into marriage, a way to embroil him in scandal, but Miss Harvey had looked even more shocked than he and completely mortified at her predicament. It was going to make for an interesting breakfast.

Standing, he walked over to the window. Perhaps she'd fled already, too embarrassed to face him. That would make things simpler. Although on the few times he'd conversed with Miss Harvey she'd seemed pleasant and engaging, he had come to Kent to get away from all of that. He'd come for solitude and peace, not society.

Looking out he grimaced. Not much chance of her having left in the current weather. It looked as though it had been snowing all night and even now there were light but persistent flurries. It would seem he and Miss Harvey were stuck together at least for the next couple of days. He doubted Heydon and Caroline would make it back home any time soon either.

'Just you and her,' he murmured, trying not to think of the moment her body had pressed up against his under the sheets.

Quickly he dressed, noting the fresh set of clothes brought in by one of the maids as she'd come to set the fire. Miss Harvey's wet bundle of clothing had been removed without a word.

Downstairs the servants were moving quickly and efficiently and he was greeted by Perkins, the elderly butler.

'Breakfast is served in the dining room, my lord,' Perkins said, pausing to lower his voice. 'I must apologise for the…er…misunderstanding last night. Young Tomlinson was aware we were expecting a guest, but didn't realise you had already arrived. When Miss Harvey knocked on the door in the middle of the night…' Perkins trailed off, a genuinely worried look on his face.

'No harm done.'

'Thank you, my lord.'

Thomas walked into the dining room, pausing in the doorway. Miss Harvey was already sitting near the top of the table, a newspaper spread in front of her. For some reason her presence surprised him—she struck Thomas as a late riser—but he supposed it was well into the morning now and he was the one out of his normal routine.

'Good morning, Lord Hauxton,' she said looking up and smiling sweetly as he entered the room. Her tone was calm and even, her gaze unwavering. It was almost enough to make him believe the encounter the night before had been purely of his imagination.

'Good morning, Miss Harvey. I trust you slept well.'

'I did, thank you. The beds here at Hailsham Hall are always so comfortable. Did you sleep well?'

'No.' He saw her eyes widen in surprise at the bluntness of his answer and felt a trickle of satisfaction as the colour began to creep into her cheeks. Thomas didn't know why he wanted to provoke her. Perhaps it was because he'd spent all night tossing and turning, unable to get the image of her out of his mind.

He meandered over to the sideboard set with a selection of breakfast foods, taking only a cup to pour some tea into. Although she had returned to her newspaper with ferocious concentration Thomas could sense Miss Harvey watching him out of the corner of her eye. He sat casually across the table from her, leaned over and plucked a piece of toast from the rack that was set in front of her. Slowly he buttered it and took a bite. Only then did he look up.

As his eyes flicked up, hers snapped down and he had to hide a smile. Instead he ate his way through the first piece of toast and promptly took another. The ride through the snow had made him ravenous and the toast was improving his mood little by little.

'Hungry?' Miss Harvey asked when he was on his fourth slice.

'I've worked up an appetite.' He saw her raised eyebrows. 'Riding in the snow last night.'

'Of course.'

'So what are you doing here, Miss Harvey?' Thomas asked, seeing her suck in her breath at the directness of the question. He knew he had a reputation for bluntness, for forgetting to observe many of the social niceties. It wasn't that he'd been raised poorly—he might not have been born to be Earl, but as the third son of the Earl of Hauxton he'd still received a fine education. He'd always been this way, finding himself growing irritated as people sidled round the issue at hand when a few straight words would sort the thing out. Thomas didn't mind having a reputation for bluntness, he found people were more likely to get to the point quicker and waste less of his time.

'Visiting my cousin and her husband.'

'An impromptu visit?' He'd noticed the dress that didn't quite fit properly. His luggage was somewhere in the Kentish countryside, but something told him that Miss Harvey's luggage hadn't been detained by the snow, more likely not packed at all.

'I like to be spontaneous.'

'In this weather?'

'It's hardly a blizzard.' They both turned to look out the window where the snow was falling heavily and swirling round creating drifts across the garden. It might not be a blizzard yet, but it wasn't far off. 'It wasn't a blizzard when I left,' she corrected.

'A spontaneous trip to see Lord and Lady Heydon, even though they're away visiting your aunt.'

'I am informed they were due back yesterday,' Miss

Harvey said with steel in her voice. She might be young, but she was no shrinking wallflower. 'If the snow hadn't made their journey impossible, they would have arrived before me. And you, Lord Hauxton, what brings you to Kent?'

He hesitated, suppressing the absurd urge he had to tell her the truth. He didn't know Miss Harvey well, not much more so than the fifty other young debutantes that giggled and fluttered their way through the balls and dinner parties of the *ton*. There was no need to tell her of the despair that had seeped over him these last few months, not a depression or melancholy, but the feeling that, despite his best efforts, he was going to spend the rest of his life alone. In the six years since his late wife's death he had mourned her and honoured her, then had tried to move forward with his life.

First he had proposed to Caroline, only withdrawing his proposal when he saw she was hopelessly in love with Heydon. Then he had travelled a little, before returning to England resolved to find a new wife. He was by then thirty-three, hardly a young man any more, and he felt the weight of his inheritance and title sitting on his shoulders. Jemima had come next, a sweet young woman who he'd been courting and had proposed to a few months after meeting her. One week later she'd died suddenly, dropping down dead while out shopping for a new dress for their wedding. He'd left England again after that, journeying to Portugal on a pilgrimage of sorts to the area where he'd spent much of his time on the Peninsula during the war. For a while he had toyed with not coming back, but his duties and responsibilities could not be ignored so here he was, back in England and finding it hard to settle.

'I'm in search of peace,' he said quietly. Many people would have taken it as a rebuff, but Miss Harvey seemed to soften in response to his words.

'Then we have something in common.'

'You are seeking peace?' He tried to keep the incredulity from his voice. Although he knew he was making assumptions he could hardly see young Miss Harvey as having experienced loss or heartache. Surely she would be shielded from the worst life had to offer.

'You find that unlikely, Lord Hauxton?'

'I admit I'm intrigued. What do you seek peace from?'

'Perhaps peace is the wrong word. I seek a sanctuary.'

He waited in silence for her to continue, but she just shook her head.

'Let's talk of something more cheerful. The last thing anyone wants at breakfast is morose company.'

He'd been quite enjoying the brief glimpse of the woman underneath the society lady, but wasn't going to press the matter. Some things were just private.

She stood, inclined her head in his direction and began to excuse herself, stopping only when there was a scampering of feet and a series of barks, followed closely by a streak of dark fur as Caroline's dog launched itself into the room.

'I do beg your pardon,' a harried-looking housemaid said as she ran after the dog. 'Bertie, come back here.'

Thomas could have sworn the dog in front of him grinned before dodging around the legs of the chair

Miss Harvey had just vacated and jumping up to place his big front paws on the skirts of her dress.

'Bertie, you old fool,' Miss Harvey said, laughing as she scratched his head enthusiastically, expertly avoiding a lick from his lolling tongue. 'I thought Caroline had brought someone in to teach you a little obedience.'

The dog barked and edged a little higher.

'Evidently not a successful endeavour,' Thomas murmured.

At the sound of his voice Bertie's head turned in Thomas's direction. Quickly the dog bounded the few steps towards him and jumped up, tail thumping on the floor as he wagged it.

'Hello, Bertie old boy,' Thomas said, rubbing the bloodhound's ears.

'I am terribly sorry, my lord,' the housemaid said, her cheeks pink. 'He's been so energetic since Lady Heydon left and, what with being trapped inside with the snow...' She trailed off.

'Anyone would go a little mad,' Miss Harvey finished for her, coming over and taking Bertie by the collar. 'I think we can manage some fresh air for you today.'

The maid looked horrified at the prospect of having to walk the dog in the eight inches already covering the garden. 'Of course, Miss Harvey,' she said dutifully.

'Not you, Polly. I'm sure Lady Heydon has some boots I can borrow and a nice thick coat. I would enjoy a little fresh air.'

'Don't be a fool. You'll slip and break a leg.'

Miss Harvey turned and regarded him with a cool

stare. 'I wasn't asking for your permission, Lord Hauxton, or your opinion.'

'The paths are completely covered, the ground covered in ice under the layer of snow. If you walk out alone, you could slip and fall and not be discovered before you died from exposure.'

'It's hardly the Arctic.'

'Inclement weather is not something to be taken lightly.'

She regarded him for a moment, her head cocked to one side, and then smiled. 'Are you saying you'd like to accompany me, Lord Hauxton?'

What he would like would be to spend the morning in front of a roaring fire with a good book in hand, *not* freezing his toes off in half a foot of snow.

'I would,' he said curtly.

'Splendid. Polly, if you could find some suitable outerwear for me I would be much obliged.'

The maid curtsied and hurried off, looking relieved to be free of Bertie for at least a few minutes.

'I shall meet you in the hall in fifteen minutes.'

He watched her go, trying to decide if it would be *too* impolite to insist he and Miss Harvey occupy different wings of Hailsham Hall after this morning.

Henrietta tapped her foot impatiently, glanced at the clock visible on the mantelpiece in the drawing room, then bent down and attached the lead to Bertie's collar. Lord Hauxton might be only two minutes late, but she had sensed his reluctance to accompany her, his sense of duty forcing him to step in rather than a desire for her company. It wasn't as though she needed his escort, it was only a little stroll and they wouldn't ever be out of sight of the house.

As Henrietta opened the door, a gust of cold air swept in and she had to brace herself to keep from shivering.

'Come on, Bertie,' she said, expecting the dog to race outside as he always did. Even Bertie seemed to hesitate at the prospect of a walk in snow that almost entirely covered his legs, so it was a shock when he darted out, pulling Henrietta behind him. The boots she was wearing were a little on the large side, but had good grip. Even so, she started to slide across the top step as soon as her foot hit the ice. Her heart jumped inside her chest and her free hand began to scrabble at the wall, but she knew she was going to fall. There was no way of stopping it—the momentum from her and Bertie was just too great.

Just as she felt her upper half begin to topple, strong arms came and looped around her waist, lifting her from the ground for an instant before setting her back firmly on two feet.

'In a hurry, Miss Harvey?' Lord Hauxton sounded impossibly calm and collected. As Bertie pulled on the lead again he quickly took it from her hand and steadied her once again to stop her from toppling. Her body was pressed against his and for a moment she was taken back to the night before when she had climbed into bed next to him. She felt something stirring deep inside her and knew the safest thing would be to shrug him off, but was unable to do so without risking slipping again.

Thankfully Lord Hauxton took a step back after a couple of seconds, releasing her before offering her his arm to lean on.

'Bertie was impatient.'

'That makes two of you,' he murmured so quietly Henrietta wasn't sure she had heard him correctly.

'*You* were late.' Normally she wouldn't dream of being so rude to an earl, but there was something about Lord Hauxton that made her want to return his directness.

'My apologies, Miss Harvey, I wasn't aware you had any other pressing engagements this morning.'

She was forced to lean on him as they descended the steps, but thought of pulling her arm free at the bottom, only to find her feet slipping on the layer of ice beneath the snow. Making a statement was all very well, but she didn't fancy being stuck in Kent with a broken leg and no way of a doctor getting out to her.

Taking a deep breath, she tried to let go of all the stress and strain from the last few days. Whenever she felt particularly on edge she liked to picture a palette of paints and the brush strokes she would use to mix them. It was a cathartic process and even in her mind she could feel the soft movements that gave such vivid results.

Underneath their feet the snow crunched and crackled and Henrietta felt her irritation lifting. It might be freezing with more snowflakes whipping about her exposed cheeks, but there was something rather beautiful about the estate grounds obscured beyond recognition by the snow.

'You've recently been out of the country, Lord Hauxton. Did you travel anywhere pleasant?'

She felt him stiffen a little beside her and wondered

what in the innocuous question had made him feel uncomfortable.

'I went to Portugal,' he said eventually.

It was a slightly odd choice of destination. No doubt after the war almost a decade ago Portugal was now a peaceful place, but you still didn't hear of many people choosing to travel there.

'For pleasure?'

'No.' Most people would offer some sort of explanation, but she was fast coming to realise Lord Hauxton wasn't like most people. He didn't seem to see the need to use unnecessary words or impart every last detail of his life on casual acquaintance.

'For business, then?'

'No.'

She fell silent. There were things in her life she didn't much wish to talk about so she would afford him the same courtesy she wished people afforded her. They walked on for a couple of minutes before Lord Hauxton spoke unexpectedly.

'I was stationed in Portugal in the war. I lost good friends there.'

'It was a pilgrimage?'

'Of sorts. They were buried in haste after falling in the fighting. I was injured right near the end of the war and never had the chance to ensure there was a fitting memorial.'

Henrietta felt the tension in Lord Hauxton's muscles as he spoke. It might be a good few years since the fighting had ended, but she doubted the horrors or the memories lessened with time.

'Forgive me, but it is a little unusual for the heir to an earldom to join the army.'

'I was never meant to be the Earl. When I left for war I had two healthy older brothers. My parents were still reluctant to let me go, of course, but I was young and eager to make my own way in the world.' He smiled ruefully. 'It is the curse of all younger brothers everywhere—that desire to prove oneself.'

'What happened to your brothers?' Even as she asked the question she felt a wave of dread wash over her. Although she couldn't remember the details, she knew it had been something tragic, something that had wiped out Lord Hauxton's entire family. She could recall a fellow debutante during her first Season whispering behind a hand. *There goes the Unlucky Earl.*

'A house fire.'

Henrietta risked a glance at Lord Hauxton's face. His jaw was set and tense, his brow slightly furrowed. It was the expression of someone who thought they were doing a good job of not showing the emotion that threatened to overwhelm them, but the subtle signs were still there all the same.

'I'm so sorry.'

'Thank you.' He spoke quietly, but did not look at her, and Henrietta turned her attention back to the snow-covered ground in front of her.

'Did you do what you set out to in Portugal?' she asked eventually.

A small smile flitted across Lord Hauxton's features—it was momentary, but there all the same. 'Yes. It was a successful trip. Cathartic.'

Henrietta felt Lord Hauxton tense as Bertie pulled on the lead.

'I think he's eager to get free,' she murmured with a smile. She loved Bertie as if he were her own, every last mischievous inch of him.

'If I let him off this lead, he'll dart off into the snow and think it's a game if we try to catch him.'

'You know Bertie well.'

Lord Hauxton paused for a second, crouching down to brush the snowflakes from Bertie's fur.

'Far too well. I've been duped by this innocent face one too many times before.'

Bertie barked happily at the attention. They'd been walking for almost ten minutes, but hadn't managed much progress in the snow. They were about two hundred feet from the house, in the part of the grounds that contained the rose garden, although it was impossible to tell what lay underfoot where they were walking.

'We should turn back soon.' Lord Hauxton glanced over his shoulder as if calculating the time to get back to the warmth of Hailsham Hall.

'Two more minutes.' Despite the freezing temperatures and the difficulty moving through such deep snowdrifts Henrietta was enjoying the walk. It felt good to take deep breaths of fresh country air, so different from the smells of London.

'I always enjoy the countryside,' Henrietta said quietly.

'You don't spend much time out of London?'

'No, my parents…' She closed her eyes momentarily as she thought of her mother's face as she discovered Henrietta at the artists' studio, then pushed the image to one side with a heavy resolve. 'My parents prefer to stay in London even in the height of summer. Our country estate is small, the London town house our main residence. How about you, Lord Hauxton?'

There was that hesitation again, as if not sure how much of the truth to tell. She realised her folly even before he spoke. The house fire that had killed his family would, of course, have decimated his family home.

'Forgive me,' she said quickly, 'I didn't think.'

'We had other estates.'

Henrietta felt the gulf stretching out between them despite her hand pressed into his arm. She had a tendency to rush in, to speak before thinking things through, and with a man such as Lord Hauxton it wouldn't win her any favour.

*Win her favour*—quietly she laughed at the idea. It was proof that she had been in London twirling her way across ballrooms for far too long when she thought of winning favour from a man she wasn't sure she even liked.

Rebelliously her mind flittered back to the image of him wrapped only in a blanket the night before. His torso had been toned and defined, his skin smooth, and she'd had the inexplicable urge to run her fingertips over the bulges of muscle in his upper arms. She might find him abrupt and even on occasion rude, but she couldn't deny he was an attractive man.

Thankfully Bertie wrenched on the lead and stopped *that* particular train of thought.

'Come on, Bertie,' Lord Hauxton said, using a much softer tone of voice with the dog than he had with her all morning. 'Time to go home.'

Bertie barked as if agreeing and began pulling furiously on his lead, wagging his tail as he kicked up the snow. Seeing a new game, the bloodhound picked up his pace and ran, halted by the sharp tug of the lead as he reached its limit. For a moment Bertie looked put out, but then started wagging his tail again and began to dash around Henrietta and Lord Hauxton in circles. Lord Hauxton dropped the end of the lead, but it was too late. Bertie had been too quick and Henrietta felt the leather tightening around their legs, pulling them closer together.

'Bertie, stop,' she shouted, knowing even if the dog stopped now there was a good chance they would all still end up in an undignified pile in the snow.

The lead tightened and Henrietta felt her dress catching around her legs and her calves buckling. She turned her panicked face up to Lord Hauxton, saw him grimace and then wrap his arms around her, pulling her on top of him as he toppled backwards.

There was an involuntary exhalation of air as her body landed on top of his, but she hoped the snow had otherwise cushioned his fall.

For a moment they both lay completely still. Henrietta's mind still hadn't caught up with events—only a few seconds ago they were both standing, about to walk back to the house, and now they were pressed together in the snow.

She looked down. Her hands were flat against Lord Hauxton's chest and underneath her fingers she could feel the rhythmic beating of his heart. Her hips were directly on top of his and Henrietta felt a spark of desire shoot through her. Despite the debauched lifestyle her mother thought she lived, Henrietta had never been in such close contact with a man before. Apart from the night before in Lord Hauxton's bed.

At that thought she felt her breath catch in her throat and she began to struggle to free herself. The lead was still wrapped around their legs, binding them together, and Bertie was complicating matters by dashing from side to side, seemingly intent on tightening the bonds that held them.

She tried to lift herself up, but her hands slipped in the snow on either side of Lord Hauxton's torso and she came crashing back down. Underneath her Lord Hauxton suppressed a groan.

'I'm not that heavy,' she muttered, trying to ignore the pained expression on his face.

'Light as a feather,' he murmured, although she could hear the strain in his voice.

'Are you hurt?' She suddenly had terrible visions of him having landed on a hidden rock, snapping his spine and rendering him paralysed.

'Just a little bruised.'

'Thank you,' she said quietly. His eyes flicked up to meet hers and he gave the briefest nod of acknowledgement, but didn't look away.

He *had* saved her, choosing to pull her on top of him and take the brunt of the impact himself. It had been quick thinking, too. Lord Hauxton had reacted even as she'd stood and panicked.

His eyes were a deep green, the sort of eyes she always wished she had instead of her much more common brown ones. At this distance she could see the tiny flecks of gold that circled the pupils and the tiny creases at the corner of his eyes that hinted he did smile, even if her company didn't seem to bring it out in him.

'I think you're going to have to move first,' he said after a few seconds.

Aware that she'd been gazing into his eyes for far longer than was appropriate, she tried to move too quickly, ending up jolting backwards and then scrabbling for purchase in the snow. Their legs were still tied together and every time she tried to wriggle to loosen the lead she felt her body brushing up against Lord Hauxton's in a very intimate manner.

'Bertie, come here,' Lord Hauxton called, his tone authoritative. The dog ignored him, standing just out of reach.

'One of us is going to have to reach down and unloop the lead,' Henrietta said as she craned her neck to see if it would be any easier behind her. She had an image of Lord Hauxton having to run his hand down her body, unable to see anything, just having to feel his way with his fingers. She didn't want to examine the thrill that shot through her too carefully so instead continued quickly. 'I'll do it.'

She slipped her hand down between their bodies, the angle meaning it had to be palm down, sliding across Lord Hauxton's torso. Even through the thick coat she could feel his taut muscles and the warmth of his body. She paused momentarily as she reached their waists, knowing she could easily brush against something she shouldn't. Underneath her she felt Lord Hauxton shift, but dared not look up into his eyes.

Quickly she reached down further, her hand catching on Lord Hauxton's waistband where his coat had flapped open and to her horror almost slipped inside. Her cheeks burning, she readjusted and lifted her hips so she could start to fumble with the lead.

'I've almost…' It was well and truly tangled, not helped by Bertie still being attached to one end and moving around excitedly all the time. 'I just need a little more give.'

She knew what she had to do, but for a minute her mind rejected the idea and she frantically tried to come up with some other way.

'I need to slide down a little further,' she said quietly, not daring to meet Lord Hauxton's eye. After the disaster of the previous night and now this she was more acquainted with Lord Hauxton's body than she had ever been with any other man.

'Whatever you need to do.' He sounded a little tense, but she reasoned she had been lying on top of him for a good few minutes now. She was not heavy, but it still must be uncomfortable for him.

Slowly Henrietta wriggled down his body, raising her bottom up in the air and shortening the distance between her arms and her feet. To be able to reach the lead properly she had to rest her cheek down on top of him and was acutely aware that she was now lying with her head right on his waistband.

'Nearly there.' She tried to sound confident, but her voice came out as a nervous squeak.

With a final fumble of her hands she managed to unhook where the end of the lead had become looped and free them. As she did Lord Hauxton shifted almost imperceptibly as his legs became free and Henrietta felt her body topple and collapse down on top of him again.

Wondering if life could get any more embarrassing, she quickly struggled to her feet, sliding on the ice underneath the snow, but managing thankfully to keep her balance. Next to her Lord Hauxton rose with much more dignity and started to brush himself down.

'I think that might be enough excitement for today,' Lord Hauxton said, catching Bertie's lead and giving the dog a stern look. He offered Henrietta his arm and together they started back towards the house, Henrietta keeping her eyes resolutely fixed on the ground rather than the man she had just spent the last few minutes pressed up against.

## Chapter Three

Surreptitiously Thomas glanced at Miss Harvey in the mirror to check she hadn't sprouted horns in the last few seconds. He was now certain she'd been placed here to taunt him and surely that could only be the work of the devil.

First she'd pressed her curvaceous naked body up to him in bed, then she'd made sure the image of her completely naked was firmly imprinted on his brain by managing to drop her sheet as she tried to flee the room. Earlier today when they'd toppled to the ground together she'd proceeded to wriggle and writhe on top of him in a most distracting fashion and then that hand...

He blinked. It *had* been innocent, he was sure of it. Miss Harvey didn't have the calculating look of a more experienced woman, she wasn't doing it purposefully to stir up desire, but when she'd ever so gently laid her cheek just on the waistband of his trousers he'd had to tense his whole body and try to force his mind to start thinking about anything else but how few layers separated her lips from his skin.

All of that he could have forgiven, but *this* was a step too far.

He was currently lying in the bathtub in the beautifully ornate room Heydon and Caroline had created solely for the purpose of bathing. His own properties didn't have a bathroom like this—instead the tub was carried to a bedroom and filled up with hot water there. This was much more sensible and many times he'd thought he must convert one of the bedrooms in his principal estate into a room such as this. Although in his bathroom he would install a lock.

After their rather unsuccessful trip walking Bertie in the snow and the five minutes he'd spent on his back half-buried, he had requested the maids heat some water for him to have a bath. Happily they had obliged and now he was submerged in half a foot of gloriously warm water.

Just as he'd leaned back and closed his eyes the door to the bathroom had opened and, instead of one of the footmen as he'd expected, bringing him a towel and clean set of clothes, Miss Harvey had stepped inside.

There was a folding screen set up in front of the bath to protect the bather's dignity from anyone passing in the hallway if the door was opened, so Miss Harvey didn't immediately see him. She was humming to herself and pulling the pins from her hair, letting the dark brown locks flow free over her shoulders.

He cleared his throat, trying not to chuckle as she caught sight of him in the mirror, her eyes widening and her mouth dropping open even though no sound came out. For a moment she didn't move and then she moved far too quickly, banging into the washstand before flinging open the door and fleeing from the room.

Alone again, he sank further down into the bath, submerging for a few seconds before coming back up to the surface. This situation with Miss Harvey, this forced proximity, couldn't be helped. They both had sought sanctuary at Hailsham Hall and they both were stuck there at least until the snow melted. With the clouds still heavy with snow and the estate cut off from the outside world it looked like it would be a few more days until either one of them could leave.

'She's just a woman,' he murmured to himself. An attractive young woman, but just a woman all the same.

He allowed himself thirty more seconds of blissful warmth in the bath and then stood, taking one of the folded towels piled on a marble-topped table. His clothes were wet from the tumble in the snow, so instead he just wrapped the towel around his lower half to cover himself. It was unlikely anyone would see him on the short walk to his bedroom.

Opening the door, he stepped out into the hall.

'I didn't mean to walk in on you,' Miss Harvey said. She'd been hovering outside and spoke before she registered his half-naked state. He watched as her eyes trailed over his body, lingering longer than they should before snapping back up to his face.

'Perhaps we could continue this conversation once I'm dressed.'

Miss Harvey nodded and turned quickly to walk away.

'Shall we say tea in the library in ten minutes?' he called after her. He didn't wait for her answer, instead walking in the opposite direction to his room, making sure he turned the lock once he was inside so he had no more surprise visitors while he was getting dressed.

Henrietta sat down on a comfortable armchair, perching on the very edge. She tapped her foot, the nervous energy surging through her, then stood and started pacing again.

The past two days had been the most mortifying of her life. Not only had she climbed naked into bed with a peer of the realm, now she'd walked in on him bathing, too. Admittedly the screen had been positioned to hide most of the Earl from her view so all she'd actually seen was his head and the very top of his chest, but he wasn't to know that.

Forcing herself to sit back down, she jumped as Lord Hauxton entered the room. He looked calm and composed and much more dressed than the last time she'd seen him.

'I'm not trying to force you into marrying me,' she blurted out before he could even sit down.

He regarded her with a long, assessing stare.

'Good. Now we have cleared that up, shall we have some tea?'

Henrietta could only watch as he started to pour the tea from the pot a maid had brought in a few minutes earlier at her request.

'I was worried you might think…' She trailed off, unsure of how to continue.

'You were worried I might think you'd engineered climbing into bed with me, dropping your sheet by the door, getting Bertie to tie us together and walking in on me in the bath?'

It sounded so bad when he listed everything that had happened the past few days.

'Yes.'

'But you didn't.'

'No.'

'Then there is nothing to apologise for and nothing to concern yourself over. Sugar?'

She shook her head and took the cup as he passed it over, grateful to have something to do with her hands.

'I have known some calculating women in my time, Miss Harvey. Women who seek to trick and seduce their way to an advantageous arrangement.' He paused for a second, looking up and meeting her eyes before continuing. 'I know you are not one of them.'

'Thank you.'

'Besides, I know how close you are to Lady Heydon. She may have mentioned I don't plan to marry again.'

'No, she hasn't.'

Relaxing back in her chair a little, she regarded the man in front of her. Caroline had always said he was a good man, one of the best, and Henrietta could see it underneath the layer of gruffness. Many men would not have been so generous, but he had accepted the events of the last few days had been nothing more than poorly timed coincidences and had quickly moved past it, allowing her to do the same.

'Is there a reason?' She'd never been able to keep quiet when she should. It was none of her business why Lord Hauxton had decided he wouldn't look for another wife.

For a long moment she didn't think he was going to answer, then he sighed and took a sip of the tea. 'Do you believe in fate, Miss Harvey?'

'Yes.'

'So do I. Not that everything we do is predestined, but that certain things are inevitable. I've been widowed for almost six years now and of course I haven't been thinking about remarrying for all of that time, but I have for the last couple of years.'

She knew he'd proposed to Caroline before Caroline and Heydon had realised they were madly in love with one another and vaguely she was aware of another fiancée, someone more recent, although she couldn't remember the details. Not for the first time she wished she had paid more attention to her mother's inane gossip—sometimes it did contain useful snippets of information, snippets that might mean she didn't blunder in and say something wrong.

'The first woman I proposed to after Emily's death ended up marrying my closest friend.' He smiled wryly. 'Not that I begrudge them their happiness.'

Henrietta stayed quiet, waiting for Lord Hauxton to continue. It was more conversation than they'd ever shared before and she was afraid that, if she started talking, he might shut down and return to the few-word answers she was more accustomed to getting from him.

'Then last year there was Jemima.' He shook his head. 'You probably didn't know her. Her family were from Bath and she spent most of her time there, preferring it to London.'

'Jemima Greenway,' Henrietta said quietly, remembering the story now. She glanced up and saw the flash of pain in Lord Hauxton's eyes and wished she could reach out and offer him some comfort.

'I courted her for a few months before I proposed. There seemed no rush, we both knew where it was leading.' He set his teacup down on the table and leaned back in his chair, shaking his head as if unable to bear the full force of the memory. 'She died a week after we got engaged.'

From what the gossips had said at the time, Jemima had just dropped down dead one day while out shopping for her wedding dress with her mother. One moment she had been excitedly looking at reams of material and the next she had collapsed to the ground.

'I'm so sorry, Lord Hauxton.'

He nodded in acknowledgement, but didn't look at her.

'I'm thirty-four. I've proposed three times in my life.' He left the sentence there, but Henrietta knew what he'd left unsaid. He'd proposed three times in his life and none of the women he'd proposed to were sitting there next to him.

From some it would sound like self-pity, but Henrietta could see Lord Hauxton wasn't the self-pitying type. He'd made his decision to remain single and unmarried from now on and that was just how it was going to be.

Henrietta almost started to say that she wasn't going to marry either, but held the words back. Her reasons, although important to her, would sound trivial when compared to the loss and heartache Lord Hauxton had been through.

'How about something a little stronger?' He stood,

walking over to the bookshelves that lined the walls. Set into a recess, between the rows of books, was a decanter and a tray of glasses.

'Brandy?'

'Please.'

Silently he poured out the drinks, lifted his glass in a wordless toast and swallowed a mouthful of the liquid. Henrietta did the same, emptying her glass after a few mouthfuls.

'Another?' He looked mildly surprised, as if he hadn't expected her to handle the liquor so well.

'Yes, please.'

He watched her this time as she lifted the glass to her lips and Henrietta had to suppress a smile. Too often people assumed she was nothing more than a normal, dull debutante, only concerned with which dress to wear to the next ball or who they hoped would ask them to dance. Not that she normally minded. For three years she'd relied on people never looking too closely to give her the freedom to pursue her passion.

At that thought the tears began to well in her eyes and she hurriedly took another sip of brandy.

'I wouldn't have thought you a brandy drinker, Miss Harvey,' Lord Hauxton said as she placed the empty glass on the little table between them. 'It seems I was wrong.'

'Why not?'

'Most young women prefer wine or punch.'

She pulled a face. 'I can't stand the punch they insist on serving at most balls. Far too sickly sweet.'

'So where did you get your taste for brandy? I may

not be well acquainted with your father, but I can't see him plying his only daughter with hard liquor.'

Henrietta closed her eyes for a moment, wondering if her mother had informed her father yet of the subject of the argument they'd shared. The look of disgust and disbelief had been hard enough to take from her mother, but a similar look from her father would destroy her. He had always been her champion, her ally, but even his kindness wouldn't be able to stretch to forgive what she had done.

'There are some things a young woman finds it best to keep from her parents.'

'Brandy,' Lord Hauxton said. 'And now I'm intrigued. What else?'

'Anything that makes one stand out from the crowd. The *ton* don't want their young women to be individuals, they want perfect replicas of the perfect woman.'

'What do they view as the perfect woman?'

She reached out and ran her fingers round the rim of the glass, wondering how they'd strayed on to the one subject she didn't wish to talk about.

'She must be demure and respectable. Able to make conversation, but not voice any opinions that are too controversial. She must always concede her views to a husband or parent. And she must only have interests that the rest of society deem reputable.'

'Reputable?'

'Cross stitching or playing the piano or painting damn watercolours.' Henrietta looked up, realising the venom that had filled her voice.

'Damn watercolours,' Lord Hauxton repeated quietly. 'I'm not sure I'm familiar with damn watercolours.'

Henrietta felt some of the anger draining from her and after a moment was unable to stop a smile from creeping on to her lips. She did have an inexplicable hatred of watercolours.

'I'm sure some people find them *thrilling* to paint with,' Henrietta said, meeting Lord Hauxton's gaze. 'And it's not so much the paints I dislike, but the insipidness of what you're expected to paint when using watercolours.'

He leaned forward in his chair as if he were really interested in what she was saying.

'What are you expected to paint?'

'Flowers or rolling hills or perhaps flowers *on* rolling hills.'

'Is there something you would rather paint?'

Henrietta let out a loud exhalation of air, trying not to dwell on the painting she'd spent so much time on. The painting her mother had cut to shreds.

'Real life. Not the idealised version, the perfect landscapes with a pretty maid skipping through the cornfields. Something more...' she searched for the right word '...truthful.'

Lord Hauxton sat back in his chair and regarded her with eyes that were filled with a shrewd expression. 'You paint?'

Henrietta nodded. It wasn't something she normally admitted, it had been private for so long, but she supposed the part of her life where she was able to creep off to a studio to paint for an hour or two every week was over. If she ever returned home, her mother would make sure she never painted again.

'Oil paints. Domestic scenes mainly.' It was a half-truth. She *did* paint domestic scenes, but not grand houses and posed portraits. She painted poverty and desperation mixed in with love and hope.

'That's unusual. How did you get into it?'

'A friend owned a studio, I used to go there to paint and was fortunate enough to receive some pointers from a few established artists.' It was another half-truth. Henrietta's rebellious streak had started even before she had begun sneaking off to paint every week. On one of her solo trips around London she had wandered in through the open doors of an artist's studio and become bewitched. Ever since she had lived and dreamed painting, spending all her money on hiring space to paint and purchasing materials.

'Are you good?' It was a direct question, but Henrietta was coming to expect that from Lord Hauxton.

'Yes.'

'I'd like to see some of your work one day.'

'I doubt I'll be allowed to paint again,' she said morosely.

'Why not?'

'Apparently it isn't a fitting pastime for a well-brought-up young lady.' The words still stung even a couple of days later. 'Especially not one who should be focusing on finding a husband because she isn't getting any younger.'

'Ouch. Your mother?'

'Yes. She is right, of course, about the not getting any younger, but her logic assumes I wish to marry.'

'And you don't?'

She was well aware she was revealing much more of herself than she set out to. Lord Hauxton was surprisingly easy to talk to once her tongue was loosened by a couple of glasses of brandy and it felt like a long time since she'd confided her true feelings in anyone.

'No. I can't think of anything worse. Marrying a man you barely know, giving him control over you and everything you do. Do you know most people get married after spending only a few hours in each other's company? How are you meant to tell in that amount of time if someone is kind or not? If they're sane or not? It would be like us getting married after spending the past day together.'

'I can see your point.' He regarded her for a moment. 'Although I think there's something more.'

'Something more?'

'Something more keeping you from marrying. The reasons you mention, they're all rather general, not very personal to your own circumstances. I'd wager there is something particular to you stopping you from marrying.'

'Something wrong with me?' Henrietta asked, feeling the anger rise inside her. He might be right, but it still sounded like an insult.

'No. I don't think there's anything wrong with you, Miss Harvey, just some additional reason you have decided not to marry.' He held his hands up placatingly. 'You aren't obliged to tell me, I know what it is like to want to keep something of yourself private.'

Before she could answer he stood and bowed, leaving her alone in the library staring after him in astonishment.

She knew the reason she didn't want to marry was because of her art. For years she'd dreamed of something more than the life that was expected of her. She might have been raised to be a wife and a mother, but that wasn't what she longed to be. When she lay in bed at night, indulging in her dreams, it wasn't a handsome husband and beautiful children she saw, it was a successful exhibition, it was people commissioning her paintings. It was doing what she loved more than anything else in the world and doing it openly and without any shame.

If she married, she knew however liberal her husband he would not permit her to continue painting as she did now. It would not be seemly for the wife of an aristocrat to mix with the sort of people she was interested in painting. No, it was better if she stayed unmarried, grew old as a spinster, at least that way there would be one less person to disapprove of her passion.

Sitting back in the chair, she closed her eyes, enjoying the warmth of the fire. Despite the difficult start with Lord Hauxton and his notoriously gruff manner he was surprisingly easy to be around. She did wish Caroline would return so she could unburden all her worries on her cousin, but spending a few days trapped in Hailsham Hall with Lord Hauxton wasn't as terrible as she'd first thought.

The memory of his warm body next to hers under the covers popped into her mind and she felt a spark of excitement which she quickly tried to suppress. She might have decided Lord Hauxton was decent company, but that didn't mean she should ever think of him as anything more than the slightly aloof friend of her cousin's husband.

## Chapter Four

Slipping into his coat and pulling the collar up so it was high around his neck, Thomas opened the front door and stepped outside. There had been a fresh drop of snow overnight and even their tracks from the day before had been completely obscured. Everything looked fresh and neat and slightly unreal as if it were a scene from a painting rather than real life.

'Not a watercolour,' he murmured to himself as he walked briskly down the steps. Miss Harvey had intrigued him yesterday with her talk of paintings and expectations and long after their conversation he'd found himself wondering exactly what it was she was hiding.

That hadn't been the only thing that had occupied his mind in the small hours of the morning in relation to Miss Harvey. Despite all his best efforts to spend his night sleeping, his slumber had been plagued by waking dreams, all of them containing Miss Harvey in various states of undress. Thanks to the events of the past few days he didn't even need to use his imagination as to what she might look like, so his mind seemed to be using its creative energy to come up with intense, all-consuming fantasies.

'Inappropriate,' he told himself. Miss Harvey had made it clear yesterday she never planned on marrying and he had made the decision he was better off alone. He might feel a strong physical desire for the pretty brunette, but she was not to be dallied with so he would have to find another outlet for the energy that was coursing through his body.

Hence the walk in the freezing temperatures. He'd thought it might help cool his desire a little and distract him from the thoughts he really shouldn't be having.

It was hard going wading through the knee-high drifts of snow and soon his trousers were soaked where the snow came to above his knees. Today, without Bertie pulling at his lead and Miss Harvey on his arm, he managed to get a little further from the house, but getting out of the estate grounds seemed impossible. It would be another few days at least until things thawed enough for a path to be forged into the village. That was if no more snow fell in the meantime.

As his toes began to throb with the cold he turned back, retracing his footsteps until he was about fifty feet from the house. His head was bent low from the snow so at first he didn't see the door open and the maid in charge of Bertie step outside. It was only when Bertie barked that he looked up, a frown already forming on his face.

'Be careful,' he called out, watching in horror as Bertie began to pull on the lead. He knew from experience the steps were particularly treacherous and icy and one sharp tug from the unruly bloodhound and it could send the maid tumbling to the bottom.

She looked up and Thomas saw the horror on her face the exact moment Bertie pulled on the lead and tugged her off balance. He was too far away to do anything as her arms windmilled and her feet scrabbled for purchase. He moved quickly, but not quickly enough, only making it to the bottom of the steps in time to hear the sickening crunch and snap as she hit the ground.

The maid gave out a blood-curdling scream and for an instant Thomas was frozen to the spot, but then the instinct that had served him so well during his fighting days in the army kicked in and he moved swiftly to her side.

'Polly,' he said, remembering the name Miss Harvey had addressed the young maid by yesterday. 'Can you move?'

She let out a little sob as an answer and as Thomas crouched down beside her he was able to appreciate the full horror of her injuries. Somewhere above them the door opened and he was vaguely aware of some other people gathering, but right now he had to focus on the distressed housemaid in front of him.

'Hush, Polly, you're going to be just fine. I know it hurts, but we need to see if we can get you inside so we can make you a bit more comfortable.'

'No, don't touch me,' she moaned, clutching at her thigh.

'What happened?' Miss Harvey asked, treading cautiously as she descended the steps. She had come out in just her dress with no coat or cloak and Thomas had the peculiar urge to berate her for risking her health in such a foolhardy manner, but he knew they had more important matters to deal with.

'She slipped on the ice.'

He saw Miss Harvey's eyes flick over the twisted body of the maid and the bright red bloom of blood spreading out from underneath her skirt.

'Polly,' she said, kneeling down and taking the maid's hand.

'We just need to lift your skirt a little to see what your injuries are,' Thomas said, motioning for Miss Harvey to be the one to actually lift up the hem. He tried not to let the horror show on his face as he caught sight of the unmistakable white of bone protruding through the skin of her lower leg.

'Do you hurt anywhere else?' Miss Harvey asked. He'd half expected her to swoon at the sight of the blood and bone, yet she seemed shocked but steady.

Polly shook her head, her face ashen now.

'Perkins, which bedroom can I take Polly to?'

'The red bedroom is made up and very close to the stairs, my lord.'

Thomas bent over Polly, making sure she was focused on him even through the pain before speaking. 'I'm going to lift you, Polly. It's important we get you inside and on to a bed so we can look at your leg and help you with the pain. It may be uncomfortable for you while I carry you in, but I'll be as fast and steady as I can.'

Polly whimpered as he placed his arms underneath her, lifting her gently. As he stood there was an inevitable jolt and Polly cried out in distress.

'We'll need some hot water, something to bathe and

bind Polly's leg with,' he heard Miss Harvey instructing the other servants. 'Anna, you and Polly are close, come upstairs and see if you can offer some comfort.'

As quickly as he could while walking steadily he took the housemaid into the house and up the stairs to the red room. Someone had already pulled back the bed sheets and he deposited her gently on the bed. He watched as Polly leaned back on the pillows and closed her eyes, the tears streaming down her cheeks.

Miss Harvey took his arm and pulled him to one side, leaving Anna to sit by her friend and smooth her hair back from her face while whispering soothing words.

'Her leg looks bad,' Miss Harvey said, biting her lip as she glanced back over her shoulder. 'I asked the footmen and they think they may be able to make it to the village, but it's unlikely Dr Beckett will be able to get back here with them. He's over sixty and not the most spritely of men.'

Cursing under his breath, Thomas shrugged off his coat and jacket and began rolling up the sleeves of his shirt.

'What are you doing?'

'The bone is protruding through the skin, it means the fracture is displaced. She has no chance of healing if the bones aren't straightened and the ends brought together.'

'You mean to set her leg?'

'If we wait for the doctor, she could lose the leg. Or her life.'

'Have you done it before?'

He shook his head. 'Not by myself, but I have assisted. During the war...' He trailed off. There were many things he'd had to do during the war out of necessity.

'Do you think you can?' Miss Harvey was whispering, ensuring Polly didn't hear her doubts.

'I have to try. Speak to Perkins, see if anyone has any laudanum. And we'll need a couple of the strongest young men to come and hold her still.'

Miss Harvey hesitated for a second, but then seemed to rally and nodded before hurrying off.

'I need you to listen to me, Polly,' he said, approaching the bed and sitting down on the edge. The housemaid's eyes flickered open and he saw the tears on her cheeks and the heavy, laboured breathing. 'I need to have a proper look at your leg and see what we can do to help the pain. I'll be as gentle as I can be.'

Minutely Polly nodded, her breathing growing even more ragged as he shifted on the bed beside her as if anticipating the spike in pain.

'Let me help,' Miss Harvey said, appearing by his side. 'I'm just going to very gently remove your stockings, Polly, then we can get this leg cleaned up a bit.'

Thomas could see the very slight tremor in Miss Harvey's hands as she reached out towards Polly's injured leg, but she didn't hesitate in gently rolling the fabric of the housemaid's stockings down, stretching the material to the maximum to lift it over the injury without catching on the wound. On the bed Polly arched her back and cried out and he was thankful when Perkins entered carrying a little bottle of laudanum.

Without touching anything, he inspected the wound. Polly's leg was swollen with an unhealthy purple hue along the bottom third of her shin. The open wound was only small, a puncture made by the fractured bone that was still protruding from the flesh.

He became aware Miss Harvey was watching him as he inspected Polly's leg and he gently pulled her to one side.

'I need to reset the bone, to bring it back through the skin and try to align it as best I can.'

On the battlefield he had often scooped up his injured men and assisted the scant medics that patched the wounded up after. Although he had never reset a bone like this before he had seen it being done. It wouldn't be easy, but if they waited for the snow to melt enough for the doctor to get through then Polly's chances of survival would be almost non-existent.

'After I've reset the bone in place, we will need to strap the leg to something to hold it in position and then bandage the wound.' Glancing over his shoulder, he was relieved to see that for now the laudanum was having an effect on Polly as her head lolled back on the pillow. It was a filthy drug, but in times like this it was better than the alternative—unbearable pain.

Henrietta felt her stomach flip over with nerves as Lord Hauxton approached the bed. Polly was drifting in and out of consciousness, but he had warned the two strong young footmen who were positioned to hold Polly still that as soon as he started manipulating her leg she would buck and scream as if she hadn't had any of the laudanum at all.

In Henrietta's hands she held the strips of fabric ready to pass to Lord Hauxton to dress the wound and bind the leg to the broom handle Perkins had produced when asked for something to splint Polly's leg to.

'Here goes,' Lord Hauxton murmured, his face grim.

Gently he took Polly's foot, nodded at the footmen and then swiftly began to manipulate the leg, pulling with his full force. Henrietta watched, fascinated and horrified as the bone began to slip back beneath the skin. Polly bucked and screamed, as he'd expected, but Lord Hauxton ploughed on, pulling on the leg until the bone fragments had straightened.

He motioned for the broom handle and bindings and quickly Henrietta set to work, tying the strips of fabric tightly as he'd instructed her to do, as Lord Hauxton held Polly's leg in position. Only when the splint was secure did he begin to lower Polly's leg.

'What's wrong?' Henrietta asked quietly, noticing the deepening of his frown.

'I'm worried the bones will slip if I let go.'

'Can that happen?'

Grimly he nodded.

On the bed Polly had stopped struggling and screaming and had flopped back on to the pillows.

'How are you doing, Polly?' Lord Hauxton motioned for the footmen to release their grip a little.

'It hurts,' she managed to utter.

'Does it feel any better?'

Polly took a moment to consider and then nodded. A momentary relief bloomed over Lord Hauxton's face and Henrietta realised how much this housemaid and her pain mattered to the Earl.

'I've realigned the bones, Polly, and splinted your leg to the broom handle. We can bandage up the wound next, but my concern is if I let go the bones may slip out of place.'

'Please don't let me lose my leg.'

'No one wants that to happen, Polly. Let me have a think while Miss Harvey dresses that wound.'

Under Lord Hauxton's supervision she cleaned the wound, wrapping the bandages around the leg and ensuring there was enough pressure to stem the bleeding.

'What are you going to do?' She spoke quietly so Polly wouldn't be able to hear.

'I think we need to keep a pulling force on the end of Polly's leg.'

'You can't stand there and hold it all day and night.'

'No, but there are plenty of people in this house and it would only be until the doctor could make it through to advise on a more definitive plan.'

'Perkins...' Henrietta turned to the butler who had been standing in the corner ready to assist if needed '...could you gather all the servants downstairs in the kitchen?' She waited until he had left to turn back to Lord Hauxton. 'How long do you think each person could do it for?'

He considered for a moment. 'Probably an hour, no more at a time. Polly, do you understand what we are going to do?'

'No.'

'Until the doctor can get here we need to keep some force on this leg to hold everything in place. Miss Harvey is going to instruct the household and then everyone will take a turn in holding your leg a little elevated and stretched.'

'It's too much bother for everyone.'

'No,' he said sincerely, 'it's not.'

Henrietta felt a swell of admiration for Lord Hauxton. He'd taken a disastrous situation and quickly and quietly done what had needed to be done, perhaps even saving Polly's life along the way. It was easy to dismiss Lord Hauxton as brusque and abrupt, but she was fast realising there was much more to him than the public persona he allowed everyone to see.

'I will go and speak to the servants now and get one of the footmen to take the first turn.' She looked at Lord Hauxton's bloodied hands and rumpled shirt and held up a hand to quieten his protest. 'You need to bathe and change.'

He raised an eyebrow and Henrietta reddened, knowing he was remembering the last time he'd taken a bath. Feeling uncharacteristically lost for words, she hurried away, risking a quick glance back over her shoulder and wondering why her heart was flipping inside her chest.

## Chapter Five

Longingly Henrietta looked at the canvas and paints stacked neatly in the corner of the garden room. Caroline and her husband had been the only people who'd known her secret. They'd once followed her to the house where she used to rent a room to paint in, away from the judgemental eyes of society. They had seen her painting and agreed to keep quiet about her secret activity.

In a bid to keep Henrietta safe Caroline had suggested she come to Kent to paint instead of sneaking off on her own in London and had bought the paints and some canvases to encourage her. Over the last couple of years Henrietta had painted when she'd come to stay at Hailsham Hall, but she hadn't given up running off to paint in the little studio in London either. There she could find her inspiration in the streets, find her models to sit for her and also have the privacy to go into her own little world and get lost in the strokes of the paintbrush.

'Thinking of starting to paint, Miss Harvey?'

Lord Hauxton's voice from the doorway made her

jump and she spun quickly, feeling as if she'd been caught doing something she shouldn't.

He looked fresh and relaxed, gone was the tension from his shoulders and the blood from his shirt.

'No,' she said resolutely, turning away from the supplies in the corner.

'I'm sure Lady Heydon would not mind.' He frowned. 'In fact, I know she doesn't paint. She's told me before how poor an eye she has for art.'

'She keeps them here for me.' It seemed an intimate confession, as if she were letting him in to a secret part of her soul.

'You must enjoy painting very much,' he said softly.

'I do.'

Lord Hauxton stepped into the room, moving over to where the fire was burning in the grate and stoking it so the flames leaped and flickered. The room was warm, almost stiflingly so. Caroline kept a small collection of exotic plants and orange trees that needed temperatures much higher than the rest of the house and as such the fire was kept lit and well stoked through most of the day.

'But you don't want to paint here?'

Henrietta closed her eyes for a moment. When her mother had destroyed her painting in London she had felt her heart rip as the canvas had. Hours she had poured into the painting had been rendered pointless in a few seconds.

'I am considering whether I will ever paint again.' It sounded overly dramatic, but in truth the statement contained only a fraction of the emotion Henrietta felt when she thought about the destruction of her passion.

'That would be a shame.'

'You don't know if I'm any good.'

He regarded her for a moment and she felt a delicious heat begin to rise up from her core. He looked at her as if he were seeing every single inch of her, his eyes taking in the physical as well as something inside, too. No one had ever looked at her like that before.

'I am not a gambling man, but I would wager you are very talented.' He paused and gave a little smile that transformed his normally serious features. 'An amateur does not look at a canvas and set of paints like you do.'

Unable to stop herself, she glanced quickly over her shoulder at the paints in the corner. Even now she knew there was a wistful look on her face.

'It would be a shame to give up something you so clearly enjoy.'

'Not everyone shares your opinion.'

'Parents, though older, are not always wiser than their children.'

'Very true. The last time I saw her my mother forbade me to paint…'

'I don't presume to know you intimately, Miss Harvey, but I cannot imagine that order went down well with you.'

She couldn't help but smile at his words. 'It didn't.'

'Unless I am missing something, I find it hard to understand what is so scandalous about painting with oil paints instead of watercolours.'

Henrietta hesitated. She hardly knew Lord Hauxton, although their forced proximity meant she was much more familiar with him than any other man in her life. Even so she felt an urge to confide everything in him.

'I've been painting for years,' she said softly. 'But

not at home. I think that is what my mother objected to the most. I would sneak away unchaperoned and she hated the idea I might have been seen in the streets of London without even a maid.'

'Why did you do it? Why not just paint at home?'

It was a simple question with a complex answer. 'I suppose I thought they wouldn't approve of my subject matter.' That much was true, but Henrietta knew there was more to it than that. She'd wanted to be free to paint whatever she had wanted without judgement, but she had also enjoyed the thrill of freedom. At first she had thrown herself into the circle of artists who also used the studio to paint. She'd accompanied them to the less salubrious parts of London, she'd drunk with them, gambled with them. After years of dainty cups of tea and small talk about fashion it had been liberating to find people who wanted to talk of art and politics and the world. She had been a curiosity to the artists, but they had accepted her in their own way.

'What do you paint?'

'Life. Real life.'

'I'm no expert, you'll have to elaborate.'

'I like to paint scenes that show how the majority live in London. A mother feeding her hungry children while her own bowl stays empty, a prostitute hanging out the window of her rooms, her face made up but her expression grim. A sailor taking his first step on to dry land after a stint at sea—that one is here at Hailsham Hall.'

'You've painted all of that?'

She nodded.

'I can see why your mother might not approve.' There

was no disapproval in his voice though, only a hint of admiration.

'She wants me to be this perfect little debutante, to find a husband, to have children and not to have a single original thought or do anything different from the hundreds of other debutantes.'

'Sometimes people are scared of what they have no experience of,' Lord Hauxton said quietly.

'She destroyed my painting. It was of a little orphan girl begging on the streets. Nothing scandalous, just real life. I'd worked on it for almost a year.' Henrietta heard the catch in her voice underneath the bitterness. 'She followed me to the studio and cut it to shreds.'

Lord Hauxton took a step towards her and then another, moving slowly until they were standing face to face only a few inches apart.

'Sometimes people are afraid of what they don't understand,' he said softly.

Henrietta looked up into his eyes, noticing how the darkness of his pupils nearly merged with the mossy green of the iris in the low candlelight. She felt her pulse begin to quicken and her heart start to thump in her chest. Her hand twitched by her side, fighting the urge to reach up and trail her fingers down his face. It would be entirely inappropriate.

She hadn't even realised she had been crying until Lord Hauxton reached up and ever so gently wiped the tears from her cheeks with the pad of his thumb.

He looked down into her eyes for a long moment and Henrietta felt her lips part and her body sway towards him. She'd never been kissed before, never wanted to be particularly, but right now her whole body wanted to feel Lord Hauxton's arms pull her close and his lips on her own.

With a deep breath and a smile that didn't quite reach his eyes Lord Hauxton stepped away, walking over to the fire again and picking up the poker, even though he had stoked it a few minutes previously.

'That is why you came here? Through all the snow?' When he spoke there was an almost imperceptible catch to his voice, but it was enough to let Henrietta know she hadn't imagined the spark between them.

Trying to ignore the feelings of disappointment, she flopped down on to a chair, her eyes following Lord Hauxton as he paced about the room like a restless cat, stealthy and light on his feet.

'Yes. She broke my heart.'

'It seems you were right yesterday, we are both seeking sanctuary here,' Lord Hauxton said quietly.

For a few moments they remained in silence and then Lord Hauxton bowed and muttered something about needing to check on Polly. Henrietta barely had time to wish him goodnight before he strode from the room.

'Fool,' she muttered to herself. A few good deeds and she was building Lord Hauxton up into something he was not.

## Chapter Six

It was late, almost eleven o'clock, and if she were sensible Henrietta would have taken advantage of the lack of company to have an early night, but she'd never been one to turn in early. Often she would sit up late with her father, discussing the world or politics. In the day he was frequently too busy to spend much time with her or her mother, but once dinner had been cleared and her mother retired to bed, then he was happy to sit down with a drink in hand and impart some of his wisdom.

She felt restless and knew if she went upstairs to her bedroom now she would only toss and turn in her sheets. At home she might slip out into their little garden with a shawl wrapped around her shoulders, perhaps taking a moment to look up at the stars, but here she would be foolish to step outside into the snow.

Instead she decided she would take a candle and wander round the house for a while. Hailsham Hall was large enough to spend twenty minutes exploring the corridors and she was unlikely to disturb anyone. Perkins, the elderly butler, had enquired a few minutes ear-

lier if she required anything and she'd insisted the rest
of the servants turn in—she hated the thought of them
staying up late just for her, especially when they would
be expected to be up and lighting the fires well before
she would ever think about surfacing from her bed.

Picking up the candle closest to her, she circled the
room and blew the other two out. She had to wait for a
moment to let her eyes adjust to the reduction in light,
but then was ready to start her wander through the halls.
First she went to the garden room, her second favourite place in Hailsham Hall, beaten only by the cosy
library. The garden room was a beautiful example of
classical design executed in a modern way. Huge pil-
lars separated the large glass windows and there were
four skylights dotted in the roof to capture even more
of the heat and light needed to keep the exotic plants
healthy. It was warm in the garden room, almost stiflingly so, but the aroma of the plants made Henrietta
think of the dense rainforests she had read about in the
books in her father's library.

She spent a few minutes wandering around the room,
running her fingers over smooth leaves and rough tree
trunks. She paused by the oranges, feeling their waxy
skins, and smiled as she remembered the delicious
freshly squeezed juice Caroline had presented her with
after the first crop of oranges had ripened on the trees.

After the garden room she decided to head to the
long gallery upstairs. It connected the main part of the
house to the little-used west wing and was where most
of their artwork was displayed, including the picture she
had painted for them. Henrietta loved walking through
the long gallery and stopping in front of each picture,

studying the brushwork and the use of colour. On one side of the gallery there were the Heydon family portraits: serious gentlemen and beautiful ladies, dressed in their finery. The portraits went back for generations, the earliest the First Duke of Heydon painted in 1422. She found the clothes they wore identified each era and gave a glimpse into the fashions of the times. Caroline's portrait was the first one she came to, painted just the year before and hanging in the gallery next to Heydon's.

On the other side of the long gallery were the landscapes and paintings that included some portraits, but not of the formal variety. Halfway along, in pride of place, was her picture.

Henrietta started with the formal portrait side, stopping in front of each one and examining it, feeling the familiar surge of pleasure she always did when surrounded by art. Some of the paintings were better than others and she always liked to cast a critical eye over the proportions and colours, knowing she could learn a lot from the artists who had been commissioned to paint the Dukes and their families through the centuries.

'I thought you were an intruder.'

Lord Hauxton's voice sounded loud in the silent gallery and Henrietta had to stifle a shriek of surprise.

'I thought everyone was in bed.' She studied him for a moment. He was fully dressed and didn't look as if he'd pulled his clothes back on in a hurry—more likely he hadn't made it to bed yet.

'What are you doing up here?'

'Looking at the pictures.'

They were standing a long way apart, he at the entrance to the long gallery and she at least a third of the way along, but even so she could feel his eyes on her, searching as if trying to understand her.

'I can't sleep if I turn in too early,' Henrietta added, feeling uncomfortable under his scrutiny.

For a moment she wondered if he might just turn around and head back to his bedroom, but she felt a thrill of excitement as he stepped further into the long gallery, moving until he was standing right in front of her.

'Would you like some company?'

She nodded, trying to ignore the way her body swayed towards his at the merest hint of proximity, and instead placed a hand in the crook of his proffered arm.

'Which is your favourite?' He gestured at the line of formal portraits stretching out before them.

'Caroline is the most beautiful Duchess, of course,' she said with a grin. 'And her portrait is pretty well executed.' They strolled a little further along the gallery. 'But I think this is my favourite of all of them.' They'd stopped in front of the picture of the Fourth Duchess of Heydon, a severe-looking woman dressed in sixteenth-century clothes and her hair hidden under a black hood and linen under-cap. The portrait was exquisitely detailed, showing every line of embroidery on her dress and every fold of material. All these things made it seem as though the Fourth Duchess of Heydon could actually be there in the room with them, but Henrietta's favourite thing about the portrait was the expression the artist had managed to capture.

The Duchess's mouth was pressed into a hard line. There was no hint of a smile or any softness in her face whatsoever. She looked to be a formidable woman—

however, Henrietta fancied she could see a sadness in her eyes, as if she were mourning for someone dear to her, the hint of regret or the glint of a tear. It might have been her imagination, but her instinct was the artist had managed to capture just the hint of emotion shown by this otherwise icy woman.

'I can see why,' Lord Hauxton said after a minute. Henrietta watched as he studied the painting, looking at every little detail, holding his candle up to inspect it. She always felt frustrated when people rushed looking at a work of art, when they gave it a perfunctory glance over and moved on. Someone had spent hours over this painting, sweating over it, probably toiling late into the night to produce something that was both impressive to look at and acceptable to whoever had commissioned it. Lord Hauxton took the time to appreciate it before passing judgement. 'I like how the artist has captured her expression. It's hard to know with someone from so long ago, but by the detail in the painting I can imagine it is a very accurate depiction of the Fourth Duchess of Heydon.'

They moved down the gallery, walking slowly and pausing in front of each portrait, giving some more time than others.

'You said you'd painted a picture for Caroline and Heydon. Does it hang in here?'

Henrietta felt a heaviness in her chest that she knew was nerves. Not many people had ever seen her paintings, at least not people who knew it was she who had painted them. It made her feel tense, the idea Lord Hauxton would see and pass judgement, even if it was only silently.

'It's on this side,' she said, indicating the opposite wall to the portraits.

As they strolled along the gallery towards it Henrietta felt as though time slowed. She was aware of the sound of her heartbeat in her ears and each breath seemed unnaturally loud.

'You've not shown many people your art, have you?' Lord Hauxton asked quietly. It was as though he'd sensed her trepidation and she forced herself to relax her hand on his arm, wondering why his attention made her feel so exposed.

'No. At least not personally. I've sold a few pieces through a friend, but no one who viewed them knew they were mine. Caroline has seen most things I've painted, but hardly anyone else knows so there has never been the opportunity, or need, to show anyone.'

She paused in front of the painting, indicating it was the one. For a long moment Lord Hauxton kept his eyes fixed on hers and then he turned slightly and looked at her work.

Henrietta found she was holding her breath as she watched his face for any little hint as to what he thought of it. She wondered why she cared so much for his opinion. She barely knew Lord Hauxton, apart from the last couple of days they'd only exchanged trivial conversation, but she was feeling more nervous than if the King himself was viewing her painting.

After a minute he turned back to her and shook his head as if in disbelief. 'You're a very talented artist, Miss Harvey, very talented indeed. I'm not the sort of man to say things I do not mean and this is one of the finest works of art I have ever seen.'

'I know it's flawed—' Henrietta said. She always saw the tiny details she wasn't happy with, the colours that were just slightly off or the proportions that were out.

'No,' he interrupted her, 'it's not flawed. The way you've captured the sailor's expression, the detail in his posture—it looks as if we are on the dockside with him, witnessing first-hand his relief at being back on dry land.'

Henrietta looked at the painting and felt a flush of pride. One of the problems with sneaking off to paint in private meant she didn't often get to hear what people thought of her work.

'Thank you,' she murmured.

'Tell me, where do you get your inspiration from? It is a striking picture, but it's hardly something you would see every day from your life in Grosvenor Square.'

'When I started painting, when I was much younger, I tried to paint all the things that are deemed acceptable for gently bred young ladies to paint.'

'The flowers on rolling hillsides in damn watercolours?' Lord Hauxton couldn't help but grin at her.

'Exactly. Or delicate little portraits of my friends, or even paintings of family pets.'

'Those subjects didn't hold your interest.'

'Not at all. It was so dull, so insipid. I longed to paint something with real emotion, something that told a story without any words needing to be uttered.'

'You went searching for inspiration?'

Henrietta nodded, thinking of the earlier half-finished paintings, pictures that had ignited her love of oil paints, but had not turned out as she hoped as she learned how to vary her brushstrokes for the rich, thick paint.

'I started wandering around London, at first the more reputable parts, but as I got bolder the less salubrious areas as well. It made me feel alive, the thrill of being able to catch a glimpse of the lives of these people I barely knew.'

'I can see how that might be intoxicating.'

Henrietta glanced up at him, flushing a little as her eyes met his and she realised he was listening intently to every word she said.

'Every so often I would see something that I would just *have* to paint. An innocuous domestic scene where there had been a flash of emotion or an exchange between two people where their feelings were obvious for the world to see, something that would swirl round in my mind for weeks until I couldn't help but pick up a paintbrush and try to reproduce it.'

'You were born to be an artist,' Lord Hauxton murmured.

Henrietta turned her face up to him, realising that for the last few moments he had been studying her and not her painting. It felt disconcerting to have those deep green eyes fixed so intently on her and she fought the urge to fidget under his scrutiny.

'It feels that way.' Her voice came out as a whisper, as if she could only make the confession very quietly. 'I feel at my happiest when it is just me and the blank canvas in front of me.'

'Most people in this world don't ever find the one thing that they excel at over all others, the one thing that makes them happy. You are very fortunate to know at such a young age.'

'It's just a shame it's not something more acceptable to society.'

'Very true.' He smiled at her then, an intimate smile that made her breath catch in her throat. 'We can't have everything, I suppose.'

He turned back to her painting, taking his time to study it again, stepping back so that he could appreciate it as a whole.

'I have a spot in my study in London, just above the fireplace. For years I've been searching for the right thing to hang there. Perhaps one day you might let me buy one of your paintings.'

Most people she would think were just being kind, but from what she had learned about Lord Hauxton over the last few days she knew he wouldn't say something like that without meaning it. He *did* admire her artwork and he wasn't making an idle suggestion that he would like to hang one of her works in his town house.

'You're too kind, Lord Hauxton.'

'No,' he said firmly. 'It's not kindness. I believe in telling the truth and not pandering too much to people's feelings—it is kinder in the long run. I wouldn't tell you I admired your work if I didn't.' He had stepped closer to her as he spoke and now there were only a few inches between them. Henrietta knew she should move away, this close she felt reckless, as if she might do something foolish. It was dark in the long gallery with just the light of their two candles and she suddenly had the urge to snuff them out and let the darkness engulf them. Then she could narrow the gap between them and brush her lips against his…

Quickly she stepped away, turning her face back towards the paintings so he wouldn't see the expression of longing in her eyes. She needed to get out of here, to get away from Lord Hauxton, before she did something she couldn't take back.

'Are you well, Miss Harvey?' She glanced up to see him scrutinising her and gave a weak nod.

'I've come over a little tired all of a sudden. Perhaps it is time for me to retire for the night.'

'A sensible idea,' he murmured. She had expected him to bid her goodnight and then she would hurry off to her bedroom, trying not to spend the whole night imagining she had been brave enough or foolish enough to kiss him. Instead he offered her his arm. 'Let me walk you to your room.'

'There's no need, I'm hardly going to come to any harm between here and my bedroom.'

He smiled at that, but kept his arm slightly extended in invitation all the same. Knowing there was no way of refusing without it becoming obvious how much he'd affected her, she returned to his side and allowed him to escort her from the long gallery.

'Thank you,' she said as they paused in front of her bedroom door.

'Sleep well, Miss Harvey.'

She watched as he strode away and cursed herself for caring that he didn't look back over his shoulder.

# Chapter Seven

'The snow is melting a little today. We might be able to get to the village and bring the doctor back.' Thomas looked at Polly's pale face and the dark rims around her eyes. He would be glad when the responsibility for her recovery was firmly on someone else's shoulders.

'Thank you, my lord.'

It was his turn to apply the pressure that stopped Polly's bones from slipping out of position and piercing the skin once again. This morning two of the maids had brought in a fresh bowl of water and redressed the wound and had told him there didn't seem to be any signs of it festering. Still, he would be glad for a medical opinion and a more definitive treatment than a rotation of people holding Polly's leg straight.

'When the next person comes to take over, I'll head out and see how passable the footpaths are. I understand the local doctor is not a young man any more.'

Polly shook her head.

'It doesn't look like there will be any more snow

today, so I hope by tomorrow at the latest we'll have the doctor here treating you.'

He looked up as the door opened and Miss Harvey glided into the room. She looked elegant this morning, with her hair perfectly pinned and dressed in a beautiful light pink dress that complemented her colouring. Thomas felt the same surge of desire as he had the evening before as they'd stood together in the long gallery. Then he'd almost kissed her, almost reached out and pulled her body close to his and kissed her until they both forgot their worries.

Luckily he had come to his senses before he did anything he couldn't take back. He'd stepped away and desperately tried to dampen down the extremely inappropriate thoughts concerning Miss Harvey. It would seem he hadn't been successful.

Silently he cursed. Last night he had tried blaming her—after all, it *had* been she who had climbed into his bed naked, giving him a memory he would never be able to forget. And then had been the close encounter in the snow where he'd felt what it would be like to wrap his arms around her and hold her close.

In truth, he knew it wasn't Miss Harvey's fault. None of the encounters they'd had were planned and it was *his* body reacting to hers rather than the other way round. Although as they'd stood together in the long gallery, illuminated by just the flickering light of two candles, he had fancied he'd seen her sway towards him as she turned her face up to his. It had looked as though she'd wanted to be kissed, although she'd stepped away quickly as if coming to her senses. Good job she had, otherwise he might have done something they both regretted.

'Good morning, Lord Hauxton,' she said, pausing momentarily as if surprised to see him. He noted the slight widening of her eyes and he knew he hadn't imagined her desire for him the night before.

'Good morning, Miss Harvey.'

'I came to check on Polly. How are you this morning, Polly?'

Before the housemaid could answer there was a loud bark followed by a pattering of feet. Bertie barged into the room, padding over to the bed.

'Bertie, come down,' Miss Harvey called, gripping hold of his collar and wrestling him back down to the ground before he could upset Polly too much. 'I'm so sorry, Polly, I'll get him out of here.' She started to try to pull the big bloodhound out of the room, scolding him under her breath at the same time. 'You can't come in here, Bertie, Polly needs her rest and most likely doesn't want you jumping all over her.'

Thomas couldn't help but smile. Miss Harvey was young and had a certain vitality about her that could be intoxicating if he wasn't careful. He hadn't come to Kent to court another young woman, he'd firmly made up his mind that his days looking for a wife were over. And Miss Harvey was far too well brought up to think of a casual dalliance. He would be much better forgetting about how her body felt pressed against his and focusing instead on deciding how he wanted to spend his next forty years.

As Miss Harvey struggled out of the room one of the kitchen maids came in, curtsying to Thomas and fussing around Polly, plumping her pillows, before carefully taking her turn to hold Polly's leg. Thomas checked that nothing else was needed and made a swift exit. He knew it was going to take a long time to make the walk into the village and he wanted to give himself as much daylight as possible.

As he left the room he barrelled into Miss Harvey who was just about to re-enter now she had persuaded Bertie behind a closed door somewhere in the house.

Instinctively his hands came up and encircled her upper arms, but their bodies still collided. She was smaller than him, her head only coming up to his chin, and slender in her build so she bounced off him with some force. Her eyes came up to meet his and he saw a flash of something quickly hidden.

'My apologies, Miss Harvey.'

'No need, Lord Hauxton, I wasn't looking where I was going.'

'I am going to venture out to see if I can make it to the village,' Thomas said as he dropped his hands from her shoulders and forced himself to take a step back. 'I envisage it taking me quite some time, so please don't worry if I am not back this afternoon.'

'You can't go.'

'Why ever not?'

'Well, it's foolish. You hardly know the area and could easily get lost in the snow.'

'Anyone could get lost in the snow.'

'Someone local is less likely to.'

'I can't ask someone else to take the risk if I'm not willing to do it myself.'

Miss Harvey shook her head vehemently. 'It's not

about avoiding the risk, it is about being sensible. *All* of the footmen have said they would be happy to go. They are local lads, brought up in the area, and they know the paths, the routes to the village.'

'And if one of them falls in the snow?' He left it unsaid, but he was thinking it would be another injury on his conscience.

'You can't blame yourself for Polly, you weren't even there when she was pulled down the steps.'

'I don't,' he said bluntly. It was true, he didn't blame himself, but he did feel a sense of responsibility.

'Then let someone else go.'

He wasn't used to being argued with. As Earl, there weren't many people who outranked him and most people were so eager trying to curry favour they didn't dare argue with him. His late wife, Emily, had always challenged him, but since her death not many people had.

'I'm quite happy to walk along to the village. I've done the trip dozens of times and it's hardly a difficult route. Once you're out of the gates of the estate it is a straight road into the village.'

She regarded him for a long moment before speaking. 'Well, if you're going then I'm coming with you.'

He laughed, stopping abruptly when he saw her expression.

'It'll be quicker if I just go on my own.'

'What if you fall into a snowdrift or a ditch? No one will know where you are and you could lie there until you freeze to death.'

'I didn't know you cared so much, Miss Harvey.'

She gave him a hard look. 'Caroline would be upset if you died while a guest at her house.'

'Ah. All the same I can't accept your kind offer.'

'It's not an offer.'

'I will be faster on my own.'

'You don't know that. I'm a very brisk walker.'

Thomas couldn't help but smile at the image of Miss Harvey trotting around Hyde Park and through the streets of London.

'It's too dangerous.'

'If it is too dangerous for me, then it is too dangerous for you.'

'I will forbid you to come, Miss Harvey.'

'Luckily you are neither my husband nor my father so you can forbid me until you're red in the face, but it won't make any difference.'

'I'm leaving in ten minutes. If you're not ready then, I will not wait.'

He knew it would take her well over ten minutes to change into something more appropriate for the snow and put on enough layers to keep the freezing temperatures out.

'Fine. I shall see you outside in ten minutes.'

Henrietta suppressed a smile at Lord Hauxton's look of absolute shock as he opened the front door to see her standing at the bottom of the steps.

'You're late,' she said, not bothering to keep the note of satisfaction from her voice. 'Shall we go?'

He nodded and side by side they set out across the snow heading for the long driveway that led to the gates of the estate. Every couple of seconds Lord Hauxton glanced over at her, a puzzled expression on his face.

'What are you wearing, Miss Harvey?' he asked eventually.

'A dress is rather impractical in the snow, it soaks up the water and gets weighed down after even just a few minutes.'

'Please tell me you've got *something* on under that coat.'

'Of course, Lord Hauxton, it is far too cold to be walking around in just one's undergarments.'

'So what are you wearing?'

In answer she undid the fastenings of her coat and opened up the front, revealing a curious ensemble. On her bottom half she had a snug-fitting pair of men's breeches that were so comfortable to wear they felt like a second skin. On top she wore a white shirt not dissimilar to the one Lord Hauxton was wearing and then a thick shawl around her shoulders.

'One of the groom's boys let me borrow a pair of trousers,' she said, shivering and quickly refastening her coat. 'I thought it a better option than a dress that drags through the snow.'

'Very sensible.'

'The breeches are inordinately comfortable. I do sometimes wonder at how unfair it is that men are allowed to walk around in relative comfort all day and women have to be trussed and tied into their dresses.'

'You're right, of course.'

'Perhaps I could start a revolution. Wouldn't it be wonderful if women could wear trousers every day if they wished?'

'Would you truly wish to?'

Henrietta considered the question. 'They are very

comfortable. And practical, of course.' She did a few lunges through the snow, demonstrating how easy it was to move in the breeches. 'I don't know if I would want to wear them every day, but it is more about having the *option* to choose them.'

'I have known one or two women who wear trousers,' Lord Hauxton said, 'although they are regarded as peculiarities.'

Henrietta sighed. It would be another thing for her mother to disapprove of. At least here in Kent, surrounded by miles and miles of snow, there wasn't much chance of her mother finding out.

It was hard work ploughing through the snow and took at least three times as long to cover the distance to the gates as it would normally. Around them everything was completely quiet, all sounds muffled by the thick blanket of snow, making the crunch of their footsteps even louder.

At the gate they paused. When Henrietta had entered a couple of nights earlier she had pulled the gate closed behind her and now the bottom was buried under at least a foot of snow.

'We may need to dig a path for the gate to open on to,' Lord Hauxton said.

Henrietta surveyed the stone wall to either side of the gate. With the snow piled up it didn't look too insurmountable. Definitely preferable than digging with their already frozen hands.

'Or we could go over the wall.'

Lord Hauxton strode over to the wall and measured it up, seeing how far he sunk into the snow.

'If I give you a boost, do you think you can climb over?'

'Of course.'

'Good.'

He motioned for her to come and join him and Henrietta felt a thrill pass through her body as he stepped in closer, moving so he could lift her up enough to enable her to clamber on top of the wall. With her boot in his hand he lifted her almost effortlessly and she was able to swing her leg over so she was straddling the top of the wall.

'Do you need a hand up?'

Lord Hauxton shook his head, gripping hold of the top of the wall and pulling himself up with ease.

'You're a man of hidden depths, Lord Hauxton. Not many earls would be able to mount a wall of this height with no assistance whatsoever.'

'I was seventeen when I joined the army, eighteen when I fought in my first battle on the Peninsula. I'd spent my days riding and fencing and sparring with the other boys at Eton. I thought I was fit, but those first few months I was lucky to get through alive.' He paused, absent-mindedly wiping some of the snow from the top of the wall with his gloved hand. 'The fitter men, the faster men, the men who could fight for hours on end without their legs collapsing underneath them and their arms aching from wielding a weapon, they were the ones who made it through to the end.'

Henrietta saw the pain in his eyes and knew he was remembering all those who hadn't made it through.

'I was eighteen, but I was determined to survive, so I worked on my strength and agility every spare moment.'

'And since the war?'

'It became apparent that the things that were important during the war were much the same as those important day to day. We only get one body and one life after all.' With that he swung his leg over and dropped from the wall, landing easily before turning back and holding out his arms.

'I don't want to hurt you.'

'You won't, Miss Harvey. Trust me.'

She jumped, propelling herself from the wall so her back didn't catch on the stones and landing firmly in Lord Hauxton's arms. He held her for a second and Henrietta didn't dare look up, remembering her reaction last time they'd stood so close to one another.

'Thank you, Lord Hauxton.'

'I wonder, Miss Harvey—are we well enough acquainted for you to drop the formality? To my friends I am Milton.'

'Milton.' She tested it out on her lips. It seemed to suit him.

'For a long time I wasn't due to inherit anything more than a small allowance settled on me by my father. Before I became Lord Hauxton, I was simply the Honourable Thomas Milton. The title still feels as though it belongs to my brother and not me.'

'I would be pleased to call you Milton, if you would call me Henrietta.' She had never invited a gentleman to call her by her given name before, but she had never spent so much time in a gentleman's company as she had in Lord Hauxton's—Milton's, she corrected herself silently.

'Henrietta,' he murmured, the name sounding far

more sultry in his deep, smooth tones than it had ever done before.

'I know, it's a terrible name. I have often wondered what possessed my parents to land me with such a monstrosity.'

'It's not so bad,' Milton said, unable to keep the smile from his lips.

'It's too long and fussy, and it's not even pretty.'

'And there is no easy way to shorten it,' Milton mused. 'Hen sounds ridiculous and Henry far too masculine. I suppose you could use Hetty...'

Henrietta screwed up her nose. It was no use—for years she'd tried to settle on a shortened version of her name she actually liked, but there wasn't anything.

'Or you could just wait for a young gentleman to sweep you off your feet and come up with an endearment for you.'

'You forget I'm planning on staying blissfully unmarried.'

'Unmarried and unattached are two very different things.' He waved a hand, moving on from the subject before Henrietta could even react. 'But I agree, for now I think you're stuck with Henrietta.'

They were walking along the road now, the snow not quite as deep here as it was in the grounds of the estate. It was difficult to make out where the road ended and the ditches to either side began, so tall were the snowdrifts, but by keeping to the centre of the winding country lane they were relatively safe.

'How long do you think it will take us from here?'

'Normally the walk is no more than half an hour, but in these conditions at least an hour, maybe more.'

'It's not as bad as I first thought.'

'No, I think a lot has melted already—look at how some of the green of the hedges are showing through.'

'Perhaps we might be able to get Dr Beckett back to Hailsham Hall with us today.'

'It would be a relief.'

For a while they walked on in silence, Henrietta risking a glance sideways every so often. Out here, without any distractions or complications, Milton was an easy man to be around. The gruff, abrupt demeanour had thawed somewhat and she wondered how much of it was a way to protect himself from the world when he had lost so much. It couldn't be easy letting anyone in when you had lost almost everyone you had ever held dear. Caroline had always said he was a man with a kind and genuine heart and Henrietta was beginning to see that for herself.

*Steady*, she reprimanded herself. So much for her steely resolve to remain independent and single. Three days spent in the Earl's company and she was already thinking what if. Her mind flickered back to when they had tumbled into the snow together. Already she had relived the moment much more than she should. Last night she'd even found herself waking from her dreams hot and bothered with the distinct memory of her body on top of Milton's, but without the thick layers in between.

'I wonder…' Milton said, breaking into her thoughts. She jumped guiltily and had to remind herself that he couldn't read her mind, there was no way he could know quite how scandalous her imaginations about him were. 'Should we stick to the road or risk getting caught in a snowdrift by trying the footpath?'

There was a pause as Henrietta realised he was truly asking for her opinion. She was not the shy and retiring type, often speaking out when she shouldn't, but men of Milton's class were brought up to think their opinion was the most important, even the only one that mattered. Especially over a woman's. It was rare to find a man who asked a woman's opinion on anything but the most mundane of matters.

They came level with the footpath and Henrietta peered down it. The snow was definitely deeper in places than on the road with drifts to the side. She doubted they would be able to tell where the footpath ended and the woods began.

'Let's stick to the road. It might take a little longer, but at least we know what is up ahead.'

Milton inclined his head and side by side they continued on to the village.

## Chapter Eight

'Come in, you must be absolutely freezing, walking all the way from Hailsham Hall in this weather.' Mrs Beckett ushered them inside, directing them to the warm kitchen at the back of the house before disappearing to find her husband.

Thomas watched as Henrietta pulled her gloves from her fingers and began to warm her hands by the fire. She had long fingers and he could imagine her holding a paintbrush with them. It had been quite a revelation when she had told him of her passion for painting. She was right, gently bred young ladies were supposed to enjoy painting watercolours—sedate scenes of the countryside or rivers. The grittier artwork, the pictures that captured a glimpse of the world today, that was most certainly a male domain. It wasn't a surprise her mother had reacted so badly—any hint of Henrietta socialising with the liberal artists, of doing anything that was outside the normal habits of a society lady, and the ensuing scandal and gossip could ruin her chances of making a good match.

For a moment he felt a sharp pang of something that felt far too much like jealousy. He had never known any artists personally, but they had a reputation for drinking too much coupled with raucous behaviour. The idea of Henrietta being swept into that world made him want to scoop her up in his arms and carry her back to safety.

'Slow down,' he murmured to himself. He hardly knew the woman.

'Pardon?'

'I might join you by the fire.'

She moved over a step and Thomas went to stand next to her. A moment later an elderly man entered the room, a pair of glasses perched on his nose and a frown on his face.

'Good afternoon, Dr Beckett.'

He held out his hand and shook Thomas's briefly, nodding in acknowledgment to Henrietta, looking her up and down, but not commenting on her unusual attire. 'My dear wife tells me there has been an accident up at Hailsham Hall.'

'One of the maids, Polly, slipped on some ice and broke her leg.'

'You're sure it is broken?'

He saw Henrietta bristle at the slight note of condescension from the doctor.

'The jagged end piercing the skin would hint at it,' she murmured.

'Then there is no time to lose. The longer a fracture like that is displaced, the longer a wound left open, the higher the chance of losing the leg. And I'm sure I don't have to tell you that an amputation is a risky business in itself.' Dr Beckett looked disgusted at the thought.

'Lord Hauxton has manipulated the leg and realigned the bones.'

Dr Beckett turned to him. 'A skill I wouldn't expect in a man of your background, Lord Hauxton.'

'I was in the war.' It was enough of an explanation for so many things. 'The difficulty we are facing is keeping the bones aligned. At present I dare not let her rest the leg down on the bed for fear of the bones slipping and failing to unite properly.'

'I will come and see the patient.'

'Is that wise, dear, in this snow?' Mrs Beckett asked, bustling in the background.

'Needs must. The road cannot be too bad if Lord Hauxton and Miss Harvey made it through.'

'Indeed.'

Ten minutes later they were walking in silent convoy back along the snow-covered road of the village towards Hailsham Hall. Thomas could see Miss Harvey had lost a little of the spring in her step and felt the same drain of energy as they covered the distance back to the estate. It was tiring walking through the snow and he was looking forward to handing over responsibility for Polly to Dr Beckett and having a long, undisturbed night's rest.

It took at least twice as long to make the return journey and at one point he wondered if Dr Beckett was going to be able to make it all the way, but as the gates of the estate came into sight the older man rallied. The snow was not as deep on the roadside and had melted a little since their outward journey, so Thomas was able to pull open the gates just wide enough to allow them to slip through. After another twenty minutes they were at the front door, greeted by the welcome prospect of hot drinks and warm fires.

Thomas eyed the bottle on the table for a second and then, without thinking too much, took hold of it and poured out two generous glasses of wine. Normally he didn't drink more than a glass or two, but tonight he felt a great sense of relief. Despite his slightly dismissive air, Dr Beckett had been very competent and had spent much of the afternoon with Polly, examining her leg and fitting up a splint-and-traction system to ensure it had the best chance of healing. The weight of responsibility Thomas felt for the young maid's welfare had lifted and he felt peculiarly carefree.

'I shouldn't,' Henrietta said as she reached out and took the glass of wine. By the light of the candle her cheeks were pink and rosy and her eyes sparkling. Despite having spent much of the day walking through the snow she seemed no worse for it. If anything, she looked invigorated.

'There's no one here to judge you.'

'Only you.'

'I wouldn't presume.'

Her eyes came up to meet his and he felt the spark that had been flying between them all day. With great effort he suppressed it. A year ago he would have rejoiced at the idea of finding a young woman he was attracted to, especially one who, it appeared, felt at least a little of the same for him. For a very long time he hadn't wanted to spend his life alone, hadn't wanted to be a perpetual widower. A year ago he had still had a little optimism left in him.

'What should we drink to?' he asked, raising his glass, but not bringing it to his lips.

'Health? Happiness?' She paused for a second. 'More snow?'

More snow. Another few days alone in Kent with pretty little Miss Harvey. Would that be heaven or torture?

'More snow,' he murmured, touching his glass to his lips and drinking deeply, all the while unable to take his eyes off her.

Henrietta looked beautiful tonight, in another borrowed dress that was a little too long in length, but expertly pinned to fit her figure. It was a deep violet with small silver stars embroidered on to the bodice area. The sleeves were long in concession to the cold temperatures, but the dress itself looked floaty and flimsy. He knew exactly what was underneath and, as his eyes skimmed over her body, even the knowledge that he was *meant* to be a gentleman couldn't stop his imagination. More than anything else right now he wanted to take her in his arms, to hold her close to him.

'Would you care to dance, Henrietta?'

She looked at him as though he were mad. 'There's no music.'

'Surely we can imagine it. Or, if not, I'm told I can hum quite a tune.'

For a long moment she just looked at him and he knew exactly the battle that was raging inside her. She wanted to slip into his arms, to allow him to spin her in a waltz, to feel his body brushing against hers. She wanted it even though she knew it was foolhardy.

'Come, it's only a dance.' It was a lie and they both knew it, but Henrietta stood all the same. Thomas felt the smooth silk beneath his fingers as he rested one hand in the small of her back and then he was distracted as she slipped her hand into his other. 'A waltz?'

She nodded and slowly they began, stepping in time, their bodies swaying to the music in their heads. As he got a feel for dancing with her he made the movements bigger, the spins a little faster. They were in the library, the space big enough for them to cover the steps, but not as roomy as a ballroom even without anyone else there.

For the first minute Henrietta's head was dipped, her eyes looking down to where their feet stepped in time, but as she relaxed into his arms he saw her chin tilting slightly and her eyes coming to meet his.

It would be so easy to bend his neck ever so slightly, to brush her lips with his own. The candlelight and flickering fire set a sensual mood and Thomas knew it was far too tempting to be swept up in the atmosphere.

He wasn't sure if he imagined Henrietta bringing her body closer to his, but with every step they brushed tantalisingly together until he could think of nothing but where his body ended and hers began.

Where there was no music there was no set end to their dance and Thomas knew he kept hold of Henrietta for longer than he should, twirling and stepping and spinning as the silent war raged inside him. It wouldn't be a complete disaster if he gave in to his desire and kissed Henrietta. They were both unmarried, unattached and by the way she was looking at him she felt the same attraction as he did.

*Control yourself*, silently he reprimanded himself. She was a woman of good birth. If he kissed her, then he would have to at least offer to marry her and, although the idea was actually quite appealing in many ways, he couldn't break his resolve so soon after deciding he was best to remain single.

They circled the library again, Thomas knowing that as soon as they stopped he would be forced to make a decision. To kiss her or not to kiss her.

It shouldn't be a hard decision—his reasons for deciding to remain single were perhaps a little unorthodox, but to him they made sense. In the last ten years he'd lost every single person he was close to, every single person he had loved. His wife and their unborn child, his parents and older brothers, and more recently his new fiancée. If he confided in anyone, he would admit he didn't think he could cope with any more heartache, which was true, but there was more to it than that, more that he didn't feel he could admit for fear of seeming irrational.

All the people he'd lost, the one thing they'd all had in common was him. He *knew* life didn't work that way, that one person couldn't bestow bad luck on everyone they grew to love, but that didn't stop him from wondering in the darkest hours of the night.

He spun Henrietta one final time, drawing her just a little closer before taking a step back and bowing formally over her hand, planting a soft kiss just below her knuckles. Thomas couldn't look at her as he stepped away, turning instead in the pretence of refilling their wine glasses.

When he turned back there was no hurt in her eyes, just a faint smile on her lips.

'I've never danced without music before. I thought it would be difficult or odd, but in fact it just makes everything more intense without the distraction of the music.'

*Intense*, the perfect word to describe how the dance had felt between them. She lifted the wine glass to her lips and took a long sip, her eyes holding his over the rim of the glass. He felt something stir deep inside him, the desire he was trying so hard to dampen down trying desperately to break free.

'Perhaps we can do it again some time,' he said, the words leaving his lips before he had a chance to censor them. They could never dance like that again. Once he might be able to resist pulling her closer to him and kissing her until neither of them could breathe, but twice? No, it would be far too risky.

'I would like that.'

He needed to escape, to find somewhere dark and quiet to strengthen his resolve. Somewhere Henrietta could not follow him.

He was about to make his excuses, to retreat to his bedroom and at least pretend to sleep when Henrietta tilted her head to one side and looked at him with a question in her eyes.

'Are you tired?' she asked.

'Why?'

'I thought we could play a game.'

Thomas had to work hard at suppressing thoughts of all the inappropriate games they could play. 'What game?' His voice came out a little brusquer than he had planned.

'I don't know, we're limited it just being the two of us, but I can't go to bed just yet, I'll never sleep.'

Thomas had never had much experience with parlour games. Of course his family had played a few when he was younger, but he had spent his young adult years away at war when many other young men were learning how to navigate through society.

'There's one I remember from childhood,' he said slowly, allowing himself the warmth of the memory of his mother sitting down to play with him and his brothers in the evening by the fire. 'It probably works better for family groups, but we can try all the same.'

'How do you play?'

'The first person recalls a memory or incident that happened at some point in their lives, the second person has three questions to determine which year it occurred in or how old the person was at the time, then they must put forward their guess.'

Henrietta cocked her head to one side and then smiled. 'It sounds fun. Shall you go first?'

Taking a minute to think, he trawled through the past few years, putting aside the more painful memories in favour of the happier moments.

'My first is a very tragic memory,' he said, holding Henrietta's eye and trying not to smile. 'It is when my pet mouse ran away. We always suspected the call of the wild was just too much with the countryside on our doorstep.'

'I've got three questions now?' she clarified.

'Yes.'

'Was the mouse your first pet?'

'Yes.'

'Had you started school at the time?'

'Good question. No.'

Henrietta thought for a moment before posing her third and final question. 'Did you cry?'

'Yes.'

'I think you were five. Young enough to not care what your brothers thought if you cried, not old enough to have been sent to school yet.'

'You're good at this, Henrietta.'

'Was I right?'

'Yes. It's your turn now.'

He watched her as she considered for a moment, noting her relaxed posture and the glow on her cheeks. She was enjoying herself, enjoying his company, and she wasn't afraid to show it.

'The first time I saw the sea…' She gave a little self-deprecating smile. 'Actually one of only three times I've seen the sea. Did I mention my parents do not travel well? We ate ices in a lovely little place overlooking the promenade and collected shells on the beach.'

'Were you young enough to still play in the sand?'

'Yes, although my mother may have thought differently.'

'Who travelled to the seaside with you?'

'My parents, Caroline and her mother, and our governess, Miss Jones. Caroline and I shared a governess for a few years.'

'Did you do anything else while you were there?'

'We paddled in the cold water and walked along the promenade.'

'I think you were nine.'

'Very close, I was ten. Ten years old and it was the first time I'd seen the sea.'

Thomas had the sudden urge to propose a trip to the seaside. It was ridiculous, nowhere coastal was inviting in this sort of weather and he didn't know Henrietta anywhere near well enough for them to even consider a trip to the same place at the same time, but still he had wanted to walk arm in arm with her along the promenade, to buy her an ice and sit in the sunshine enjoying the moment, to watch her pull off her stockings and paddle her feet in the water.

His eyes flicked to where she'd tucked her feet up on the chair beside her. She looked comfortable, at home, and he realised this would be what it would be like to have Henrietta as his wife. Relaxed and easy and happy.

Unsure where that idea had come from he quickly dismissed it. He might desire Henrietta and enjoy her company, but he wasn't looking for a wife any more.

'Shall I do another?' he suggested quickly, anything to pull his mind from the inappropriate direction it was heading in.

'Yes, please do. I'm enjoying your game, Milton.'

He liked how she said his name, liked the silky sound of it as it rolled off her tongue. He could imagine her whispering it to him as she writhed underneath him.

Quickly he coughed, trying to hide his reaction to the image that had popped into his head. He wasn't sure where it had come from and needed to banish any sort of thoughts about Henrietta in his bedroom.

'My first time on a boat,' he said, trying to focus on

the game, 'I was terribly seasick, spent the whole time hanging over the rail.'

'Where were you headed?'

'France.'

'Who were you with?'

'One of my brothers—Richard, the middle one.'

Henrietta frowned as if not sure what to make of his answers.

'What was the purpose of your trip?'

'We were running away.'

'Well, I've got no idea,' she exclaimed with a frustrated little shake of her head. 'You could have been ten or eighteen.'

'Which is your guess?'

'Fourteen.'

'I was sixteen. Richard wanted to join the army, too, he wanted to fight on the Peninsula, do his bit for his King and country. Our parents weren't keen on either of us going to the fighting.'

'What happened?'

Thomas smiled at the memory of he and his brother disembarking the boat, thinking they would make their own way to Portugal. They'd been young and naive, Richard only a year his elder.

'Our father was waiting when we got off the boat and turned us round and marched us straight back on. Found it hilarious that we thought we could just make our own way to Portugal and join the army there.'

'But you got your own way a year later.'

'I did,' he said quietly. Despite the horrors of war, the memories that would never leave him, Thomas didn't regret joining the fight. It had shaped him as a man, made him into the person he was today, and taught him to appreciate what was important in life. 'I sat down with my father and explained my decision to join the army, to seek a commission. I argued that they had an heir and a spare, so it was up to me to make my own way in life. I wanted to do this rather than follow my brothers' paths to Oxford or Cambridge.'

'Your father agreed?'

'He wasn't happy about it, but he agreed. He helped me with my first commission and waved me off when it was time for my regiment to leave.'

'Would you do it again, if you had your time again?'

'Yes. Without a doubt. The men I fought with…they became as close as family.' He'd often imagined his life having turned out differently. If he hadn't left for the Peninsula he might have been home on the night of the fire. Many long nights he'd spent wondering if he might have noticed the blaze, might have been able to alert his family and get them out in time. It was something he no longer allowed himself to do, the emotional toll of the speculation resounding for long after he had forced his mind on to other things.

'I can't imagine what it was like for you.'

'I don't think anyone who wasn't there could even begin to understand.' People often tried to compare challenging or difficult experiences in their own lives to war, but unless they'd been there, unless they'd lost comrades and witnessed the horrors of battle, then no one could really know what it was like.

'It changed you?'

'Yes. When I left I was carefree, a privileged young man who'd led a charmed life. When I returned…' He'd been broken. He'd seen things no person should and then he'd returned home to find his family ripped away from him in tragedy.

Henrietta stood and came to perch on the arm of his chair, tentatively reaching out and placing her hand over his.

'I'm sorry to bring up the memories. I never would want to cause you pain.'

Her hand was soft and warm on his and he had the overwhelming urge to bring it up to his lips and run them over the delicate skin. As he had the thought he felt his fingers twitching and it took a gargantuan effort to keep his palm flat against the arm of the chair.

'They may be painful,' he said quietly, looking up into her eyes, feeling mesmerised by the reflection of the flickering flames from the fire, 'but they are part of me, part of my life.'

'I'm sorry all the same.'

It would be so easy to loop an arm around her waist and topple her into his lap. He was sure it wasn't what Henrietta had been thinking of when she came to sit near him, but his instincts told him that she would be a willing participant.

Glancing up, he knew it was impossible, it would be wrong to kiss her when he had no intention of marrying her. Henrietta was from a good family, she had the right to expect at the very least gentlemanly behaviour.

'I find I am weary after our excursion today,' he said, draining the last of his wine from the glass. 'You will have to excuse me, I am poor company, so I think I will retire to bed.'

'Goodnight, Milton,' Henrietta said with a smile. He

saw she wasn't put out by the swift change in him, she just moved smoothly away and tucked herself back in her own armchair.

'Goodnight, Henrietta.' He paused at the door, wanting to go back, but managed to force himself through and out into the hall. Only when he was back in his bedroom with the door firmly closed behind him did he allow himself to think of the woman he'd left downstairs.

Seasons out in society, but Milton was the first man she'd felt that thrum of desire for, that inexplicable attraction and deep yearning to spend more time with him.

She ate her toast slowly, savouring the buttery flavour, and drank two cups of sweet tea to fortify her for the cold temperatures outside, before asking Anna to fetch her coat and cajole Bertie up from the kitchen.

'Shall we walk out to the gate and see what condition the road is in?' Milton suggested, offering her his arm as they descended the steps at the front of Hailsham Hall. With Bertie's lead in one hand and her other tucked into the crook of Milton's elbow, Henrietta marvelled at how quickly she had become comfortable in this strange seclusion. She would be quite contented to spend another month with just Milton and Bertie for company.

The walk was much easier than the day before, the snow still deep in places, but along the drive it had melted considerably. It was more akin to an easy stroll than the walk just twenty-four hours earlier.

'Snow like this always takes me back to childhood,' Milton said with an easy smile. He seemed relaxed today, almost carefree, and it made her realise he was still a relatively young man. The knowledge of how much he'd been through, losing his first wife and his fiancée, and earlier all his family, made him seem much older than his thirty-four years. When he smiled he looked even younger, his face lighting up with a boyish charm.

'Why is that?'

'Our home, our main residence that is, was in Nor-

## Chapter Nine

The pale wintry sunlight was streaming through the window as Henrietta woke up and for a moment she was tempted to duck her head below the covers and ignore the signs that it was probably approaching mid-morning already. At home she often slept until well past breakfast time, choosing to forgo the morning meal and instead luxuriate in her comfortable bed. She had always found it difficult to get up in the mornings, preferring to stay up well into the early hours and then sleep in if her engagements allowed it.

She lay under the covers for another few minutes, seeing if the urge to doze became stronger, but it soon became apparent that this morning she was fully awake. Out of bed, she rang for a maid, asking Anna to bring her some warm water and another borrowed dress from Caroline's collection, feeling a surge of guilt at needing to borrow even more clothes from her cousin. Caroline wouldn't mind, of course, she was far too generous a person to even think of being put out by Henrietta borrowing a few items of clothing when she was in need, but she felt guilty all the same.

For a moment she stood looking at herself in the small mirror on the dressing table. Some of the frown lines she'd noticed when she had first arrived in Kent had disappeared and she looked happier, more relaxed. She knew once the snow thawed she would have to make a decision as to her future, but for now she was quite content not needing to think of the real world out there beyond the snowy gates of Hailsham Hall.

Downstairs the house was quiet and she wondered if Milton had already risen. He struck her as an early morning person. Often the most organised and disciplined people did seem to like to get up at the crack of dawn, as if afraid the day were going to run away without them. They'd stayed up a little late the evening before, but she had been in bed before midnight and he had retired a few minutes before her.

'Good morning, Henrietta,' Milton greeted her as she entered the dining room. He was sitting at the top of the table, reclining back in his chair with a book open on the table in front of him. 'Have you seen the snow?'

Trying to ignore the little jump in her chest as she looked at him, she hurriedly stepped over to the window.

'It's melting.' It was hard to keep the note of dismay from her voice. While the snow had been thick and impenetrable Hailsham Hall had seemed the perfect refuge. When the snow melted enough for the roads to be passable again it would no longer just be her and Milton in the Kentish countryside. There would be no

more hiding from her life, no more pretending that this was her reality.

'I might walk out later this morning and see what state the road is in. Perhaps my luggage will arrive today or tomorrow.'

Morosely she nodded. Of course she would be pleased to see Caroline when she and her husband were able to make the journey from Hampshire, but it did signal the end of the wonderful seclusion. There would be no more cosy afternoons by the fire in the library, no more silent waltzes, no more almost-kisses.

She turned abruptly. It would be a good thing, she told herself. Being trapped here with Milton wasn't real life and she had always known one day the snow would melt.

'Would you like to join me? We could take Bertie. He's been causing havoc in the kitchens again.'

'I wouldn't want to leave you to suffer Bertie's torments alone.'

'Good. I will let you eat your breakfast in peace.' He stood and left the room. Only after he had disappeared did she realise Milton must have been sitting in the dining room with the sole purpose of waiting for her, to invite her to have a stroll about the estate with him. She felt a flush of pleasure at the thought and quickly tried to dampen it. So much for her resolve to stay single and independent—the first time an attractive gentleman paid her any attention and she was swooning at the thought of spending some time alone with him.

She smiled. It wasn't quite true. She knew she was passably attractive and had received her fair share of interest and even a few marriage proposals in her three

thumberland. Up north you get some incredible winters. The snow can lay a foot deep for weeks on end.' It explained why he was so comfortable in his ability to navigate the snowy landscape.

'It must be very beautiful in the snow. I've only visited once, in the summer, but I can remember the rolling hills and the stunning purple of the heather. Do you go back there?'

He shook his head. 'Not really, not since...' He paused and she saw the flash of pain in his eyes and wished she hadn't asked. 'Not since the fire. It burned Greenacre to the ground, nothing worth rebuilding.'

She could imagine it would be far too difficult for him to spend time in a place where the memories were of all the people he'd once loved and lost.

'We had other estates, one in Yorkshire and one in Surrey. I made the Surrey house my home, but I have noticed you don't get a proper winter down south.'

'This is beautiful...' Henrietta gestured to the white countryside '...but you have to admit it is a little inconvenient. I can't imagine spending half the winter snowed in.'

His eyes met hers and she felt the simmering intensity. 'Weeks spent warming yourself by a roaring fire, walks in the snow, that wonderful feeling of being cut off from the world? I couldn't tempt you?' His voice had taken on a low, seductive tone and Henrietta knew she would agree to anything he said right now.

'Perhaps I could be tempted.'

They had almost reached the gates, with Bertie straining on the lead in front of them. Henrietta felt as though she were gliding across the snow and didn't want to turn back to the house and cut short their walk.

'Perhaps I could tempt you instead with a little detour to the lake?'

'Now that I would definitely enjoy.' The lake was more of a pond, tucked at the edge of the estate to the west of the entrance gates. As long as there were no large snowdrifts they would be able to follow the perimeter path to the lake and then cut back through the formal gardens to the rear of the house. It would mean another half an hour out in the snow, but today the temperatures weren't unpleasant and she was enjoying the fresh air and the company too much to refuse.

'Do you think if I let Bertie off his lead he'll disappear and never come back?'

She would swear the bloodhound's ears pricked up at the suggestion and he started to pad along in a sedate fashion, modelling what a perfectly behaved dog would look like.

'He hasn't had a proper run around in days. It would be kind to let him off.'

Milton eyed her. 'As long as you help me catch the rapscallion when he disappears into the undergrowth without a backwards glance.'

'I promise.'

Milton paused, bending down and unfastening the lead from Bertie's collar. As soon as he was free the dog took off at speed, hurtling through the snow and barking happily.

'You may regret it, but you've made Bertie a very happy dog,' Henrietta murmured.

'My good deed for the day done already and it is not even midday.'

'You commit to a good deed a day?'

'I strive to, although some days people are just too irritating,' Milton said, suppressing a smile. Not for the first time she wondered how much of the gruff persona was a façade, an act, designed to keep casual acquaintances at arm's length.

'What sort of thing constitutes a good deed?'

'Rescuing damsels in distress, fighting footpads—you know, the usual everyday things a man must do.'

She looked at him with raised eyebrows.

'Fine, perhaps not every day, although I did chase a footpad into the slums of St Giles once when I saw him slip his hand into a man's pocket and take his purse.'

'Did you catch him?'

'No, but he threw the purse at me in an attempt to slow me down. It hit me in the face and the footpad disappeared into the maze of alleys, but I managed to return the purse to its owner.' He grinned at her. 'It was the most excitement I'd had for a long time.'

'Tell me some more of these good deeds. Do you actually try to do something good every day?'

He looked away from her for a moment, his eyes focusing on something in the distance, and it seemed as though he were having to steady himself before he spoke.

'I don't suppose you would have ever met my wife, Emily. She would have had her debut when you were still in the schoolroom. She had a kind heart, probably the kindest I've ever known.'

She heard the catch in his voice and wondered how it must feel to love someone for so long.

'She was quiet, shy, I suppose, but she would go out of her way to make people happy. I can remember her saying that there is only one life, only one world, and that we all have to live in it together. If we could make just one person's day a little better, it would make the world a little better.'

'She sounds very wise.'

He nodded. 'When she died, when I emerged slowly from the fog of mourning, I tried my hardest to be a man she could be proud of.'

Henrietta felt the tears prickling in her eyes and tried to blink them away. It wasn't her grief or sorrow to claim, it wouldn't be right for her to cry.

Milton shrugged. 'Emily was right, of course, the world is a better place if we all think of someone other than ourselves.'

'You must miss her very much.'

'I do. We were only married for three years and she's been gone for six, but sometimes I still feel like it were only yesterday I lost her.'

'Were you very much in love when you got married?'

He smiled ruefully. 'Not really. I'd known her vaguely since childhood and when I returned from the war an earl, with the responsibility of carrying on the Hauxton family name squarely on my shoulders, she seemed as good a candidate as any for a wife.' He paused, taking a deep breath as if to steady himself. 'It was only once we were married we fell in love.' He was being remarkably honest with her and Henrietta marvelled at his strength to discuss something so painful so openly.

'I was about to say you were lucky, finding love like that, but that sounds too flippant,' she said gravely.

'We were lucky. *I* was lucky. I always remind myself of that. I got to spend three years with Emily and, although losing her was terrible, I would choose loving her and losing her again a thousand times to living without her in my life and not having to go through the bereavement.'

'Do you still think of her a lot?' It was a personal question, perhaps too personal, and Henrietta glanced quickly at Milton's face before he answered.

'Little things remind me of her, often when I least expect it. Although the age-old saying is true, time is a great healer. The year after her death I couldn't imagine moving on with my life, I couldn't imagine anything but mourning her for the rest of time. But as the years have passed I find I am grateful for the time we spent together, but it is not all I can think of any longer.'

They walked on in silence for a few minutes, both focusing on Bertie jumping through the snow on the path ahead of them. There should be a great gulf between them, but somehow there was not. Milton had experienced so much more in his life and lost so much more. In comparison she had been sheltered. Her quarrels with her mother over her art seemed trivial compared to the trials he had endured in his adult life. Even so, Henrietta felt herself pulled towards him. They might have lived different lives, experienced different things, but he was one of the few people she felt at ease with.

'There,' he said as they rounded the corner and

stepped out from the shelter of a copse of trees. In front of them was the lake, glittering in the late morning sun. Henrietta had been here before as she had explored the estate both on her own and with Caroline and little Harry, but it had never looked like this before.

'It's beautiful.' The lake was completely frozen over, the ice thick and opaque, but glinting under the sun's rays. The banks were covered in untouched snow and the only footprints belonged to some sort of small bird hopping around on the surface.

Bertie barked and headed straight for the lake. Henrietta remembered too late that he loved ducks, but any sort of bird would do, and it would seem he was rather excited to see the little bird hopping about on the ice.

'Stop, Bertie,' she called out, trying to make her tone as stern as possible. He ignored her completely, dashing down the snowy bank and only stopping as his paws touched the ice.

'Come back here now.' Milton took a step towards the bank and for a moment Henrietta thought the bloodhound would obey him and pad back to their side. On the ice the bird flapped its wings and she could see the moment the excitement overtook Bertie. In comic slow slide he propelled himself across the ice, his paws slipping out beneath him more than once. As he came within two feet of the bird it flapped its wings again and flew away, landing on a nearby tree and watching the scene on the ice below.

Bertie barked and then turned back to them and Henrietta felt herself relax a little. She'd been worried the ice wouldn't hold his weight or that they wouldn't be able to persuade him back from the centre of the lake, but

now the bird had flown it looked as though he had lost
interest in the frozen lake and was intending to make
his way back to them.

As they watched Bertie tried to move towards them,
but his paws kept slipping and if anything he seemed
to be slipping backwards.

'The longer he stands in that one spot the more the
ice is melting underneath him,' Milton murmured. 'It's
making it too slippery for him to move.'

'If he stays there too long, the ice will crack.'

'I know.' Milton sounded grim and Henrietta felt a
surge of panic. She loved Bertie as if he were her own
dog and would never forgive herself if something happened to him while she was supposed to be looking
after him.

'Come on, Bertie, come back here. We can go home
and get you a nice treat from the kitchen.' Bertie barked
mournfully as he tried again to move towards them,
ending up in a heap on top of the ice.

There was an ominous creak and Henrietta felt her
whole body tense. So far there wasn't a visible crack in
the ice, but it could only be a matter of time.

'I'm going to have to get him,' Milton said, beginning to unbutton his coat.

'Don't be ridiculous, the ice is cracking already.'

'If he stays on there for much longer, he will go into
the water and, in these temperatures, he might never
get out again.'

Henrietta bit her lip. She wanted Bertie to be safe,
but it was a big risk Milton was taking. She had known
a child who fell through the ice when she was younger
and the little girl hadn't survived. The freezing tem-

peratures could stop the heart immediately if suddenly submerged.

'I'm lighter, I should go.'

'No.' Milton handed her his coat and stepped forward, edging down the bank and on to the ice. She heard the creak as he took his first step and felt as though she wanted to cover her eyes, but knew she had to keep looking. Bertie had stopped struggling and was lying mournfully about fifteen feet out from the centre, letting out the occasional whine.

'I'm coming for you,' she heard Milton say quietly and at his words Bertie stilled.

Milton moved slowly, placing each foot carefully on the ice and letting the weight of his body shift slowly before taking the next step. She marvelled at his patience—her urge would be to ran as fast as she could, scoop Bertie up and run back to firm land as quickly as possible—but she knew Milton's way was safer.

She let out a long breath as he reached Bertie and, leaning forward, picked up the shivering bloodhound. As Milton turned there was another ominous creak and Henrietta had to stifle a scream as she saw the ice crack just behind them. Milton would be aware of the shifting ice and the last thing he needed was for her to distract him.

He moved quicker now, running and sliding across the ice as it began to crack behind him until Henrietta was convinced it would swallow him up. Two feet from the edge of the lake he threw Bertie up on to the bank and Henrietta grasped the dog by his collar, pulling him in close to her. Milton jumped, too, propelling himself through the air just as the last of the ice fractured beneath him. Henrietta reached out and grabbed his hands as he jumped, pulling with all her force to make sure he didn't slide back down the bank into the freezing water. Together they tumbled to the ground, the air pushed out of her lungs as Milton landed on top of her.

'Thank you,' he murmured, shifting slightly so all his weight wasn't on top of her. A spark seemed to jump between them and even though they were lying in the snow Henrietta felt a wonderful anticipation begin to build. Milton was looking down at her, his gaze flickering between her eyes and her mouth, and Henrietta felt her lips part ever so slightly in invitation.

Gently he brushed a strand of wayward hair from her face and then, as if he couldn't hold himself back, narrowed the distance between them and kissed her. His lips were soft on hers at first, but as she rose to meet him he deepened the kiss, drawing her further towards him. She felt a delicious frisson of desire blooming and spreading through her whole body. Inadvertently she raised her hips to meet his, only realising as she brushed against him.

All too soon Milton pulled away, although only ever so slightly. He regarded her for a moment, then let out an almost inaudible groan and kissed her again. Henrietta came up to meet him, losing herself in the kiss, hardly noticing the coldness of the snow seeping through the layers of her clothes where she lay on the ground.

Just as she thought she might start floating she felt Milton stiffen above her and then jumped in terror herself as Bertie barked very close to her ear and then licked her face with his rough tongue. She scrabbled backwards in shock, hardly noticing that Milton had got to his feet.

'I'm sorry,' Milton said a little gruffly. She wasn't sure at first what he was apologising for—the kiss or the unruly dog's behaviour.

Bertie barked happily as if oblivious to the fact he'd interrupted the best kiss of her life. Not that she had anything else to compare it to, but it had left her feeling as if she were soaring through the air, her feet barely touching the ground.

Quickly, all too quickly, Milton was a foot away from her, brushing the snow from his jacket and reaching out to offer her his hand. She hesitated for just a moment, then slipped her fingers into his. She didn't want his apology, she wanted him to kiss her again.

Milton turned away, putting on his coat and quickly fastening it up before catching Bertie by the collar and re-attaching his lead.

Henrietta felt shaken and unsure of herself. She'd been almost kissed twice before, both not particularly pleasant experiences with gentlemen in their cups thinking they were much more desirable than they actually were. Luckily their inebriation had meant she'd been able to dodge the kisses, but she could still remember the sensation of warm breath on her face and insistent hands pawing at her body. Neither of those instances had she been keen to repeat, but if Milton as much as looked at her with a hint of desire in his eyes she knew she would be swooning into his arms.

Milton cleared his throat. 'I'm sorry,' he said again, the little half-smile she was beginning to know so well on his lips. 'I couldn't help myself. Will you forgive me?'

'There's nothing to forgive,' she murmured. He looked completely unshaken by their kiss, as if he went around kissing young ladies in the snow all the time.

He offered her his arm and she took it, wondering if they were just going to ignore such a momentous occurrence and walk back as if nothing had happened between them. She felt her spirits drop. It would seem only she had thought the kiss an almost life-changing moment.

## Chapter Ten

Thomas kept his eyes fixed on the house in the distance, not daring to glance to his left where Henrietta was gliding along beside him, her head dipped as if deep in thought.

The kiss had been foolish—no, more than that, it had been downright reckless. Of course he'd wanted to kiss her, he'd been wanting it every second of the last few days. That didn't mean he should have acted on it, but when he'd looked down at her lying in the snow, her hair flying loose, her cheeks rosy from the cold, he hadn't been *thinking*, just feeling. And the result was a kiss that had made every iota of desire he'd been suppressing for the last few days surge to the surface. Now it was going to be difficult to dampen it back down.

The rebellious part of him questioned whether he really needed to repress it. Henrietta had been a willing participant, more than willing. She'd pulled him close, invited him in. She might be innocent in experience, but she had wanted it as much as he did. Quickly he reminded himself he was meant to be a gentleman and Henrietta was not the sort of young woman you could have a dalliance with. She was the sort of young woman you married and it would be safer for everyone, especially her, if he didn't have any thoughts in that direction.

As they neared the house Thomas saw something moving out of the corner of his eye and as he swung to face the driveway he felt his eyes widen in astonishment. A carriage was making its way very slowly up the drive, the coachman letting the horses pick their pace and the carriage rolling along at no more than a slow walking pace.

'Is that yours?'

He shook his head. As it drew closer they were able to make out the shield on the side.

'It's Heydon's.'

'They're back.' Henrietta sounded pleased and he supposed he should feel the same way, but the return of their hosts meant their secluded little interlude together was well and truly over. It was probably for the best, but that didn't stop the swell of disappointment he was feeling.

They waited, watching as the wheels almost stuck in the snow, until the carriage drew level, and inside he could see Heydon with his son on his lap and his wife opposite. Once the carriage had rolled to a stop a footman hurried down the steps from the house, taking extra care on the spot where Polly had slipped a couple of days earlier.

As the footman opened the door to the carriage Heydon hopped down, little Harry in his arms already struggling to get free. Caroline followed, taking her husband's hand to steady herself in the snow. Last came a middle-aged woman dressed in dark colours whom Thomas assumed must be Harry's nursemaid. Bertie barked and jumped, pulling on the lead, but he kept a firm hold until Heydon took the dog from him, giving Bertie a stern glance which did absolutely nothing to calm him down.

'Auntie Henry,' Harry shouted, wriggling free from his father's grip and throwing himself into Henrietta's arms. She swooped him up, bringing him in for a little kiss and then holding the boy close to her. 'It snowed.'

'Milton,' Heydon said, reaching out and shaking his hand, then pulling him in for an embrace. 'You made it. We weren't sure if you would get here with the snow.'

'It wasn't too bad when I set off. Probably foolish to make the journey. My carriage and luggage still haven't arrived.'

Heydon grimaced. 'The snow is still pretty deep here. When we left Hampshire there wasn't much left at all. If we'd known the roads would be so covered, we probably would have delayed another day.'

'Henrietta dearest, what a lovely surprise.' Caroline kissed her cousin on the cheek and Thomas caught the look of concern in her eyes. 'We weren't expecting you.'

'It was a sudden decision. I hope you don't mind.'

'Of course not. We love having you to stay.' Caroline turned to Thomas and kissed him on the cheek, too, smiling her warm smile. 'I'm so glad you came, Milton. We've been looking forward to your visit.' When Caroline had first married Heydon, Thomas had wondered if there would be some awkwardness between them seeing as he had proposed to her first. Despite his fears there had never been a problem and he realised it was because theirs was only ever meant to be a friendship, whereas Caroline and Heydon were made for each other.

'When did you arrive?' Heydon asked him, clapping him on the back and stepping back to allow the ladies to walk up the steps to the house first.

'Mind the top step, it's dangerous,' he heard Henrietta cautioning Caroline.

'Four days ago. Just before the snow came down in earnest here.'

'And Henrietta?'

'A little later.' He didn't mention the first night he'd spent in Hailsham Hall, the shock of finding Henrietta climbing into bed next to him or the few minutes that followed. It wouldn't be fair or noble, and a part of him wanted to keep those memories just for himself, too.

'You look well, Milton,' Heydon said, clapping him on the back again. Heydon always had been an observant man. He was quiet and perceptive, always watchful. As a duke he was one of the most powerful men in the country, but unlike many of their peers he didn't flaunt his power or influence, instead choosing to quietly go about his business. It meant it was hard to fool Heydon, hard to keep secrets from him, and as such the Duke was probably the only person who knew how deeply the events of the last few years had affected Thomas. 'Although a little damp.'

'Your dog is to blame.'

'Not *my* dog.' Heydon bent down and released Bertie from his lead. 'My dear wife's. I tolerate the beast.' Bertie jumped up and licked Heydon on the face and despite his protestations Heydon lovingly gave his damp fur a good old rub. 'Now off with you, go find Polly to terrorise.'

'Ah.'

'Ah?'

'There was an accident while you were away.' Thomas grimaced, thinking of the sickening crunch and the scream that had followed when Polly had fallen. 'Polly slipped on the top step in the ice. She fell down and broke her leg. A nasty fracture.'

'Good Lord, is she all right?'

'The doctor thinks she will keep the leg, although likely have a limp when she's back on her feet. Henrietta tells me the wound is healing well, I haven't seen it today.'

Thomas noticed the slight raise in Heydon's eyebrows as he used Henrietta's given name rather than the formal Miss Harvey.

'Poor Polly. What a nightmare. Was Dr Beckett able to get here in the snow?'

'Not at first. We managed to make it to the village yesterday and bring the doctor back with us.'

'We?'

Before he had to answer, to let slip quite how much time he'd been spending with Henrietta these last few days, he was saved by the two women just in front of him.

'Milton is being modest,' Henrietta said, still holding little Harry in her arms. 'The break was terrible— all blood and bone sticking through the skin. We knew we wouldn't be able to get to the doctor, so Milton realigned the bone and set it back in the right place. He likely saved Polly's leg, probably even her life.'

'All that time in the army,' Heydon murmured. 'You're a useful man to have around. Thank you for looking after everything while we were away.'

'I'll just go up and check on Polly,' Caroline said, leaning over and giving Harry a kiss on his head. 'Would you get Harry settled back in before lunch, Katherine, but if he's not too tired he can have lunch with us.'

'Of course, Lady Heydon.' The nursemaid took Harry from Henrietta's arms and cajoled him upstairs in the direction of the nursery.

'I'm going to change for lunch,' Henrietta announced, touching her damp skirt. Luckily her coat was dark in colour and so the wetness from the time she'd spent on her back in the snow didn't show up, but she must be feeling a bit uncomfortable now. For an instant Thomas had an image of her slipping out of her dress, allowing the material to pool around her ankles. In his mind she looked up at him and met his eyes with an invitation as she stepped from the circle of her clothes.

'Come through to the library, Milton, the fire is always roaring in there and we have a lot to catch up on.' Heydon turned to the footman who was taking the coats. 'Williams, could you bring up some hot coffee? Unless you'd prefer tea, Milton?'

'Coffee would be good.'

Milton followed the Duke down to the library, unable to stop himself from glancing over his shoulder at Henrietta as she hurried upstairs.

He took one of the high-back armchairs, settling into the soft cushions and stretching his feet out towards the fire. He might not have been the one on his back in the snow, but his trousers were still damp and his toes icy inside his boots. At the time he hadn't noticed the snow underneath them and he realised how swept up by Henrietta and the thought of kissing her he had been.

'I'm sorry it hasn't been the week of solitude you were hoping for,' Heydon said mildly as he settled in the chair opposite him, also stretching out his feet towards the fire. 'I know you wanted to get away from society, from people.'

'It has been a pleasant few days none the less.'

'Henrietta is a lovely young woman. Easy to spend time with.'

Thomas nodded, non-committal. He shared most things with Heydon. Gradually over time, and often a few glasses of brandy, the little details of their lives would spill out and undoubtedly one day soon he would tell him about Henrietta and the turmoil she had created inside him in the short time they'd spent together, but right now it felt too raw, too close.

Anna, one of the housemaids, entered carrying a tray with two steaming cups of coffee and placed it down in front of them.

'Anything else you would like, Your Grace?'

'No, thank you, Anna.'

Once the door was closed both men picked up the cups, content in the silence for a while.

'How are you?' Heydon asked eventually.

'I'm well.'

'No, truly, how are you?' A few weeks ago he had met with Heydon in the club in London they both frequented. As they often did they'd sat and talked, joked about life and discussed mutual acquaintances. As the

night had worn on Thomas had admitted his restless-
ness, the creeping melancholy he sometimes felt was
snapping at his heels. He'd felt it ever since returning
from Portugal. While travelling it had been easy to
think of other things, but on his return he had been unable to escape his grief, the mourning he still felt for
his late wife and for Jemima, the woman he had hoped
would be his second wife.

Heydon had listened, had allowed him to talk without interrupting. He had ordered him another brandy
and when Thomas had finished speaking had nodded
thoughtfully. It was one of the things Thomas liked most
about his friend—Heydon didn't see the need to fill a
silence with some meaningless platitude. Then he had
invited Thomas to Kent, to spend a few weeks away
from London at the height of the Season, to escape the
endless balls and dinners, parties and charity functions.
To come and be with people who loved him, but who
would also allow him to wallow for a few weeks if that
was what he really needed.

'I admit I was struggling a little before I came down
to Kent,' he said slowly. 'But since I've been here…per-
haps it's the country air.' He knew it wasn't. He knew
it was Henrietta. It wasn't that she made him forget—
he didn't think he would ever forget the pain of losing the people he loved—but these past few days he'd
found himself actually looking forward to something
again. For months since his return from Portugal he'd
felt as though he were simply following the same old
routines with no real motivation to do more, but since
he'd been in Hailsham Hall he had felt as though he had
come alive again.

'Or perhaps the company,' Heydon said quietly. Thomas looked up sharply and had to suppress a smile as Heydon held out his hands as if to ward off the look he was receiving. 'Henrietta is certainly not a dull young woman. She's fun. Interesting. Sometimes we need to be reminded that life is there to be enjoyed.'

'She's certainly something.'

'I thought I saw something pass between you, a look—no, it was something more than that. A connection.'

'I've enjoyed her company,' Thomas said simply. 'But perhaps that's the problem.'

Heydon frowned for a moment but Thomas knew it wouldn't take the man long so didn't bother explaining himself. 'You don't want to form too much of an attachment.'

'I can't. Not with anyone and certainly not with an innocent young woman.'

'You're not cursed, Milton.' Heydon said it so quietly that Thomas wasn't sure he'd heard the right words. 'Deny it all you want, but I know it's what you fear deep down. That everyone you love dies.'

'This is a bit deep for morning coffee,' Thomas murmured.

'I know you're not superstitious.'

'I'm not at all.'

'Yet…'

He couldn't deny it. He *did* worry that if he ever opened his heart again he would be condemning that person to an early grave.

'It doesn't matter,' Thomas said after a few moments.

'It doesn't matter because I don't want a relationship. I don't want to get married.'

Heydon sat back in his chair and drained the last of his coffee. 'That's what you have always wanted. Remember when you courted Caroline. It was because you wanted a wife, you wanted a family. What's changed?'

'I can't do it again. I can't lose someone I care about again.' Heydon began to speak, but Thomas shook his head and continued. 'And I know I might not lose them, but I actually don't think I could stand any more loss, so why risk it?'

For a long moment they were both silent.

'Perhaps you are right. Perhaps it is time to start looking elsewhere for your happiness.'

Thomas nodded. It was what he planned to do, the reason he'd come to Hailsham Hall. Here he could plan his new future in peace. He could plot out what he wanted to do with the next forty years of his life now he had decided not to marry and raise a family. First he thought he might travel a bit more, perhaps somewhere exotic, somewhere hot. Then, who knew?

'Lunch is almost ready, darling,' Caroline said as she swept into the room. 'Stop gossiping like two old women and let Milton go get changed. I don't know what happened in the snow, but both you and Henrietta look like you rolled around in it.'

Thomas stood, glad he didn't have the sort of complexion that blushed easily, or a guilty expression that could give him away.

'The blame is squarely on your dog, Caroline. He almost had me in the lake and Henrietta went over backwards in her effort to catch him, too.'

'But he's been so much better behaved recently. I think the obedience lessons really are starting to pay off.'

He watched as Heydon reached out and pulled his wife to him, waiting until she toppled into his lap before kissing her on the cheek.

'That dog will never be well behaved.'

'I will take my leave and get changed. I'm hopeful my luggage will turn up later, but for now I am once again in your debt for something clean and dry, Heydon.'

He left swiftly, smiling to himself at the tableau by the fire. He might not hope for domestic bliss for himself, but he was pleased Heydon was so happy with Caroline even after three years of marriage.

## *Chapter Eleven*

Henrietta stepped back, making sure Milton didn't see her as he strode out of the library and up the stairs. She hadn't planned on listening to the men's conversation, but as she'd walked back downstairs from getting changed into something dry the words had drifted out and she'd found herself unable to step away.

*I don't want a relationship. I don't want to get married.* They were the first words she'd heard and she had frozen on the spot. He'd said more, of course, something about not wanting to lose anyone else, and Heydon had advised him to look somewhere else for his happiness, but all she had really taken in was *I don't want to get married.*

When Caroline had swept down the stairs Henrietta had quickly darted around the corner out of view, her emotions too raw to be able to face her cousin just yet.

It shouldn't matter, but as she stood there with her hands shaking she realised that it did. However much she had told herself she wasn't falling for Milton these last few days, that had been a complete and utter lie.

Every minute she'd spent with him had added to the fantasy, the dream that the spark she felt would bloom into something more, something permanent.

She'd allowed herself to hope even though he'd told her exactly the same thing a few days earlier. He'd told her he wouldn't marry again, that he wasn't looking for another wife, but still she had allowed herself to dream.

'You don't want it anyway,' she muttered to herself, but she knew it was a lie. All the time there hadn't been anyone to capture her interest it had been easy to be free-spirited and resistant to the social pressure to conform, but as soon as she was faced with a man she felt an attraction to, the desire to settle down, to become a wife and a mother, overshadowed anything else.

'You're an artist,' she whispered. 'There's more to you than belonging to a man.'

She repeated the words over and again, but they felt hollow. She wasn't an artist, not really. She might paint, pour her heart and soul into the canvases she produced, but she knew there was more to it than that. As a woman of a certain social class she would never be able to exhibit her paintings, never gain the recognition from the art world she dreamed of.

Steeling herself, she stepped out from behind the corner. She wouldn't wallow. Although they had been acquainted before, she had only really known Milton for a few days and a few days was not long enough to feel anything more than a passing desire, even if her heart felt peculiarly heavy in her chest right now.

She was the first into the dining room, choosing to stand by the window and observe the snowy vista rather than sit down before everyone else arrived. After a few minutes she heard the door open behind her and she expected Caroline's light footsteps, but instead instinctively she knew it was Milton.

'I hope you've warmed up,' he said, coming to stand next to her, close but not too close as to be inappropriate.

'I have, thank you.' She cursed her rebellious heart as it started to pound in her chest as he leaned a little closer. 'My dress was soaked, wetter than I had realised.'

'I apologise. I didn't even consider your comfort.' She glanced up at him, saw the frown on his face and realised he was finding this difficult. He might have decided nothing could happen between them, but that didn't mean he could dampen the fire that burned between them.

'I didn't notice, not while…'

'Me neither.'

She saw it then, the flare of desire in his eyes, and knew he was thinking about kissing her again. Even when he knew he couldn't. She felt powerful for a moment, then with the memory of the words she'd overheard, the power seeped away and, underneath, all that was left was the sadness.

'Ah, you're here already,' Caroline said, gliding into the room, followed a few seconds later by her husband. 'Milton, your coach and luggage have arrived. It's being taken up to your room now.'

Henrietta tried not to look guilty, tried not to spring away from Milton. They hadn't been caught doing anything, just having a normal conversation while looking at the view. Still she slipped around Milton's firm body and came and took her place at the table next to her cousin.

'Mama,' Harry shouted as he whizzed into the room. The little boy had so much energy and he gave Henrietta a cheeky grin as he clambered up on to the chair at the head of the table.

'Young man,' Heydon said, giving his son a mock-stern look, 'who is sitting in my place?'

'Me!' Harry said gleefully.

Heydon smiled indulgently and sat down in the place to Harry's left, just across from Caroline. 'It seems I've been usurped,' he said to Milton who came and sat next to him.

It was one of the things Henrietta liked most about coming to stay with Caroline and Heydon. They could throw a formal dinner party fit for royalty, but when it was just family they weren't pompous or too rigid in tradition. They didn't fuss about gentlemen only sitting next to ladies at the table or mind when the head spot was claimed by the youngest member of the family. It felt wonderfully relaxed, wonderfully homely, as if they were dining in a rustic farmhouse rather than one of the finest houses in England.

'Don't think I'm not ecstatic to have you here, but why the unplanned visit? If I'm not mistaken, you came without any luggage at all,' Caroline asked as steaming bowls of soup were placed in front of them. 'Not yet, Harry darling, it's hot. We have to blow on it.' She turned back to Henrietta while still keeping one eye on her son. 'Unless we have a *very* similar wardrobe, of course.'

Henrietta smiled. Caroline had been born to be a

mother and could carry two conversations easily, seamlessly switching between the two without losing her place in either.

'I ran away.'

'What happened?'

'Mother found my latest painting.'

'The one with the little orphan girl?'

Henrietta nodded. It had been the painting she'd been most proud of. Nearly a year to complete and almost finished, just the last few finishing touches to go.

'She followed me to the studio one afternoon. Apparently she thought I had a lover…' Henrietta swallowed '…but I'm reliably informed a lover would have been more palatable than the truth.'

'She found out everything?'

'Soup,' Harry chattered happily in the background, plunging his spoon in. Without losing any focus on Henrietta, Caroline took a napkin and tucked it into the front of his little shirt, smoothing it down to protect his clothes from the coming onslaught.

'She said I was foolish and selfish and stupid and she told me she had never felt so disappointed in me.'

'Did she see the painting? How good it was?'

Tears welled in Henrietta's eyes and she tried to blink them back. She would not cry over this again, too many tears had been spilt already.

'She saw it. She took a knife to it and cut it to shreds.'

'No. Oh, Henrietta, I'm so sorry. I know how hard you worked on that.'

She nodded, not wanting to speak, not wanting anyone to hear the emotion in her voice.

'You can stay here for as long as you want, of course

you can.' This was one of the things she loved about Caroline. As the responsible older cousin she should be urging Henrietta to go home, to make amends with her mother, but Caroline *understood*. She knew how important it was to Henrietta to have something of her own, to be someone except Henrietta the not-all-that-successful debutante.

'I'm never going back there,' Henrietta said, knowing she sounded petulant and immature, but unable to help herself.

'However long, you always have a home with us.'

'Thank you.'

'Will she come here?' Milton asked from across the table and Henrietta looked up to find his eyes on her. It was an unsettling feeling, the warmth that rose up from somewhere deep inside her, and she fidgeted, hoping Caroline didn't notice how one little look could unnerve her.

'My mother? I hope not.' She grimaced. Her mother didn't travel well, eschewing the carriage in London whenever she could and putting off any longer journeys for months at a time if she could get away with it. Here in Kent Henriette should hopefully be safe.

'Surely she will want to clear the air,' Heydon said, offering her an encouraging smile.

'You didn't see her face when she was saying all those horrible things.'

Absently Caroline leaned over and planted a kiss on Harry's head, wiping some of the soup off his face with a spare napkin before turning back to face Henrietta.

'You'll have to paint it again,' she said firmly. 'It was too good to let it be destroyed.'

'I can't paint it again.'

'Nonsense. Of course you can. It was a beautiful painting, Henrietta, stark and real and haunting.' Caroline had seen it a few weeks earlier when visiting London before they'd gone on to see Caroline's parents in Hampshire. She always dropped in to the little studio where Henrietta rented a room to paint once a week and store her supplies.

Henrietta shook her head. 'I'm not being awkward. I actually don't think I could paint it again. Those first few weeks of starting a new painting, I can't explain it, something takes over me, an energy, a sort of frenzy. I don't think it would be like that a second time.'

'But you should paint,' Milton said quietly. His expression was serious, his eyes waiting for hers to meet his gaze. 'The same painting or something new, whatever you wish, but it would be a tragedy if this episode stops you from painting.'

'Milton, you're a gentleman,' Caroline said quickly, an enthusiasm burning in her eyes.

'I like to think so,' he murmured, but she ploughed on as if she hadn't heard him.

'Henrietta and I have always debated her decision to paint, to pour so much of herself into art that is… controversial for a young lady. I think our fear, and her mother's fear, is a gentleman would not look upon it as a suitable pastime for a potential wife.' She paused, looking at Milton with an encouraging smile. 'But you're a gentleman and you think it's a good idea?'

Henrietta waited for his response and as always he didn't rush to answer, instead preparing what he was about to say.

'Most gentlemen are fools,' he said eventually. 'Most gentlemen don't know what they want from a wife before they start looking. They have these ideas about suitability and accomplishments. They approach the whole thing with a list of what they would like as if they are in the market for a new carriage or a racehorse. They don't understand what is actually important in a marriage, what makes it more than some regrettable business decision.'

Henrietta found herself leaning forward in anticipation of his words. He was right, of course, young ladies were trained to play the piano and paint watercolours and embroider, *these* were seen as useful skills for them to take to a marriage even though they had no practical use. Most matches were made for the sake of money or power, but the men behind the decisions seemed to forget they would have to live with their wives for the rest of their lives.

'What the gentlemen seem to forget is that the marriage might last thirty or more years. That is a long time to live with anyone, especially if you have little in common. *I* would much rather a wife whom I was going to spend all that time with had something more than pleasantries and platitudes in her head, something that made her happy, something that made the years interesting.'

'Even if that something was not a usual pastime for a young lady?' Henrietta asked.

Milton looked at her then, giving her that half-smile that she already knew well, the one that threatened to make her knees wobble when she was standing up.

'Who gets to decide what is acceptable and what is not?'

'Perhaps I could send you to London to talk some sense into my mother,' Henrietta murmured.

'I don't think you should give up your painting, Henrietta,' Milton said softly, speaking as if it were only the two of them in the room. 'But perhaps you should consider how you can continue to do what you love but still allow yourself the possibility of having the other things you may want one day, too. A marriage, a family.'

Next to her Caroline was nodding vigorously. It was the message her cousin had been trying to give her for a long time now, that she should continue painting but not sneak off to do it, not jeopardise her safety or her future.

Milton continued. 'I suppose you have to ask yourself what you like most: the painting, creating a work of art that no one else can, or the risk and the lifestyle of doing it all in secret.'

Henrietta felt the rush of blood to her cheeks. It was true that she did enjoy the illicitness of it, the feeling that for once she wasn't stepping the same path as every other debutante from a good family in London. She enjoyed it, but that wasn't the reason she did it. If necessary, that side she could give up.

'You're far too perceptive, it's hard to be irrational when you're around.'

He grinned at her and Henrietta could feel Caroline and Heydon's eyes flicking between them, assessing this informality and drawing conclusions from it.

'It doesn't matter,' she continued, sitting back as her soup bowl was whisked away and a fragrant chicken dish placed before her. 'I'm not going back to London to live in the same house as my mother, so I won't be able to go to the studio to paint anyway.'

'Paint?' Harry asked, his eyes lighting up. 'Harry paint.'

'Perhaps later, darling, we're having lunch now and I'm not sure if Katherine has recovered enough from the journey to cope with painting this afternoon.'

'She did look a little green,' Heydon murmured.

'I'll paint with him,' Henrietta volunteered. She loved spending time with Harry, loved the way everything seemed magical when seen through a two-year-old's eyes.

'Would you? He would love that.'

'Of course. Perhaps we'll put something down to protect the floor, but it'll be a lot of fun.'

'Thank you.'

Henrietta peered at Caroline as she heard the note of relief in her voice. Caroline was much more involved in her son's day-to-day life than many mothers of their class. Harry had a nursemaid, but Caroline spent at least half the day with the little boy, showing him the insects in the gardens in the summer or reading him stories snuggled up by the fire in the winter. She looked tired, Henrietta realised, tired and pale. Perhaps it was just the journey, it was a long way from Hampshire in the snow and they'd had to stop overnight at a coaching inn, but Henrietta watched her cousin's posture, the delicate hand she was inadvertently resting on her lower abdomen. Silently Henrietta smiled. Later she would ask Caroline whether she was carrying a little brother or sister for Harry, but she suspected she knew the answer already.

'Will you be staying with us for Christmas, Milton?' Caroline asked, turning in her chair so she was facing

Milton for just a second before hurriedly scooping another spoonful of dinner up on to the fork for Harry.

'Let me do that, my love,' Heydon said, taking the
fork from her much to Harry's delight.

'No, I'll head back home before then.'

'You won't be alone for Christmas?'

Milton shook his head, but Henrietta saw the second
of hesitation and knew it was a lie.

'You have to stay until our Christmas ball at the very
least. It is on the twentieth of December.'

'I don't wish to impose. That's over a month away.'

'You know we love having you here.'

'Thank you.'

Henrietta felt the surge of turmoil inside her. Another
month under the same roof as Milton. Now Caroline
and Heydon were home it wouldn't be as intense, but it
was still intimate. They would sit together at mealtimes,
probably play cards in the evening. Part of her was already anticipating the moments when his body might
innocently brush against hers, even though she knew
nothing could come of it. The kiss had been a one-off,
something never to be repeated, even if she couldn't
stop reliving the moment in her mind.

Quickly she took a sip of her wine, holding the glass
up to her lips for a moment longer than was needed. She
would have to be cautious now, Caroline was perceptive and knew her better than anyone else. She would
pick up on the little glances, the blushes, the pauses in
conversation.

Henrietta knew Caroline would encourage her, but
that wasn't what she needed right now. Before lunch
she'd heard Milton say he would never marry again, he'd

been quite clear and certain. Now she had to examine the disappointment that had filled her and decide how she was going to move on with her life.

It also showed her that perhaps her intent to stay single wasn't as resolute as she'd previously thought.

'Henrietta?' Caroline was looking at her with concern.

'Sorry, I was lost in my thoughts. Did you ask me something?'

'I was wondering if you might help me prepare everything for the Christmas ball. As usual I've invited far too many people and I'm overwhelmed already with all that is needed to be prepared.'

'Of course.'

Caroline was one of the most organised people she knew, so Henrietta was certain the request was more that her cousin thought she needed distracting than Caroline actually needing help.

'You've got a good eye for the aesthetic, perhaps I could leave you in charge of the decorations. I've asked the gardeners to start collecting holly and we grow our own mistletoe for the ball each year, but perhaps you could co-ordinate the rest.'

'I'll make a start straight away.'

The normality of the conversation had served to calm the flutters in her chest and as Henrietta glanced across the table to where Milton and Heydon had their heads bowed together in conversation she promised herself she would stop obsessing over Milton, force him from her mind and start focusing on the other things in her life.

## Chapter Twelve

'You're a fool,' he muttered to himself as he walked slowly along the hallway towards the drawing room. From inside there were happy hoots of laughter as Henrietta took charge of Harry for an afternoon of painting. Heydon had gone to settle his wife upstairs with Caroline pleading exhaustion from the journey. She had looked a little pale at lunch and Thomas felt the familiar panic he always did when there was even a hint of someone being unwell.

He paused outside the door. What he *should* do was turn around and walk away. Perhaps retreat to the library for the afternoon, choose a book from the shelves and lose himself in it. Or take a brisk walk in the snow, or… Anything but push open the door and go into the room with the woman he couldn't stop thinking about.

'Good afternoon. Is this a private lesson or can anyone join?'

The servants had spread what looked like a couple of old sheets on the ground and Henrietta had set Harry up with one of her canvases and a paint brush. Already he was enthusiastically splattering paint on to the canvas, using his hands to smear it around as much as the brush. Sitting perched on the edge of one of the sofas was Katherine, Harry's nursemaid, no doubt ready to scoop him up and dunk him in a bath as soon as he got bored with the paints.

Henrietta looked at Thomas, as if deciding whether to shoo him out of the room or invite him in.

'Have you painted before, or are you a complete novice?'

'I don't think I've ever held a paintbrush in my life.'

'What would you like to paint?'

'Something simple. Easy. I know my limitations.'

'Harry is painting Bertie, a picture for his mama and papa. Perhaps you might like to do something similar. Animals are good for a first foray into art.'

'I'm not sure I want to compete with Harry.' He crouched down next to the little boy. 'That's amazing, Harry, it looks just like Bertie.'

Harry nodded seriously and then dabbed another paintbrush full of paint on to the centre of the picture.

'Perhaps a flower, then? We don't have anything for you to copy, but I'm sure you can paint a flower from memory.'

Henrietta started to set up another canvas, picking a few paints and squeezing them out on to the wooden palette, all the time encouraging Harry. She was a good teacher to the little boy, allowing him to do as he wanted, but heaping on the praise to bolster his confidence.

'Done,' Harry declared after a few more minutes.

Both Thomas and Henrietta crowded round, looking at the smear of paints on the canvas.

'That is wonderful, Harry darling,' Henrietta said, leaning in and giving him a kiss on the top of his head. 'Your mama and papa are going to be so pleased with their present. Shall we let it dry and then we can hide it until Christmas?'

Harry nodded and then lunged towards Henrietta, painted hands spread. She embraced him, seeming not to notice the smear of paint left on her cheek as he pulled away.

'Let's get you cleaned up and then perhaps we can sit by the fire for a story,' Katherine said, taking his hand and leading him from the room.

For a moment it was silent and Thomas was acutely aware it was just the two of them alone again.

'Your lesson,' Henrietta said at last, stepping towards the canvas she had set up. 'First you need to make a rough sketch of what you want to paint—some people do a full drawing, others just some guiding lines to check the size is right—but you'll need something drawn before you start to paint.' She handed him a pencil and motioned at the canvas.

'What are your favourite flowers?' he asked.

'Irises,' she said without hesitation.

'Irises,' he mused, starting to sketch out a thin stem and delicate petals. He wasn't a naturally gifted artist, but he had spent many of his school days drawing little sketches on the paper he was meant to be copying down his lessons on. He could draw a flower without showing himself up too much.

Thomas felt Henrietta's eyes on him, watching his hands as they moved over the canvas.

'Aren't you going to paint?'

She shook her head, but there wasn't the certainty that had been there when he'd asked her the same a few days ago.

'What next?' He had drawn a rough sketch of an iris that filled most of the canvas.

'Now you paint.' She showed him how to blend the thick, oily paints, how to dab a little on to the canvas and then change the colour ever so slightly for the next stroke to give the flower a natural look. 'You can use the brush stroke to create different effects by exerting different amounts of pressure.'

As if without thinking she reached out and placed her hand over his own, demonstrating how to create long smooth strokes and short textured areas. She was standing close to him now, so caught up in the painting that he didn't think she had even noticed their bodies were almost touching. He could feel the heat of her skin where her fingers rested on top of his and smell the fragrant lavender scent of her hair.

It would be so easy to lean in and run his lips over the soft skin of her neck, to murmur in her ear, to pull her body to him. Already he knew how well her body moulded to his, how perfectly they seemed to fit together. It would just be a matter of a few seconds and a few tiny steps and she would be in his arms.

As if sensing his thoughts, Henrietta suddenly turned and looked at him. The movement meant her head was even closer to his, her lips mere inches away. In the warmth of the drawing room her cheeks were already flushed, but this close he could see her lips were rosy, too. Rosy and kissable.

'I know we shouldn't,' he murmured, waiting for her to be the one to step away, knowing that he couldn't be the first to pull back. He *knew* kissing her was wrong, knew she deserved more than a kiss from a man who couldn't commit to her, but he still couldn't bring himself to move away.

'We shouldn't,' she echoed, but didn't pull away from him.

Time slowed, every second filled with delicious anticipation, building and building until Thomas couldn't stand it any longer. He reached out and spun Henrietta to face him fully, at the same time taking a step in closer to her and kissing her. His hands encircled her waist, pulling her in, and he kissed her long and hard, feeling her mouth moving under his, inviting him in.

Their bodies were so close he could feel the thumping of her heart even through the layers of her clothes and he had the overpowering urge to strip through the layers to get to her skin. Restraining himself, he instead raised a hand to the bare skin just before her shoulder, caressing the velvety softness and imaging what it would feel like if he were to dip his fingers under the neckline of her dress and trail a path over the swell of her breasts.

'You don't know what you do to me,' he whispered in her ear as he pulled away slightly, taking the opportunity to run kisses down the line of her jaw and on to her neck. Henrietta let out a little gasp of pleasure and sank into him, allowing him to push the material of her dress off her shoulders just a little.

Even as he kissed her he knew he should stop. Henrietta was younger than him, probably inexperienced in anything more than a stolen kiss or two, and she was well within her rights to expect marriage after being kissed like this. A marriage he couldn't offer her. These last few years he'd tried his very hardest to be a good man, a moral and upstanding man, but right now he couldn't do the right thing. He couldn't step away.

Henrietta let her head fall back, opening up her neck to him, and Thomas moved his hands to follow the course of his lips, tracing over her collarbones and resting in the hollow of her neck. As she looked up at him there was a raw desire in her eyes and he knew if he wanted to he could lay her down here in the drawing room and explore every inch of her body without a single protest from Henrietta. She would welcome it, encourage it even.

It was, oh, so tempting. He could already feel the desire surging and pulsing inside him. It would just take a few expert movements and he could have her dress pooling around her ankles.

With a shuddering breath he stepped away. She deserved better than that, better than a man who took what he wanted, but couldn't commit to her.

Thomas tried to ignore the confusion and hurt in her eyes, instead giving her a breezy smile.

'You're irresistible,' he murmured, 'I'm sorry, I couldn't stop myself.' He knew it was unforgivable, to treat such a moment, such a connection, with such glibness, but he had to put some distance between them. If she looked up at him with even a hint of desire, then he didn't think he would be able to do the honourable thing and walk away.

He saw the minute clenching of her jaw, the shuttering of her eyes and, after a moment of searching his face, she turned away, hastily rearranging her dress.

'I'm not some young, inexperienced debutante,' she said, suddenly turning back to face him. 'I'm not going to press you into an engagement just because we've shared a kiss or two.'

'I didn't think that of you…' The lie tasted like ashes in his mouth and he trailed off at the expression on Henrietta's face.

'I told you the other day I do not wish to marry. I do not wish to chain myself to a man who would have ultimate control over my life. I want more than that for myself.'

He nodded, but he could hear the hollowness of her words. She might believe them on one level, but he could see the yearning in her eyes as she looked at Harry, the maternal instinct that was impossible to quash. A family was only obtainable after a marriage, at least in their social class, which meant one day Henrietta would decide her yearning for children would overcome her misgivings about taking a husband. He knew the feeling well. He had wanted children of his own, so much it hurt to think about the daughter he had lost at the same time as Emily, and even after that pain he would risk it all again for the chance to hold his child in his arms. Or at least he would have until recently. Now, no matter how much he wanted a family, he wouldn't risk anyone losing anyone else he loved, his heart couldn't stand it.

'I am perfectly capable of conducting a dalliance without getting overly attached.'

'Is that what this is?' He asked, taking a step towards her, but halting as she took one back. 'A dalliance?'

'Two adults who desire one another, who do not want a commitment. What else would you call it?'

He looked at her silently. Despite her protestations she still looked young and innocent, too young and innocent to be having this conversation. Even if she told him she wanted it, even if she welcomed him into her bed with open arms, he knew he had to protect her.

'A dalliance,' she repeated, quieter this time, her gaze holding his. 'Two consenting adults who feel a mutual attraction enjoying a physical connection.'

She couldn't know what she was proposing, but even so he felt his body tighten at the idea of spending weeks kissing her, touching her, tumbling her into bed. He'd never had a mistress, never felt the need, but right now he could imagine the appeal.

'You don't know what you're saying,' he said quietly. Henrietta couldn't be proposing an affair, women of her social class just didn't do that, at least not before marriage. Their virtue was too precious, too much of a commodity.

She held his eye, outwardly calm, but he could see just the faintest flicker of uncertainty in her expression.

'What do you propose, then? We go back to behaving like strangers, stiff and formal?'

The idea was ridiculous. He felt as if he knew Henrietta better than he'd known anyone for a long time. He couldn't go back to the formal manners society would expect of them.

'Or ignore the attraction between us and pretend we're friends.'

'We are friends,' he said.

She regarded him for half a minute in silence, then nodded. 'Friendship, then.'

Thomas blinked, wondering how he'd just managed to negotiate away from the thing his body was craving the most. He wanted so much more than friendship, he wanted to gather Henrietta in his arms, carry her to his huge four-poster bed and not emerge for a week. Better still, he wanted to whisk her off in his carriage to his estate, lock the doors behind them and not emerge for a month.

'Friendship.' He nodded, wondering if he was going to be able to be in her presence for the next month, not able to touch her or kiss her, without going mad. 'Although…'

Henrietta fixed him with a hard stare. 'Friends do not go around kissing each other.'

'How did you know what I was going to say?'

'I saw the look in your eyes.'

'I wasn't aware I was so transparent.'

He was saved from Henrietta's answer by a soft knock at the door and Anna the housemaid slipping inside. They weren't standing even remotely close together and Henrietta had straightened her dress from their embrace a few minutes earlier, but still he felt as though he sprung away from her guiltily.

'There's a carriage approaching, miss. Lady Heydon wanted me to let you know.'

'A carriage?' Henrietta looked flustered as she moved towards the window.

He moved to stand beside her, saw the panic and misery on her face.

'It's my mother.'

ances, to clear their minds, to focus only on what was important to them now.'

'Sound advice for battle, I'm sure,' Henrietta murmured, 'but this whole thing is about past grievances.'

'True. I'll just remain quiet, some silent support.'

Trying to silence the angry monologue that was already running through her head, outlining all the arguments as to why her mother was being unreasonable, Henrietta took Milton's proffered arm and together they walked towards the morning room. She should feel awkward with him by her side after what had happened only a few minutes earlier, but at present her main preoccupation was her mother.

'Henrietta,' Mrs Harvey exclaimed as they walked into the room.

'May I present Lord Hauxton, Mother.' She knew they had met before, but the formality was a shield, something to delay the inevitable conflict.

'Pleased to see you again, Mrs Harvey.'

Henrietta's mother looked momentarily thrown to see Milton, looking between Henrietta and him with a puzzled expression, but she rallied in a matter of seconds.

'Lovely to see you again, Lord Hauxton. I'm afraid I'm going to have to beg forgiveness and ask for a private word with my daughter. We have some important matters to discuss.'

'I have asked Lord Hauxton to stay, Mother.'

Mrs Harvey's eyes narrowed as she surveyed her daughter. 'Do not be foolish, Henrietta. We have *private* matters to talk about.'

'Lord Hauxton is the embodiment of discretion.'

# Chapter Thirteen

Henrietta felt a violent shaking deep inside her and wasn't sure if she should blame it on the exchange she'd just had with Milton or her impending confrontation with her mother. After her resolve at lunchtime to stop thinking about Milton, to push away any desire she felt, she was disappointed in herself with how long she'd held out. A few minutes in his company and she had completely forgotten she was meant to be focusing her thoughts on anything but the man beside her.

The kiss had made her feel as if she were floating up into the air and she knew Milton felt the same. The physical aspect of their attraction couldn't be denied.

She felt her cheeks flush at what had come next, her offering herself to him only to be completely and utterly rejected. Remembering his words, his insistence that he would not marry again when she had overheard him speaking to Heydon, she had offered him the alternative, a dalliance, an affair. And even that he had rejected.

Shaking her head, she took a deep breath, trying to

steady herself. She probably should be thanking him—young women from good families did not enter dalliances before marriage.

'She shouldn't have come here,' Henrietta murmured, watching the approaching carriage with dread. She'd thought she was safe from her mother in Kent, especially with the snow. It was too soon to see her again. Even if she came with a sincere apology Henrietta didn't know if she would be able to forgive her just yet. But she knew her mother—the reason for the visit wouldn't be to apologise.

Henrietta glanced at the man standing beside her and straightened her back slightly. She would try to be as magnanimous as he was, try to emulate his behaviour when he tried to perform a good deed every day. If her mother had come to apologise, she would hear her out, if she had come to reconcile, she would consider her proposition.

'Shall I show her in here, miss?' Anna asked quietly. 'Or put her somewhere else?'

Henrietta shook her head. 'Not here. She mustn't see the paints.'

'Show Mrs Harvey into the morning room,' Milton said, taking charge of the situation. 'Neutral ground,' he murmured to her as Anna left the room.

'I can't see her.'

'I am not sure your mother is going to give up until she has spoken to you. She's travelled a long way.' He spoke calmly, rationally, and next to him Henrietta felt like a petulant child.

'I might say something I can't take back.'

'Would you like me to accompany you, calm the situation if things are becoming too heated?'

It would be unusual to allow a virtual stranger into the middle of their family quarrel, but Henrietta realised Milton would bring much-needed calm and perspective when she was likely to be anything but rational.

Before she could decide, the carriage had pulled up outside, rolling to a stop on the thin layer of remaining snow. It really had started to melt quickly now. Probably by tomorrow there would be hardly anything left.

From the window she watched as her mother stepped down, taking a moment to look up in satisfaction at the façade of Hailsham Hall. It had been the most talked-about event of the Season when Caroline had married Heydon and become a duchess. She knew her mother yearned for the same sort of match for her daughter. Perhaps not a duke, as they were few and far between, but an earl or a viscount, someone titled and important who could trace each side of his family tree back through the nobility at least half a dozen centuries.

Coming from humbler beginnings as the daughter of a vicar, her mother had already climbed a few social stations in society. Henrietta had often wondered if that made it even more important to her that her daughter made a good match.

Quickly she stepped back as her mother's gaze swept in her direction. She needed a few more minutes to compose herself before she faced her mother's disappointment.

'Before we went into battle a very wise officer used to give this little speech to the troops,' Milton said quietly. 'He would tell the soldiers to let go of all past grief

'Henrietta.' Her mother's tone was sharp, but this only made Henrietta want to stand her ground more. She had to suppress a smile of relief as Milton took a spot by the window, planting his feet firmly apart as if to say it would take four horses to drag him away.

'I have nothing more to say to you, Mother.'

'Don't be ridiculous. This *farce* will end now. You will pack your bags and come back to London with me.'

'No.'

'I command it. I am your mother.'

'And I am an adult, perfectly capable of making my own decisions, and I choose not to go with the woman who destroyed something I'd been working on for months.'

'I am not going to argue with you again about those damn paintings, Henrietta.'

She knew her mother must be angry by the language, she could count the number of times she had heard her mother cursing on one hand, and three out of five had been since she'd discovered Henrietta's pastime.

'So you haven't come here to apologise?'

'Apologise? You want me to apologise to you? After everything you've put me through. Everything you've risked.'

Henrietta blinked. Normally she got on relatively well with her mother, as long as they didn't spend too much time cooped up together. The older woman was a little self-centred, but Henrietta had always found that a positive—it meant she hadn't noticed when her daughter had started to creep away once a week.

'Everything I've risked?'

'Your future. Your reputation. *Our* reputation. If

the news got out that you'd been running round London unchaperoned, painting pictures of the slums and those who inhabit them, you would be shunned. No man would marry you, no woman would invite you to dinner. It is not a seemly pastime for a woman in any circumstance, but what makes it worse is how you've gone about it.'

Henrietta felt herself bristle and knew it was partly because her mother spoke the truth—she had been secretive in what she was doing. Now she could pretend it had been to prevent a reaction like this, but she knew deep down part of her had enjoyed the thrill, the break from the monotony of her normal life.

'You seem to think I care about all those things, Mother.'

'Of course you care.' Her mother raised her voice. 'You might think it is amusing to be single and unmarried now, but what about when all of your friends have settled and had children? What about when you're the only unmarried forty-year-old, stuck at home because no one will have you? You'll care then.' Mrs Harvey shook her head. 'We are not going to discuss this again, Henrietta. It is over. Finished. You will come back to London with me and you will forget about your silly paintings.'

Tears flooded Henrietta's eyes and she tried to blink them back. She had always known that she could never succeed in her art in the same way she could if she were a man. If she were a man, she would be lauded, encouraged to pursue her vocation, free to follow her creative dream. As a woman she was stifled in so many ways.

'No.'

'What do you mean "no"?'

'I will not come back to London and I will not forget about my paintings.'

'I am warning you, Henrietta Harvey, don't make me do something you will regret.'

'What more can you do, Mother? You destroyed the painting I'd been working on for the best part of a year. I poured everything into that and you just shredded it as if it were nothing.'

'It was nothing. A silly painting by a silly girl.'

'No.'

'I know you have done others. So you will come back to London or I will find the others and I will destroy them, too.'

Henrietta looked at her mother, wondering where the kindness had disappeared to, the compassion. They had argued before, but never like this. It was as though she were seeing a completely different person standing in front of her.

'You wouldn't,' she said flatly. 'It would be counterproductive. None of the people who bought the paintings know it was me who painted them. You would only be drawing unnecessary attention to them.'

Her mother reached out to grab her arm, but Henrietta brushed her away. Next to the window she saw Milton stir as if ready to pounce between the two women.

'You will be disowned. And you can't stay with Caroline for ever.'

With a great indrawing of breath Henrietta turned and began to walk away. She had hoped her mother had come to apologise, hoped they could perhaps work something out, but it had just been an extension of the argument they'd had back in London.

'Don't walk away from me, Henrietta. I will speak to your father and he will compel you to come home.'

Sharply Henrietta turned, unable to hold back some of the pent-up emotion. 'You say you care for me, that you care for my reputation, my future, but how is any of this caring? You destroyed something that meant a great deal to me and threaten to destroy more. You tell me I will be disowned, that I will have no place in the world…' She paused, shaking her head. 'I may have been a little foolish in how I went about finding the time and space to paint, but *this* is why. You never would have let me.'

In a blur her mother closed the gap between them and struck her on the face. It was a sharp, hard slap that made her ears ring and her neck snap back.

'Henrietta,' Milton said, immediately by her side. He put a hand to her cheek and for an instant she sank into it, appreciating the coolness of his skin against the burning of hers. She raised her eyes to his, trying to convey that she would be all right even though the words could not come. He nodded once, then spun to face Mrs Harvey.

'Leave,' he commanded.

Henrietta saw her mother hesitate and immediately Milton took her firmly by the arm and guided her from the room. Henrietta didn't hear what he said to her mother in the hallway, but the older woman left without a fuss. From the window Henrietta saw her climbing back into the carriage. Now she was alone she felt the tears spilling on to her cheeks and within seconds her whole body was racked with great sobs.

'Hush,' Milton said as he came back into the room, immediately taking her into his arms and allowing her to bury her head in his shoulder. He didn't try to murmur false platitudes, instead calmly stroking the back of her neck and allowing her to cry. It should feel awkward, being in his arms again so soon after their last kiss and the confrontation that had followed, but Henrietta found it comforting more than anything else and allowed herself to be enveloped in his arms for far longer than she probably should.

When she eventually pulled away he stopped her from moving too far, tilting her chin with one of his fingers and having a good look at her cheek.

'I don't think it will show,' he said after a moment. 'But it will probably be sore for a while.'

'I can't believe she slapped me. She's never struck me before. Not even as a little child.'

'Her emotions were running very high. Although that is not an excuse.'

His fingers were still on her chin and she felt the urge to step in closer. Even now, even with the shock and anger flowing through her, she couldn't stop herself from feeling a flicker of desire for the man standing in front of her.

'I'm sorry,' he said quietly.

'For what?'

'I should have reacted quicker.'

'You couldn't have anticipated my mother would behave like a woman possessed. No one could have.'

'Still, I was here to ensure things didn't escalate and I wasn't very successful.'

Henrietta felt the tears falling afresh on her cheeks and ever so gently Milton reached up and wiped them away with the pad of this thumb.

'You will work it out. It was just too soon.'

'I don't know if I ever want to see her again. You heard what she threatened to do.'

'Empty threats. You're right, why would she draw attention to the paintings that are already out there without anyone knowing you were the one who painted them?'

'Perhaps to teach me a lesson. To show me that it will not be tolerated.'

'Is your mother really that vindictive?'

Slowly Henrietta shook her head. She didn't think so, at least a few weeks ago she would have laughed at the idea of her mother doing something as destructive as slashing her painting or demanding Henrietta return home with her, but it felt as though the woman who had just been in the morning room with them was a stranger.

'I don't think so, but then again I didn't think she would act as she has. We've never quarrelled like this before.'

'Where are the paintings? Are they well hidden?'

Henrietta looked up sharply. He sounded rather like he was planning on charging round London gathering up her artwork to keep it safe from her mother.

'I sold three, not personally, of course, but through another artist who uses the same little studio to paint. One was to a family in Mayfair, another to Lord Melbrooke and the last to a woman by the name of Mrs

Hobbs, a widow I think. And then there is the one hanging in the long gallery here.'

'That one is safe at least.'

She paused biting her lip. 'The last painting is still at the studio. One of the other artists is going to try to sell it for me, but at the moment it is still sitting in storage.'

'You think your mother knows about it?'

'It would be the first place she would look.' Henrietta felt sick at the thought. Having one painting destroyed was bad enough, but two would be devastating. The painting in storage was of a mother feeding her children while her bowl remained empty. It was one of her favourites and had taken her a long time to paint.

'I think the paintings that have been sold should be safe. You're right—it would be counter-productive to draw attention to them now. And your mother is hardly going to defy Heydon to take the one from here. It's the one left at the studio that is at risk.'

'I have to go back. I can't let her wreck another one.'

Milton surveyed her for a long moment, then nodded.

'I will accompany you.'

'Don't be ridiculous. There's no need.'

'There's every need. You have no idea what conditions the roads are in on the way back to London and, if it snows further, you could be stranded.'

He wasn't wrong, she would be foolish to go on her own, but he wasn't the right person to accompany her. At the very least two days to travel there and back, probably more likely four in total when you took into account the time spent in London, spent together in close proximity. She wouldn't be able to bear it.

'I'm sure Caroline…' She trailed off, thinking of her

cousin's pale face and the suspicion that she might be pregnant. Henrietta knew she couldn't ask Caroline to endure another couple of days in a carriage when the best place for her was here at home. 'Or even Heydon,' she said lamely. Heydon would, of course, accompany her if she requested, he was a good man, a kind man, but it would be selfish of her to take him away from Caroline when she needed him. Her cousin's first pregnancy had been straightforward, but since having Harry there had been two losses early in pregnancy.

She waved a hand dismissively. 'I'll think about it.'

Milton inclined his head, then quietly left the room in that assured way of his that Henrietta knew meant he was planning on accompanying her no matter her views on the subject.

## Chapter Fourteen

'Congratulations!' Henrietta hugged Caroline, taking care not to crush her. 'I knew it. I could just tell by how you were holding yourself.'

'It's too early to know anything for sure, of course.' Caroline was being cautious with her optimism after the two miscarriages she'd suffered in the past year.

Henrietta nodded, knowing it would be empty words if she told Caroline everything was going to be all right. No one knew that, not until the baby was safely in her arms.

'James is ecstatic, of course, I think he has these dreams of a huge family even though neither of us is getting any younger.'

'You're hardly an old matron.'

Caroline beamed and placed a hand protectively on her belly. She'd told Henrietta that by her reckonings she was about four and a half months along, just enough for a little bump to start showing under her clothes, cleverly hidden by the layers to the casual observer.

'Now, tell me everything your mother said.'

Groaning Henrietta slumped back on the bed, allowing a full minute to pass before she started to speak.

'I thought she might have come to apologise, you know. Beg my forgiveness for destroying the painting.'

'But she didn't?'

'Not at all. She demanded I stop being a silly little girl and return home with her, then threatened to destroy all my other paintings if I didn't.'

'Words said in anger often are not followed through.'

Henrietta nodded. Caroline was right, but she couldn't risk it. It was hard to explain, this need to protect what she had created. Each painting had taken hours upon hours of hard work and concentration, but that wasn't it really, it was more the emotional toll, the part of herself that she poured into each picture. *That* cost her. That was worth protecting.

'I've never seen her like this before.'

'No, she's normally calm and relatively reasonable. Do you think it is the scandal she fears the most?'

Shrugging, Henrietta propped herself up on her elbow.

'She said both times that she cares for my reputation, that she doesn't want the scandal to engulf me, but how can she proclaim she cares for me and then destroy something that is so important to me?'

'Have you thought how you would feel if your reputation was sullied by this?' Caroline asked quietly. Henrietta wouldn't take the question from anyone else, but she knew Caroline was asking with love and an open mind, ready to support her whatever she decided.

'I don't want to marry,' she said, feeling the heat rush to her cheeks as she couldn't keep the image of

Milton from her mind. *Liar*, the voice inside her head screamed. She hadn't wanted to marry until the past few days—now if he asked her she would fall over herself to accept. 'I didn't want to marry,' she corrected. 'At least I didn't think I did.'

'Your reputation is about more than finding a suitable husband.'

'I know, being shunned from balls and dinner parties and all that. I do know that, but I can't bring myself to care too much. It's all a little tedious anyway. Perhaps I'd be better just declaring myself an eccentric, scandalous artist and actually giving people something to talk about.'

Caroline cocked her head to one side for a moment as if she were seriously considering the idea. 'Society does love an eccentric…but it would put you into that role, that is all you would become, and there is so much more to you than that, Henrietta.' She paused, running a brush through her hair thoughtfully. 'You said you *didn't* want to marry. Has something changed?'

Henrietta groaned again and flopped back so she was lying completely flat on the bed. Caroline always ferreted out her secrets, even the painting and sneaking off to the studio every week. Caroline had been the only one to find out the truth for years.

'Milton is a very nice man,' Caroline said mildly.

*Nice* didn't seem to be the right way to describe him, it seemed too bland.

'And you have spent a lot of time alone with him. Sometimes feelings can develop.'

'There might have been a moment,' Henrietta confessed.

Caroline's eyes were shining as she turned in her seat and waited for Henrietta to continue.

'A moment?'

'A kiss.' She closed her eyes. 'A few kisses.'

For once Caroline was lost for words, her mouth opening a little, but no words coming out.

'A few kisses?' she managed to repeat eventually.

'Two. It's so stupid, I know nothing can happen between us, but I can't stop thinking about him.'

'He's in your mind every moment of every day?'

Henrietta nodded.

'Do you think you're falling for him?'

It was too hard a question, not because she didn't know the answer, but because she knew there couldn't be a happy ending.

'Before it happened, before anything happened between us, he told me a little about his life. How he's lost so many people, how he plans to stay single and alone because he can't bear the idea of losing anyone else.'

Caroline nodded as if she'd heard the same from him.

'I know nothing can come of it, nothing but a little flirtation, a little infatuation, but I am hoping for something that can never be.'

'He might change his mind.'

Henrietta shook her head. 'He was so certain, so firm. I don't doubt that he feels the same attraction, but I know nothing can come of it.'

'And that is breaking your heart.'

It seemed so silly to be feeling this about a man she had only ever exchanged polite conversation with before the past week.

'Things change, Henrietta, the convictions and re-

solve we have ebb and flow. Look at me and James—
we were friends for years before he realised he felt the
same way about me as I had always felt about him.'

'I don't think Milton will change how he feels and I
can't blame him. I can't imagine losing that many people. I can understand the need to protect your heart from
any more pain. Who am I to ask him to risk it again, all
for someone he barely knows?'

'But you want to?'

Henrietta closed her eyes and remembered the pure
joy when he'd taken her in his arms and kissed her.
She hadn't been able to think of much else. Every time
they were in the same room together her whole body
tingled and her heart swelled. She didn't know if it was
an infatuation or something more, but she couldn't stop
daydreaming of a future together, a future they could
never have.

'How shallow does that make me? I've always said
I don't want to marry, that I don't want to tie myself
to a man who will have control over everything I do.
Then an attractive man shows me a bit of interest and
I'm falling over myself to change my mind.'

'Milton's different,' Caroline said slowly. 'He
wouldn't control you, he wouldn't want to. If you wished
to paint, he wouldn't even see it as his place to approve
or disapprove. He's a decent man. I didn't know him
with his first wife, but Heydon tells me theirs was a
partnership.'

Henrietta nodded. It was perhaps why she had so
readily dismissed the concern of being controlled by
her husband. Many men would feel it their place to con-

trol what their wife got up to, but Milton would be supportive whatever she decided.

'He's too good.' She sighed, squeezing her eyes shut for a moment.

'Not too good. Just what you deserve.'

'But I'm not what he wants.'

'Nonsense. He's just scared. Understandably.'

'I don't want to force anything.'

'Then don't. Either it will happen or it won't. All you can do is to be open to it if it does.' Caroline smiled. 'It puts his offer to accompany you to London in a slightly different light.'

'How do you mean?'

'It would give you two some time together. Cooped up in a carriage with nothing else to do but be with one another. I think perhaps I will need James to stay here with me after all.'

The idea of days spent in Milton's company, just the two of them, left Henrietta feeling equal parts excited and apprehensive. Caroline was right, there was no way to force the matter. Either Milton would realise he cared for her and put his misgivings aside, or his desire to protect his heart from any more hurt would be too much to overcome.

'I've got the perfect dress for travelling,' Caroline mused, walking over to her large wardrobe. 'It would complement your colouring perfectly.' She took out a beautiful deep green dress with darker and lighter panels in the heavy skirt. Henrietta got up and fingered the material, eyeing up the deep neckline and pulled-in waist. It would leave little to the imagination.

'I thought you said not to force the matter.'

'This isn't force, this is making sure he has all the right information to make the correct decision.'

'It's lovely, but I can't wear one of your finest dresses. You've lent me so many already.'

'You know I don't mind you borrowing anything, Henrietta. And this is for a very good cause.'

It *was* a beautiful dress and the thick material would keep her warm on the journey.


'Are you sure you don't want me to accompany them?' Thomas heard Heydon mutter to his wife.

Caroline shook her head serenely, murmuring something about Henrietta being in safe hands. Thomas glanced at her guiltily. If only Caroline knew how wrong she was. Far from safeguarding Henrietta's reputation these last few days, he'd actively sabotaged it, not through malice but a lack of self-control. Now he was setting off in a carriage with her with no real chaperon and a long journey on the muddy roads ahead of them.

'We'll be back in a matter of days.' Henrietta hugged Caroline gently and then turned to Thomas with a serene smile. 'Are you ready?'

He took her hand, helping her up into the carriage and waiting until she was settled on the seat before jumping up himself. They weren't completely alone, with Esther, the young woman who was normally Caroline's lady's maid, accompanying them. She, however, suffered from motion sickness if she sat inside the carriage and so had opted instead to sit up top with the driver, covered in a few layers of blankets to keep warm.

Still, even with the veneer of respectability it meant

he and Henrietta would be alone in the carriage for the entire journey with no one to witness what went on.

Silently he reprimanded himself. *Nothing* untoward was going to happen. He was a gentleman and surely he had enough self-control not to ravage Henrietta while cooped up together for a few hours.

Carefully he settled into his seat, not looking up until he was sure Henrietta was focused out of the window, waving to Harry who was demanding he be allowed to travel, too.

Thomas glanced up, feeling his body tighten as his eyes swept over the beautiful green dress she'd chosen for the journey, the dress that seemed to accentuate every curve of her body. She had a cloak thrown over her shoulders to keep her warm, but at present it was not pulled together at the front, giving him the perfect view.

Resolutely he turned away, joining Henrietta in looking out the small window as the carriage pulled away. He fancied he saw a gleam in Caroline's eye as she waved goodbye, but couldn't work out what the secret smile meant.

'Thank you for accompanying me,' Henrietta said as she sat back in her seat, pulling her cloak around her. 'I know it isn't how you hoped to be spending your time.'

He gave a soft smile. She wasn't wrong. When he'd planned this escape to Kent it had been with the intention of taking some time to consider his life, his wants, his plans. Deciding what sort of man he wanted to be going forward, what he was going to focus his time and energies on now he had decided he wasn't going to be the husband and father he had always hoped he would be.

In truth, he'd hardly given the matter any consideration. His thoughts had been consumed by Henrietta. He had either been with her or thinking about her, or at night having very vivid dreams about her. Not once had he put his mind to deciding what to do with his life, instead trying to work out ways to get close to Henrietta and then cursing himself for his weakness.

She picked up a book from the small pile she'd placed beside her, flipping to a marked page about halfway through. Sensible girl, bringing something to occupy her mind. He didn't have anything and would spend the journey resolutely trying not to look at the woman across from him.

'Would you care for a book?' Henrietta asked after a few minutes, indicating the two left in the pile on the seat beside her.

'What are you reading?'

'An account on the many expeditions of the African Association in their quest to chart Africa. I have to say their success rate has never been very high.'

'Ah, John Ledyard and the like. I remember learning a little about them in school.'

Henrietta leaned forward and turned the book around, showing him an illustration of a river winding its way through dusty banks.

'Fascinating, don't you think? What I wouldn't give to see how the people native to that part of the world live.' She'd acquired a dreamy, faraway look in her eyes and he instinctively knew she was thinking about painting.

'You'd like to paint them?'

'I'd like to capture how they live, what their everyday life is like, what hopes and dreams they have. *That* would make quite an exhibition.'

He sat back in his seat, his knees brushing against hers in the confined space and making them both jump apart guiltily.

'I've been thinking about that.'

She looked at him with confusion. 'You've been thinking about painting the people of Africa?'

'No. I've been thinking about exhibitions. Art exhibitions.'

She looked at him with guarded interest, as if she wouldn't allow herself to get too invested in what he was saying before she knew the whole of it.

'What about them?'

'You should do one.'

She laughed and he noted the slight bitter tone. 'Don't be ridiculous. There's my reputation to consider, remember.'

'You shouldn't marry someone who won't support your passions. So any man put off by your painting isn't the right husband for you.'

'I'm not marrying anyone.'

Thomas brushed away her comment and ploughed on. 'And the same can be said for the rest of society. Any person who judges you to be inferior just because you're different, instead of celebrating your talent, well, then do you really need them in your life?'

'It's easy to think like that as a wealthy titled man. You're expected to break the rules, society indulges you.'

'Perhaps they would indulge you, too.'

'Hardly.'

'You're a beautiful young woman, Henrietta, well

connected in life and with great talent.' He thought of the painting of Henrietta's hanging in the long gallery at Hailsham Hall. It wasn't merely good, it was incredible, as mesmerising as any painting he'd ever seen in any church or private gallery. 'If you put together an exhibit, then you wouldn't have to hide this massive part of you any longer.'

He saw her bite her lip and wondered if she would confide her fears in him.

'What if people thought my work just mediocre?'

'It wouldn't happen. Everyone has critics, of course, people who would criticise no matter what you produced, but I think it could be very well received.'

She looked at him long and hard, then shook her head wonderingly. 'You're too kind, Milton—has anyone ever told you that before? Too good and too kind.'

'Is that a bad thing?'

'No.' She reached out as if to take his hand and then caught herself. 'It just makes it very hard not to—' Henrietta cut herself off sharply and looked out of the window.

Thomas knew what she was going to say, he could complete the sentence in his head. *It just makes it very hard not to fall for you.* He'd seen how she had been looking at him, felt the way her body responded to his kisses. There was more than pure desire here, there was a deeper connection, one that he was still trying to deny.

They sat in silence for a while, with Henrietta returning to her book and Thomas trying very hard not to spend his whole time staring at her.

## Chapter Fifteen

'If we stop for no more than an hour, my lord, we can be in London by nightfall.' The coachman busied himself with the horses as Milton turned back to help Henrietta down from the carriage.

'Just a quick stop for lunch and then it won't be too much further to London.'

She stretched, arching her neck back. She wasn't a great fan of travelling by carriage, much preferring to ride when she had the option, but with the threat of more snow still a real possibility it had been more prudent to take the carriage. Looking around, she saw the muddy wheels of the carriage and grimaced, another reason horseback would have been foolish—the snow had left the roads in a terrible condition, covered with thick mud making for a bumpy ride in the carriage, but even more dangerous on horseback.

'Shall we see what they have inside?'

It was a regular coaching inn, busy with travellers passing through on their way in and out of London. Her mother might even have paused here the day before on her round trip. They went inside, but were informed all their private dining rooms were occupied.

'I'm ever so sorry, my lord, we've had such a rush on today.' The landlord was wringing his hands at the thought of having to turn an earl away.

'We can sit out here,' Henrietta declared, looking around the dingy bar area. It was clean, at least, although afforded little privacy. There were a few locals sitting at the bar itself and a couple at one of the tables.

Milton surveyed the area and then gave a nod, allowing the landlord to direct them to what he assured them was his finest table.

They didn't wait long for the meal to be set before them, accompanied by two glasses of heavy red wine. Henrietta had just lifted her glass to her lips when she was aware of a group bustling towards them.

'Miss Harvey, what an absolute surprise. I said to Mama that's Miss Harvey sitting out there and I knew I just had to come over.'

'Mrs Wellingbrooke,' Henrietta said, trying not to grit her teeth. Rebecca Wellingbrooke was one of the cruellest young women in society and one of Henrietta's least favourite people to socialise with. She had tried to sabotage Caroline and Heydon's relationship a few years earlier, hoping to snag Heydon for herself. After failing miserably, she had married the very wealthy Mr Wellingbrooke, a man forty years her senior. She had been overheard lamenting that he hadn't yet died and made her a wealthy widow, but her ailing husband at home didn't stop her from making the most of her position in society.

Milton rose to his feet and inclined his head in greeting.

'Mrs Wellingbrooke, you're looking well.'

'How kind of you to notice, Lord Hauxton,' she said, giving him a calculating look and fluttering her long eyelashes. 'Are you travelling together?'

'We have both been staying with Lord and Lady Heydon, it seemed silly to take two carriages back to London,' Henrietta said, trying to make her tone care-free. The last thing she needed was Mrs Wellingbrooke spreading gossip about them.

'Of course. Are Lord and Lady Heydon with you?' She looked around dramatically. It was obvious they weren't, unless they were hiding under the table or in the stables.

'No.'

'So it is just the two of you?'

'Yes.'

'You're right, of course, not to be bothered by what other people think. There is absolutely nothing wrong with travelling in a carriage with a gentleman, especially when the whole world knows you would be poorly matched. No need to worry about scandal.'

'Indeed,' Milton said stiffly, sitting back down and taking a mouthful of wine. 'How is your husband, Mrs Wellingbrooke?'

'Dear Mr Wellingbrooke is suffering with his gout, but he tells me I'm such a comfort to him I quite make him forget his pains.'

'You must be eager to get back to him, then?'

'Indeed.' Mrs Wellingbrooke's face hardened a little at the veiled dismissal. 'Will we be seeing you at any of the Christmas balls, Miss Harvey? Or have you decided to eschew them this Season?'

'Why would I eschew them?' Henrietta asked, trying to keep her calm. She didn't know why some people had to be quite so horrible all the time. It wasn't as though she'd ever done anything to Mrs Wellingbrooke to make her dislike her.

'Oh, I must have heard from someone that you were stepping back this Season, having a little break from the relentless cycle of balls and parties that we put ourselves through in the quest to find a husband. Is it three years you've been out in society now?'

'Yes.'

'Well, never mind, Miss Harvey, there's someone out there for everyone.'

With a sickly sweet smile Mrs Wellingbrooke bade them farewell and glided away, leaving Henrietta and Milton sitting in silence until she was safely out of the door.

'What an awful woman,' Milton said, picking up his glass and taking a large gulp of wine as if needing to fortify himself after the encounter.

'She's like a caricature of all the scheming, nasty society women.'

'Didn't she have her sights set on Heydon at one point?'

'Indeed. When he was just realising how he felt about Caroline. She tried to sabotage their relationship.'

'Her marriage is hardly the coup of the century.'

'To Mr Wellingbrooke? No, I suppose not. He is awfully rich, of course, but very old. And I know she was hoping to marry someone with a title.'

Henrietta fell silent, trying to work out why Mrs Wellingbrooke's words had hurt so much. Henrietta *had* been out three Seasons without getting married, but that had been her choice rather than a lack of interest. She shouldn't care what society thought of her and, if she were ever to take Milton's advice and start painting openly, even perhaps exhibiting her art, she would have to learn to ignore all the nasty, insinuating comments from people like Rebecca Wellingbrooke.

'She is a horrible woman,' Henrietta said slowly, 'and hardly anyone actually likes her, but people do listen to what she says.'

Milton watched her attentively as she paused, trying to put into words the thoughts in her head.

'I know I shouldn't care, that I should be able to ignore the gossip and cutting remarks. If you want to be even slightly different, then you have to expect it.'

'But you can't?'

'It still hurts. I might not want to marry, but having someone insinuate that you're a failure because of it, even if deep down you know they're wrong, well, that hurts.' She shook her head. 'Perhaps I'm shallow, caring so much what other people think.'

'You're not shallow.' Milton's voice was low and intense and she felt a delicious shiver as he placed his hand on the table next to hers so his fingers brushed against her skin. 'Never think that.'

'I'd love to put on an exhibition, to paint what I want to paint and do it openly. To be able to say to everyone I socialise with *this is me, this is what I do*, and not care if they approve or not.'

'Not many people in this world can. We all care in some way what others think of us.'

'It's suffocating. If I didn't care how things looked,

I could have spent the last few years painting openly, not sneaking off to snatch a few hours here and there.'

To her surprise he took her hand then, grasping her fingers in his on top of the table for anyone to see. He squeezed gently, waiting for her to look at him before speaking. 'You're young, Henrietta, still finding your place in the world. You have years ahead of you to become the woman you wish to be.'

For a moment Henrietta fell silent as she contemplated his words.

'The woman I wish to be,' she murmured. An artist, open about her work and proud, but also a wife, a mother. She wanted it all. And she wanted it with this man.

Shifting slightly in her seat, she felt her knees brush against Milton's, sending a jolt of energy through her body. She knew he felt it, too, by the slight stiffening of his posture and widening of his eyes.

They were interrupted by the landlord coming to clear their plates, Milton discreetly slipping his hand away from hers without drawing any attention to it. As the landlord walked away Henrietta edged a little closer to Milton. Perhaps he was right, she was still young and had the chance to make herself into the person she wished to be. And right now she wished to be the woman he desired, the woman he couldn't stop thinking about.

Their legs brushed together again and this time Henrietta didn't make any effort to move away, instead looking up at Milton and holding his gaze.

'What sort of woman do you think I should strive to be, Milton?' she asked, her voice low.

It was a few seconds before he answered, his voice barely more than a whisper. 'You might doubt yourself, but I think you're almost perfect just as you are.'

'Almost perfect?'

'You wouldn't want to be entirely perfect. That would be dull.'

'I definitely don't want to be dull.'

'Henrietta…' he said, but seemed to think better of saying any more. She watched him for a moment and then smothered a sigh. She was trying to rush things, to force something that couldn't be forced. With a bright smile she stood and stretched, breaking the connection between them.

'We should get going, the coachman said we would reach London by nightfall if we push on.'

Milton motioned for her to go on ahead while he paid. She was already sitting in the carriage by the time he came out, her book in her hand. She might not be able to focus on the words, but at least it provided some distraction from the man across from her.

## *Chapter Sixteen*

Keeping completely still, Thomas risked a glance down at Henrietta as she was slumped beside him. The journey had become a nightmare after lunch, with the roads so muddy they had been stuck behind two carriages that had lost their wheels and needed lifting out of the road. Far from reaching London by nightfall, they were still only on the outskirts and it was well into the evening. After a brief discussion with the coachman they had agreed to push on with the journey, but the carriage was feeling increasingly cramped and Thomas longed to stretch his legs.

About an hour ago Henrietta had begun to nod off, her head bobbing up and down as she kept almost falling asleep. After a few amused minutes of watching her, he'd offered his shoulder and Henrietta had quickly accepted.

Now he was sat in the small carriage with Henrietta's body pressed against his, her head a reassuring weight on his shoulder. He was so tempted to lean over and place a kiss on her smooth brow, but he knew that was a liberty too far. It would be far too easy to let one kiss lead to another and before he knew it he would be falling for her.

Forcing himself to look out of the window, he tried to work out exactly where they were. He had travelled this journey on multiple occasions, although normally during the daytime. The darkness was disorientating and it was a few minutes before he realised they were closer to his town house than he had first thought.

The plan was for Henrietta to stay at her cousin's London house. Even while Lord and Lady Heydon were in Kent they maintained a skeleton staff in Grosvenor Square. Henrietta had a letter from Caroline asking them to make her up a room for the night. He would drop her off there first and return to his house for a night's sleep, before they went about the business of rescuing her painting tomorrow.

Gently he shook Henrietta awake, knowing she would want a few minutes to collect herself before she had to leave the carriage.

'It should only be five or ten minutes now,' he said, suppressing a smile as she yawned sleepily. She looked adorably disorientated as she woke and for a long while she stayed pressed against him as if enjoying the closeness and warmth.

'Was I asleep long?'

'Perhaps an hour.'

'Thank you for lending me the use of your shoulder.'

'It was my pleasure.'

'What is the plan for—' Henrietta was cut off as the carriage lurched to one side, throwing them both violently to the left. She let out a little involuntary scream which was cut short as her body hit the side of the carriage. It felt as though the movement went on for a long time, but it could only have been a couple of seconds before the carriage settled at its new angle, forty-five degrees to the ground.

'Are you hurt?' He picked her up from the floor of the carriage, steadying her as she clambered back on to the tilted seat.

'No—no.' Henrietta ran her hands over her body as if she couldn't be sure. 'No,' she confirmed after a few seconds. 'Are you?'

He hadn't been thrown in quite the same way as she and, apart from the jolt which had made him tense every muscle, he was unharmed. 'I'm fine.'

Once he was satisfied she was settled back in the seat he pulled himself up and peered out of the window, testing the door of the carriage to see if it would open. With a loud crack it splintered, but with a little force he was able to open it enough they would be able to slip out if needed.

'Are you hurt, my lord?' The coachman's worried voice came from up on top of the carriage.

'No, we're fine. How about you and Esther?' At least inside the carriage they were protected by the framework of wood. The driver or Esther could have easily been thrown clear of the carriage when it lurched.

'Just a little shaken. The wheel's come off.' The coachman appeared at the door, crouching down and peering in, his face white with worry.

'We need to get out.' Thomas turned to Henrietta. 'If I go first, I can help you out if you are able to slip down.'

Henrietta nodded and cautiously he slipped through

the partially open door. The angle of the carriage meant he had to duck and weave a little, but as the carriage hadn't overturned it wasn't too taxing.

As he turned around he saw Henrietta already following him and reached through the gap in the door to pull her out.

For a moment they all just stood there, looking at the carriage. The front left wheel had come off completely and was now lying about twenty feet away where it had rolled to a stop. The horses were standing placidly as if they had hardly noticed the carriage they were pulling had been so badly damaged.

'I'm so sorry, my lord,' the coachman said, his hands running absently over the wreckage of where the wheel once stood. 'We hit a rut and the wheel just splintered.'

'No one is hurt, that is the main thing. What do we need to do with the horses?'

The driver looked around for a moment as if collecting himself. 'We need to unharness them and get them away from the carriage. We're going to need some help. Esther, be a good girl and see if there are any strong lads in that inn across the road who will lend a hand.'

Esther hurried off and immediately the coachman set to work, all the while murmuring to the horses to keep them calm. Thomas stepped up and took the first of the horses once it was unfastened, leading it a little distance away from the rest. It was cold now they were out of the carriage and he had to stamp his feet to try to warm himself.

Within a few minutes Esther had returned with six young men, all eager to earn a few coins in exchange for some heavy lifting. They followed the instructions quickly and within a few minutes the horses had all been unhooked from the harnesses and were being led away in the direction of the Heydons' town house. The carriage had also been shifted to the side of the road, left to be dealt with in the morning. Esther was leading the procession with the driver at the back, supervising the young men who seemed in high spirits.

'That was all sorted rather quickly,' Henrietta said, surveying the wreckage of the coach by the side of the road. A few people had stopped to watch while the horses were being uncoupled, but now the spectacle was over they had moved on, leaving just Thomas and Henrietta in the dark street by themselves.

'The advantage of having a deep purse to draw on.'

'Very true.'

'Come, we should get you settled into your residence for the night.' He offered her his arm, thankful for the slight warmth of her body as she stepped in closer to him. There might not be any snow on the ground in London, but the air temperature was freezing and there was an icy wind blowing.

'Thank you.'

They set off walking, following the route the men and horses must have taken, but already there was no sign of them. The streets were quiet, a testament to the cold conditions—most sensible people were sitting by their fires or tucked up under their blankets to keep out the icy night.

'Have you ever been in an accident like that before?'

Henrietta shook her head. 'Not in a carriage. I was thrown from a horse once when I was younger—I caught myself on the branch of a tree and sustained quite a gash.' Her fingers danced up to her scalp and she indicated an area just in her hairline above the nape of her neck. 'I suppose I was quite lucky there was no more damage. How about you?'

'No. I try not to travel in carriages much as a rule, I don't like the way they make me feel trapped inside. So no carriage accidents for me.'

'Will it be difficult to fix the wheel?'

'I shouldn't think so. It didn't look like there was too much damage to the actual carriage. A new wheel and a little patch-up work on the body of the carriage and it should be fine.'

They walked on in silence for a few minutes, their pace rapid to try to combat the cold, but even though it wasn't the most pleasant of conditions Thomas felt a peculiar lightness to his step. He was walking through London with a pretty and interesting young woman on his arm. The sky was clear and the crescent moon shone brightly and there were even a few stars sparkling in the darkness.

Nights like this were dangerous. They made a man feel invincible, as if he could do anything, risk anything. He had this sudden urge to sweep Henrietta into his arms and kiss her right here in the middle of the street. It would be rash—even though there was no one about, they were in a neighbourhood where someone they knew could easily be passing and would see their indiscretion—but even so he almost shrugged off that concern. For one night he wanted to be carefree, to not worry about what was deemed acceptable by society, to not worry about guarding his heart from any further damage.

'You look deep in thought,' Henrietta said, a small smile on her lips as if he amused her. 'What are you thinking about?'

'Kissing you.' He shouldn't have said it, but the words were out before he could stop them, a testament to the recklessness that was raging inside him.

'Kissing me?'

'More specifically taking you in my arms and kissing you until you forgot who and where you were.'

Her tongue flicked out between her lips and he could tell by the expression in her eyes that it wasn't an unwelcome suggestion.

'I was thinking about the kiss we shared in the snow,' he said quietly. 'And how I would very much like to repeat it.' He smiled at her. 'Although perhaps without the near dip in the icy lake and the soaking clothes from the tumble in the snow.'

'We shouldn't.' She didn't sound very convincing and her words were betrayed by the spark of desire in her eyes.

'No, we probably shouldn't. That doesn't stop me from wanting to.'

He placed his free hand over hers where it rested in the crook of his elbow and slowed his pace, feeling the wonderful anticipation of the build up to the inevitable kiss. They would stop and turn to one another and then slowly he would pull her in towards him.

'Don't look round,' a low voice came out of the darkness. 'And no sudden movements or I'll slip this knife between your ribs.'

In surprise Thomas glanced down, feeling rather than seeing the point of the blade through his clothes.

He'd been so preoccupied with his desire he had lost his caution and his wits. They might be in a respectable part of London, but it was still a London street at night, still a hunting ground for the criminal and immoral.

'Do exactly as I say and no one need get hurt.' The man had a deep voice and an accent Thomas couldn't quite place.

Next to him he could see Henrietta shifting slightly and suddenly he knew she was going to do something rash. It would be entirely in character, she would have the opinion that a criminal must not be allowed to triumph, even if it meant putting her life in danger. With a firm hand he gripped her arm and tried to give her a warning look, but she was a little preoccupied with straining round to try to catch a glimpse of their assailant.

'I said don't look round,' the man growled, transferring the point of the knife to poke into Henrietta's back.

'Steady. She's just nervous, nothing more. Tell us what you want.'

'Your money and any trinkets this pretty little lady is wearing. Rings, necklaces, I'll have them all.'

'No, you will—' Henrietta said.

'Hush, darling, it is only money after all,' he said, adopting his most supercilious tone. Henrietta looked at him as though he had gone mad, but after a moment her eyes narrowed ever so slightly. He wanted to appear like the average aristocrat, with too much money and too little physical prowess. That way the footpad would be lulled into a sense of security Thomas could use to his advantage.

'Fine,' she shrilled, beginning to unfasten her coat,

making a great show of it to distract the man standing behind them.

Thomas's eyes flicked down to the knife and he saw the footpad had moved it away from Henrietta a little to allow her to access her jewellery. He watched for a moment, waited for the second the knife wavered in the criminal's hand, then struck out with three fast blows. The first slammed the man's wrist against a wall, hitting with such a force the knife clattered to the ground and Thomas felt some of the bones crack underneath his fingers. The howl that came from the man's mouth sounded otherworldly and pierced through the silent night. The second was a powerful uppercut to the footpad's chin that made his head snap back. The third was a punch to the stomach, eliciting a low groan as the man doubled up and then slid to the floor.

Quickly Thomas kicked the blade away out of the man's reach.

'Henrietta, the knife,' he instructed, glad to see her moving without hesitation to pick up the weapon that was lying a few feet away. She gripped it tightly in both hands, holding it out in front of her.

Slowly the footpad struggled to his feet, eyeing Thomas warily. Without taking his eyes off him, the man spat blood to his left and then began to back away.

Thomas took the knife from Henrietta, making sure the footpad saw him do so, and watched until the criminal disappeared into the darkness.

'We need to move,' he said, tucking the knife away and taking Henrietta by both arms. He ran his eyes over her, checking she wasn't hurt, and then with a satisfied nod took her hand and began to pull her along.

'Has he gone?' He heard the slight tremble in her voice and nodded quickly to reassure her. Henrietta had been brave, almost foolishly so, while the footpad was threatening them, but as often happened the enormity of the situation had only dawned on her now the main risk of danger had passed.

'For now. I think it's likely he's run away entirely, gone somewhere to lick his wounds, but there is a chance he could be hanging around, waiting for us to let our guard down.'

She glanced uneasily over her shoulder.

'My house is only a few streets away. We'll head there.'

They moved quickly, almost running through the streets. If he had been alone, Thomas probably wouldn't have worried too much. The likelihood of the footpad returning was low, but with Henrietta in tow he wasn't happy about even the slightest risk. Now he just wanted to get her safely behind a locked door.

It took them just under ten minutes to get to Thomas's house and he gave an audible sigh of relief as they hurried up the steps to the front door. The house was dark, but as he rapped on the door there was the glimmer of candlelight almost immediately.

His butler opened the door, the surprise registering on his face as he realised his master was back unexpectedly.

'Lord Hauxton, we were not expecting you for another couple of weeks.'

'It's a quick visit,' he said, ushering Henrietta inside. He felt himself relaxing as she stepped over the threshold into the safety of the house. While she started to take off her coat he stood on the steps and surveyed the street. It didn't look as though they had been followed by the footpad, but Thomas would instruct the servants to keep a close eye on the people passing by the house the next few days. 'Could you arrange for some supper to be served, just something light we can take in my study. And make sure the fires are lit, I feel chilled to the bone.'

'Of course, my lord.'

Thomas ushered Henrietta through to his study. It was his favourite room in the house, cosy and warm in the winter with two comfortable armchairs that could be pulled close to the fire. For a few minutes there was a bustle of activity around them, with a couple of the housemaids dashing in and out lighting the fire and bringing candles to illuminate the room. Henrietta stood by the fire at first, arms outstretched, curling her fingers as if trying to capture the warmth. He sat in one of the armchairs watching her, waiting for them to be alone to speak.

'Brandy?' He remembered the night when they had first drunk brandy together, when he had first caught a glimpse of the true Henrietta under the poised façade of a debutante.

She nodded, gratefully accepting a glass once he'd poured and taking a long sip. The brandy was delicious and just what was needed. Even after just the first mouthful he could feel it warming him from the inside.

Once a light supper of bread and cheese and some cold meats had been brought in the servants quietly closed the door and left them alone. For a moment Henrietta remained silent, then she let out a soft exhalation. He could see the tension slowly start to seep from her shoulders and realised she had been shaken by their encounter with the footpad.

'You're safe now,' he said quietly, coming to crouch down in front of her, taking one of her hands in his own.

'You must think me foolish.'

'Not at all. It was an ordeal and you coped tremendously well. Not many women would have remained calm when threatened by a knife like that.' He smiled at the memory of her indignation at having the knife pressed against her ribs. It was unclear what made some people respond with such foolish bravery when threatened, but Henrietta had done just that.

Gently he stroked her hand, knowing he should move away. The situation was far too dangerous, far too tempting. They were alone in his study, unlikely to be disturbed with only a few of his servants in the house. It would be so easy to get carried away in the moment.

With a great effort he stood and stepped away, busying himself with readying a couple of plates of supper for them. When he glanced round Henrietta was staring off into the distance. As he watched her he knew he wouldn't be able to deliver her to the Heydons' town house and then just abandon her, not when she was clearly so shaken. Pushing the thought from his mind, he resolved to eat first and plan later—everything felt easier on a full stomach.

## Chapter Seventeen

Henrietta forced some of the bread and cheese down her, knowing she would wake grumpy and starving in the morning if she didn't, but she ate the bare minimum to sustain her. It wasn't that the food was unappetising—the bread was deliciously crusty and the cheese tasty—she just had a nauseous feeling in her belly that she couldn't seem to settle.

'Have you ever been attacked like that before?'

Milton looked up in surprise as if he'd half forgotten she was there. 'Not quite like that. I was threatened with a gun by a highwayman a few years ago, but he was scared off by another approaching carriage so I didn't have to exert myself.' He shook his head ruefully at the memory. 'And I have been pickpocketed twice, once in London and once in Paris.'

'I've never been pickpocketed or threatened like that before today.'

'Good. It isn't a pleasant experience. Once is more than enough.'

'It's not as though I've always stuck to the more salubrious areas either. When I started sneaking off to paint I socialised a little with some of the other artists and they took me to some questionable places. Even there I never fell victim to anything.'

'There are a fair number of criminals in London, but many of them stay around what they know, the places familiar to them.'

'Do you think he followed us here?'

'No, but I have alerted the servants to be vigilant.'

She paused, feeling the hammering of her heart in her chest, then looked across at him. Milton looked relaxed and comfortable reclining in his armchair, so relaxed he was starting to put her at ease.

'I don't want to go,' she said quietly. 'I don't want to go to Heydon and Caroline's town house. I don't want to be alone.'

For a moment he studied her. 'If you're sure…'

'No one even knows we're in London, not one apart from a few servants. What are the chances anyone will find out?'

'Very low.'

'I would feel safer here with you.'

'Then I agree, you should stay here…' He paused for just a moment longer than was natural. 'I will ask the servants to ready one of the guest rooms.'

She nodded, staring into the fire. It was probably inadvisable, staying in the same house as Milton—if anyone found out, the scandal would be of immense proportions. Gentleman that he was, Milton would probably propose, despite his protestations that he would not ever marry again. She felt a flush of concern. She wanted him, but not under those circumstances.

Quietly she reassured herself. No one would find out. Milton's servants were hardly likely to tell anyone and Heydon's were discreet. Tomorrow she would send for Caroline's lady's maid, Esther, and ask her to attend her here. Then she could leave as if she had just been paying a call.

Milton disappeared for a few minutes, no doubt asking the servants to make her up a guest room.

Henrietta stood. She felt restless, as if she would never be able to settle. When Milton returned to the room she was pacing up and down in front of the fire.

For a moment he regarded her from the doorway and then seemed to make a decision and made straight for her.

She felt the surge of anticipation rush through her body as he stood right in front of her and took her hands by both of his, forcing her to stop her frantic pacing.

'Talk to me.'

She was distracted by the comforting strength of his hands as they enveloped hers and, even though she knew it was dangerous, allowed herself to look up into his eyes. They seemed a deeper, darker green in this light, with the flickering flames glinting off them.

'I feel nervous, as if I'm balanced on the edge of a knife blade.'

'Is it because of what happened this evening?'

She considered, then shook her head from side to side in an indecisive gesture.

'Partly, I suppose. I feel shaken by that, but I think I'm nervous about tomorrow, about potentially running into my mother, about not being able to save my painting.'

'Anything else?'

His hands were cool in hers and she suddenly felt an overwhelming heat rising up inside her.

'Perhaps.'

'Perhaps?'

'I know I shouldn't be staying here.' Her voice was barely more than a whisper. 'I know it is foolish to risk my reputation like this, even if it's unlikely that anyone would ever find out. I know…' She trailed off, unable to put the rest into words.

'What else do you know?' Milton prompted her, his voice low, almost seductive.

'I know it's dangerous to be staying under the same roof when I feel like this.'

'Like what?' He took a step closer to her and now their bodies were almost touching. Milton was still holding both her hands and it felt a wonderfully intimate position.

Henrietta tilted her chin up, distracted by how close his lips were to hers.

'Like I want to kiss you.' She shook her head. 'No, more than that. I want to spend the night with you.'

She saw the fire in his eyes, the way he looked at her as though he wanted to devour her. It made her want him even more. Never before had she felt so attractive, so wanted. It was intoxicating.

'We have to be sensible.' He sounded as though he wanted to be anything but sensible.

'I know.'

'We have to think of the consequences.'

'I know.'

He shook his head ruefully. 'Then why is it so hard?'

Gently he let go of one of her hands and she was convinced he was going to step away. Instead, he raised his fingers to her cheek, sending wonderful shivers down her spine as he trailed them lightly over the soft skin.

'A kiss surely wouldn't be too bad,' Henrietta murmured.

'We've kissed before,' he agreed. 'And the world didn't end.'

The wait seemed an eternity, stretching out in wonderful anticipation as he stepped in a little closer, his hand looping around her waist and resting in the small of her back. All the time she couldn't tear her eyes from his and then he ever so gently brushed a kiss on her lips.

'The world's still here.'

'So it is.' She could hear the smile in his voice and then all rational thought was lost as he kissed her again. Henrietta felt as though they were rising away from the ground, as if it were just she and Milton and nothing else solid or substantial in the world.

She wanted this moment never to end and almost melted into Milton as he pulled her even closer to him. Henrietta let go of the little voice that was telling her she was being foolish, and just let herself enjoy the moment. Too soon she would have to return to reality, return to her real life—right now she was going to appreciate every single second.

'We need to stop,' Milton said, pulling away only a fraction. She could still taste him on her lips, still feel his breath on her skin.

'No,' she said, more decisively than she thought possible. 'We don't.'

He leaned back a little further, searching her face

for a sign that she was sure, that she wasn't about to regret anything.

Then with a groan he kissed her again, his hands sliding down her back and over her body, pulling her to him until it was as though they were just one person.

Milton broke away slightly, bending and kissing her neck, her collarbone, the bare skin of her chest. She wanted him to touch her where no one else had ever touched her, to run his fingers over every single inch of her body.

With a little gasp of surprise she stiffened slightly as he began to push down the neckline of her dress. He must have noticed, as he stopped, looking up at her instead.

'Don't stop,' she whispered. It was further than she'd ever allowed herself to go, but it felt completely right, completely natural.

Milton spun her round, lifting the strands of hair that had pulled loose and kissing the nape of her neck. She arched backwards, closing her eyes as he expertly began unlacing her dress. The fastenings that often took her maid ten minutes to loosen were undone in a matter of seconds and she shivered slightly as the cool air hit her skin. Milton took his time, trailing his lips down the length of her back, murmuring how beautiful she was, how perfect.

When he reached the dimples at the base of her spine he straightened, spinning her round and looking into her eyes, then pushed the material from her shoulders. It fell, pooling around her feet, so she was only clad in a thin chemise and petticoats. Again he made short work of these and for a moment she wondered how many women he must have undressed to make him so rapid. The thought was pushed from her mind when he took a little step back, opening the space between them, and shook his head with a smile on his face as he looked at her.

'You don't know how many times I've imagined you like this. After that first night...' He trailed off.

Henrietta knew she should feel self-conscious, knew she should probably be trying to cover herself with something, but it felt natural to have his eyes on hers, natural to stand there with nothing on.

'You're beautiful. More than beautiful. Perfect.'

Over the years since her debut she had been complimented before, but it had always seemed empty, as if it were rote or routine, what the gentlemen were expected to say. Milton was the first man she had ever believed, the first man who she felt truly saw her and thought what he saw was beautiful.

'You're still dressed,' she said, pulling at his jacket. He allowed her to strip him of his jacket and waistcoat, but when her fingers began tugging at his shirt he placed his hand over them and stilled her hand.

'If you undress me, I may not be able to stop when I should.'

She frowned. She hadn't really thought where this would all end up. No, that was a lie, she'd imagined it a thousand times, but right now, caught up in the moment, she hadn't stopped to consider the end result. Or the consequences.

Before she could ask him what he meant he was kissing her again, taking her in his arms and slowly easing her down to the floor in front of the fire.

Henrietta felt her body arch and writhe underneath his touch. He trailed his fingers over her arms and shoulders, then dipped his mouth to catch one of her nipples between his lips. She let out a low moan as jolts of pleasure shot through her body and then almost cried out with disappointment as he pulled away. He kissed and nipped and teased every part of her body, all the while building the wonderful anticipation, drawing lower across her abdomen, until she felt his kiss on her most private place.

Henrietta stiffened and Milton reacted by stroking her legs, her abdomen, until once again she relaxed. This time when he lowered his mouth she groaned in pleasure.

Slowly he dipped his fingers inside her, stroking and caressing alongside his kisses, until Henrietta felt a wonderful tension building inside her. Faster and faster he began to move, seeming to sense the building sensations until she cried out in pleasure, the waves of heat pulsing through her body.

For a long moment Henrietta couldn't move. She lay in front of the roaring fire with her eyes closed, her head lolling to one side.

Milton lay down beside her, resting a hand on her hip and tracing lazy circles on the soft skin.

'You don't know how hard I am finding it to stop,' he said, a rueful smile on his lips.

'To stop?' she asked, forcing her eyes to open.

'I know I have to, but you make it so hard. I don't think I've ever wanted anyone the way I want you.'

Henrietta rolled over on to her side so she was facing Milton, taking a moment to run her eyes over his smooth features, his strong jaw and the bewitching green of his eyes.

'Does it make a difference?'

He raised an eyebrow in question.

'Well, you say we have to stop. But is *that* so much worse, so much more, than what we've done already?'

He didn't answer for a minute as if really considering the question.

'If we make love, we will have to marry and, as much as I care for you, Henrietta, I can't do that.'

'Why?'

'I just...'

She shook her head. 'No, not why can't you marry, but why would you have to marry me if we make love?'

'You might get pregnant.'

'Unlikely, not from just being together once.'

'It's not just that...' He shook his head, looking away for a moment. 'I would *have* to marry you. It's just the way things are.'

She tried not to acknowledge the shrivelling hope that was dying inside her. Even though she knew he would never marry, even though she even half understood his reasons why, she still secretly had hoped. It had been the kind of hope she hadn't even acknowledged to herself, but it was hope all the same.

Suddenly feeling very exposed, she started to gather her clothes to her. Milton caught her wrist.

'I'm sorry,' he said when she finally looked at him. 'I know we shouldn't have gone so far.'

'There's nothing to be sorry for. I don't regret anything—nothing at all.' She paused, wondering whether to say more. 'I don't expect anything from you, Milton. You don't have to worry about me making you feel guilty, pushing you to marry me. I understand where we stand.'

'I know.'

She stood, stepping into her dress without bothering with her chemise and petticoats. Suddenly she had the overwhelming urge to cry and she definitely didn't want to do it in Milton's company.

'Let me help you,' he said, springing to his feet and helping her pull her dress up. He wasn't anywhere as quick securing the fastenings as he was at undoing them, but in a few minutes Henrietta felt dressed enough to brave a dash upstairs to find her bedroom.

'Which room is mine?'

'I can show you up?'

'I'm fine. Just tell me which one it is.'

'The second door on the left at the top of the stairs.'

'Thank you.'

Thankfully she didn't run into any of the servants while dashing through the house clutching her petticoats. Once she was in the bedroom, she locked the door behind her and then rested her head against the wood panelling. Her breath was coming in fast gasps and she was trying hard to keep control of herself.

'It doesn't mean anything,' she whispered to herself, repeating it as if it were a mantra. 'It doesn't mean anything.'

It was the truth—to Milton it didn't mean anything, not really. She knew he cared for her, he'd said as much. It wasn't just desire on his part, but that didn't really matter. Even after everything they'd shared downstairs he'd held some of himself back from her, refused to let go completely and abandon himself to the moment.

Slowly she moved away from the door and started to unfasten her dress. It was difficult to untie it all by herself, but she didn't want one of Milton's servants helping her. After a few minutes she stepped out of the dress and placed it neatly hanging over the back of the chair. The room was warm, but with nothing on she still shivered and quickly pulled her chemise over her head.

Taking the candle from the little dressing table, she went over to the bed and placed it on the table. Then she climbed under the covers and blew it out.

The darkness was almost overwhelming and Henrietta wriggled further under the covers. As she closed her eyes she thought back to the moments in Milton's study, the way she'd felt when he'd kissed her, when he'd laid her down in front of the fire. She hadn't realised then that he meant to give her pleasure, but take none in return.

'Stubborn man,' she muttered. It was no different what they had done. If anyone found out she had even spent a chaste night in his house her reputation was ruined—once he'd begun undressing her all pretence of respectability was lost.

Henrietta closed her eyes, knowing full well she wasn't going to be able to sleep, and tried not to imagine how it would feel to have the weight of Milton's body on top of hers.

## Chapter Eighteen

Pacing backwards and forward, Thomas threw back the glass and finished the brandy with a grimace. It was no use, he would have to drink the whole bottle to make him forget how Henrietta had felt underneath him, how soft her skin, how sweet she had tasted.

Not that he wanted to forget. Those few minutes in his study would stay with him for ever, taunting him, but also reminding him he was alive. Ever since meeting Henrietta it had felt as though he were slowly awakening from a long sleep. He realised that after the events of the last few years he'd closed in on himself a little, isolating from the world and trying to protect himself from any more heartache.

It had been necessary at the time, but now he was realising he needed to build a future for himself.

For an instant he saw Henrietta smiling up at him from the bed sheets and he had to quickly banish the idea. He knew if he married her they would be happy. It would be hard not to be happy with Henrietta by his

side, but he just couldn't risk it. That happiness was
what could make losing her even more painful.

Slowly he undressed, trying not to think of what
Henrietta was doing now. She was only a few feet away,
albeit through the thick wall dividing the bedrooms.

Slipping into bed, he wondered if he had made a
mistake. She had looked so disappointed when he'd
stepped away, when he'd told her they couldn't do any
more than they had already. He knew she wasn't experienced, knew she was an innocent when it came to men,
but she had still been willing to give herself to him.

'You're a fool,' he muttered as he blew out his candle.
He would curse his scruples for years to come.

It had taken Thomas a long time to fall asleep and
even then he had slept fitfully, so he was only half doz-
ing when he heard the door to his room open and soft
footsteps crossing the floor.

'Henrietta?' he whispered, knowing it could only
be she. The maids might come in after dawn to set the
fire, but they wouldn't be creeping round in the middle of the night.

'I couldn't sleep,' she said, her voice coming out of
the darkness.

Thomas was about to reply when he felt the edge of
the bedcovers lift and her slip into bed beside him. She
was warm and soft as she moved in closer to him and
for a moment he was so stunned he couldn't move. He
wondered if he were still asleep, but he knew if he were
dreaming she would have come to him naked.

'What are you doing, Henrietta?'

'I couldn't sleep,' she repeated. 'I kept thinking of

you.' Her body pressed up against his and he felt rational thought beginning to slide away. Frantically he tried to keep hold of it.

'And you thought you'd come and see if I were awake?'

'Exactly. I was lying there thinking about earlier, about what I should have said to you, and I realised I have enough regrets in my life. I don't want to add another one to them.'

'You regret something?' It was hard to follow her train of thought while her breasts were pressed against him, her arm slung possessively across his abdomen.

'I regret not telling you how I feel and what I want.'

'How do you feel?' His body was screaming for him to ask her what she wanted, because he was pretty certain he wanted the same thing, but he had to make sure she wasn't going to declare her love for him and tell him she hoped one day he would change his mind about marriage.

'I've never felt this way about anyone before,' Henrietta said quietly, her breath tickling his neck. 'Whenever you walk into a room I can't think of anything but you. It's distracting. I didn't know you could feel attraction like this, desire like this.'

He knew he should be relieved that she was talking about the purely physical, but he felt a small pang of disappointment. Quickly he pushed it away, not wanting to analyse what it meant.

In the darkness she wriggled next to him and he felt a fresh bolt of desire coursing through his body. Gently she touched his face, running her fingers over the coarse stubble from the day.

'I understand why you don't want to marry, honestly I do. I can't imagine losing so many people you love and I can understand feeling the need to protect yourself against any more loss.' She paused for a second and then pushed on quickly before he had chance to reply. 'I'm not asking for marriage from you, Milton, I would never do anything to make you unhappy, but we're here together now. If anyone finds out I spent the night in your house, my reputation will be ruined whether we locked ourselves in separate wings or spent the night in drunken debauchery.'

She wasn't wrong. Gossip and scandal were a strange thing, caring nothing for facts and pulling only the most sensational to the attention of society.

'The way I see it either somehow society will find out I've been here or they won't. If they do, it will be assumed that you have taken my innocence and I will be damaged goods. If they don't…well, then there is nothing to worry about.'

'We will be careful tomorrow and my servants are discreet.'

'Exactly. So I was lying in bed wondering why, when we're already under the same roof, we're denying ourselves what we really want.'

He opened his mouth to start explaining what he had said earlier, but before he could get anything out she kissed him, her lips soft and sweet and pulling every rational thought from his head.

'You don't have to marry me,' she said again as she pulled away slightly. 'I want this, you want this. I don't want to think about anything but tonight.'

He knew there was no resisting her, the words were

already burrowing into his brain and taking hold. The idea of just thinking of tonight, of what they both wanted, was intoxicating. It had been a long time since he last acted rashly, doing what he wanted instead of what he knew was right, but tonight he was going to do just that.

In the darkness he ran a hand over Henrietta's hip, bunching the cotton of her chemise and exposing the skin underneath. Where he could not see anything it was as if his other senses were heightened. He fancied he could hear the whisper of fabric as it brushed against her skin, feel even the lightest of touches as her hands skimmed over his back.

Seeking out her lips in the darkness, Thomas kissed her again, revelling in how sweet she tasted and how soft her lips felt. Taking the hem of her chemise, he tugged it up, breaking away from Henrietta for just a second to lift it over her head, and then there was nothing between their bodies.

Thomas often slept naked in bed, preferring the feeling of freedom over the restrictive bedclothes available. Tonight when he'd slipped between the sheets he hadn't even imagined he would be sharing his bed, but his nakedness did mean Henrietta's touch was already driving him wild.

The darkness seemed to embolden her and she ran her fingers over his torso, his abdomen, circling out and over his hips and on to his legs. He mimicked her movements, teasing with his touch and feeling her body instinctively press in closer to his.

'I couldn't stop thinking about you,' Henrietta

whispered as he broke away and rolled her over on to her back.

'Good.' Under the sheets he manoeuvred himself so he was on top of her, feeling the press of her hips as she silently urged him not to stop. He wanted her badly, but knew this was their one night together, his one chance to enjoy every inch of Henrietta's body.

He did just that, running his lips over her skin, making her writhe and buck beneath him until she was begging him for more. Only then did he position himself over her and gently press forward.

Henrietta gasped and stiffened, but slowly her body relaxed and her hips began to rock underneath his. He tried to keep his movements slow and measured, wanting to draw it out for as long as possible, wanting it to last for ever, but it was impossible. His desire took over and their bodies came together faster and faster until Henrietta cried out and he felt himself stiffen as the waves of pleasure engulfed him.

For a long moment he couldn't move, all he was aware of was the sound of his blood thumping in his ears and the ragged quality to his breathing, but as he slowly began to recover he moved off Henrietta, lying down next to her. She curled up next to him, placing her head on the spot where his chest met his shoulder.

They lay in the darkness, neither of them speaking, for a few minutes. Next to him Henrietta's breathing was slow and even and he wondered if she had fallen asleep, but eventually she wriggled a little and flung an arm across his chest.

'Is it always like that?'

'No.' Over the years he'd made love to plenty of

women, but never had he felt such intense passion, such all-encompassing desire.

'Can I stay with you tonight?'

He couldn't imagine letting her go at all so he squeezed her a little tighter in answer.

'Let me lock the door, then we won't be surprised in the morning.'

It was a struggle to get up out of his warm bed and move away from Henrietta, but he forced himself to feel his way over to the door and turn the lock. He moved quickly back to bed, pulling Henrietta on to his chest as she had been before and dropping a kiss on her hair.

## Chapter Nineteen

Henrietta had half expected to be disorientated when she woke, but she had slept deeply and peacefully and came around slowly, so by the time she'd opened her eyes she remembered the events from the night before.

Glancing over to the sleeping form in the bed next to her, she had to suppress the urge to trace her fingers over his features. Milton was sleeping soundly, a little half-smile on his lips. The frown lines, so often a feature when he was awake, were smoothed away and he looked younger and more carefree.

Carefully she wriggled in closer and placed a gentle kiss on his lips.

Henrietta had an image of waking up to him every morning, of spending lazy days in bed together, emerging only when absolutely necessary. Quickly she tried to push the image away, repeating to herself it was just not meant to be.

'You look very serious,' Milton murmured as he opened his eyes.

She felt serious. Through the crack in the curtains

she could see the pale dawn light beginning to filter through and she knew their time together was drawing to a close. She had promised him a night of pleasure with no consequences, but all she wanted to do was wrap herself around him and beg him to let her stay. It wasn't dignified and it wasn't fair to either of them.

'I should probably go back to my bed,' she said as she sat up.

Milton's arm moved quickly, pulling her back down on to the pillow next to him.

'There's no rush. No one is looking for you, no one is expecting you.'

'Your servants…'

'Know better than to disturb a guest at this hour. A few more minutes won't hurt.'

Even though she knew it was a bad idea she allowed herself to be enveloped by the warmth of the bed and the caress of the man lying next to her. Every moment she spent here with Milton was another moment her mind was building up this sense of false hope. She knew he had nothing more than this morning in his mind when he pulled her back under the sheets; he was just thinking of the pleasure they could give each other before they had to get up and pretend the last few hours had never happened.

Propping himself up on his elbow, Milton kissed her between her eyebrows. 'You're frowning.'

'I don't want this to be over,' she said quietly.

'It's not over yet.' He kissed her, wiping all rational thought, all doubt from her mind. It wasn't hard to suc-cumb to him even though she knew it was likely setting herself up for an even harsher heartbreak in the long run.

Milton snaked a hand behind her back, stroking her smooth skin, every caress making her forget her doubts a little more. He was right, it wasn't over yet. Even one more minute was worth staying for.

Deciding she would just abandon herself to the moment and regain her rational self later, she pressed her body against Milton's. He lifted her hips and she swung herself upright so she was straddling him. Henrietta knew she should feel self-conscious with his eyes on her body, but instead she felt powerful, beautiful.

Milton pressed up into her and Henrietta slowly lowered herself down, feeling as if they fitted perfectly as their bodies came together. His hands gripped her hips, but with a grin she pushed them off, taking control of the speed she moved at.

Instead Milton reached up, playing with her breasts and sending jolts of pleasure through her, making her buck her hips faster and faster.

She flicked her hair to one side, feeling the moisture starting to drip down her neck as she moved faster and faster. All too soon she felt the tightening inside her, followed by wave after wave of heat gushing through her. Milton stiffened underneath her, letting out a low groan and holding on to her hips for a long moment.

After a minute Henrietta manoeuvred herself off and hovered near the edge of the bed. She should clean herself up and dash back to her own room, but when Milton caught her gently by the arm and pulled her back under the covers she wasn't strong enough to resist. His arms were just too welcoming, the warm bed too appealing.

\* \* \*

She must have dozed for the sun was much brighter through the chink in the curtains when she awoke. Milton was awake, tracing a finger over the soft skin of her upper arm.

'What is the plan for today?' he asked when she moved against him, pulling the covers up to shield her nakedness.

'Go to the studio, hope the woman who rents out the rooms is there, go in and get the painting.'

'Then straight back to Kent?'

She nodded. Straight back to Kent. Straight back to reality. She would love to spend another night here at Milton's house, but it was only delaying the inevitable. It would make it harder in the long run if they spent too much time together like this, harder when she had to go back to pretending there was nothing but friendship between them.

'Straight back to Kent,' she said with more resolve than she felt.

Feeling a sudden rush of emotion, a mix of sadness and anger at how unfair everything was, Henrietta wriggled out of Milton's arms and stood, collecting her chemise and throwing it over her head quickly.

'You're going?'

'Yes.' She couldn't say any more, knowing her voice would betray her emotion.

'Henrietta.'

She shook her head, unable to look at him.

'Henrietta, talk to me.'

'I need to get back to my room.'

'Let me walk you.' He stood up and out of the corner of her eye Henrietta couldn't help catching sight of him. He was all hard muscle and smooth lines and for a second she was distracted. Firmly she made herself turn away.

'I can find my way back to my room.'

'Tell me what's wrong.'

She shook her head, walking briskly over to the door, knowing she had to get out of the room within the next ten seconds or she might break down in front of Milton. Her pride wouldn't allow her to do that.

'I will see you for breakfast,' Milton called after her as she left the room.

Quickly Henrietta hurried down the corridor, slipping into her bedroom before any of the servants could catch sight of her. Once inside she turned the lock and collapsed back on to the bed and allowed the sobs to rack her body.

Thomas paced backwards and forward in front of the window in the dining room, spinning on his heel every time there was any little sound that might indicate Henrietta was entering the room. It had been an hour since she'd fled his bedroom, an hour of mulling over every last moment of the night before. He knew he'd been wrong to let her into his bed, but what man would have been strong enough to say no when she was climbing right in next to him? She'd been warm and willing and it had been what he had fantasised about for days.

'You're weak,' he chided himself. A strong man would have taken her by the hand and walked her chastely back to her bedroom. He snorted. No man was that strong.

'Is something funny?' Henrietta asked as she sailed into the room. He studied her, marvelling at the perfection of her appearance. No wonder it had taken her an hour to appear. There wasn't a single hair out of place, a single crease in her dress. She looked as if she had stepped out of a painting. He frowned. It was too perfect and he had the impression she had donned her armour for battle. It wasn't the breastplate and greaves of a knight of yore, but her own version of armour all the same.

She was wearing the same green dress from the day before, a deep moss-green garment that was well fitted around the bodice area and then skimmed out from a high waistline. She looked beautiful in it, poised and regal, and he found himself unable to tear his eyes away.

'Nothing important. Shall we eat?'

A light breakfast had been laid out on the table and now Henrietta had appeared one of the maids had instructions to bring fresh coffee and toast. Thomas pulled out Henrietta's chair, his hand brushing accidentally against her arm as she sat and he had the funny feeling she was going to pull away as if she were burnt. Instead he didn't think she even registered the contact and he slipped into his chair with a heaviness in his chest.

His attempts at small talk were thwarted by Henrietta's monosyllabic answers, so after a few minutes they fell into an uneasy silence. All the time Thomas was cursing himself for letting things get this way between them. He should have known they couldn't have one night of passion and then continue on with their lives as if nothing had happened.

Henrietta might have come to him, willing and eager, but she *had* still been an innocent.

She ate little, picking at her food with a distracted uninterest, then stood to excuse herself after only a few minutes.

'If you have other business to attend to, I can make my way to the studio myself,' she said, not meeting his eye.

'The only reason I came to London was to accompany you.'

She reddened a little and then gave a short, sharp nod. 'Very well. Will you be ready to leave in half an hour?'

'Of course.'

Henrietta nodded again and then swept from the room. Her posture was stiff, her face expressionless, but Thomas fancied he heard a low sob as she fled up the stairs. The sound sent a shard of pain through his heart and he was on his feet before he could stop himself.

He almost rushed after her, but stopped himself. She didn't want to talk to him right now. Perhaps in half an hour, when they were away from the house with the distractions of London around them he might be able to raise the subject.

Slumping back in his chair, he wondered what he would say. What was there to say? Henrietta might protest she didn't want any more from him, she might even believe it, but when it came down to it he knew she cared for him more than she should. After the incredible intimacy of the night before it would be difficult to go back to never touching one another, never sharing their innermost thoughts and feelings. He was finding the prospect depressing and Henrietta wasn't the one with the motivation to stay single.

*You could marry her.* The thought popped unbidden into his brain. It wasn't the first time he'd thought it, although he'd always tried to quickly dismiss it. The idea was just too appealing that if he dwelled on it for too long he might end up doing something he would regret.

He could marry her. It would be marvellous, days spent strolling through the park with her on his arm, discussing estate business, perhaps travelling a little, taking her to the exotic locations she wanted to visit to paint. Then long nights in one another's arms, making love until they fell into an exhausted sleep.

The idea was tempting and for a long time it had been trying to burrow itself into his mind. He knew he would be happy with Henrietta. A life with her, married with children, that was the life he'd always wanted for himself, what he had been searching for over the many years since his first wife's death. If he'd met Henrietta a few years ago, he would have had no hesitation in storming up to her room, throwing open the door and asking her to marry him.

Shaking his head, Thomas stood and began pacing the room. He couldn't do it. No matter how much he wanted to. If he asked her to marry him he would be opening up his heart to her and then…

The idea of losing her was devastating. He *knew* nothing was definite in life, but he couldn't be hurt again if he didn't let himself love.

Even though he knew he couldn't marry her the idea stayed lodged in his mind.

'Enough,' he muttered to himself, striding out of the

room. He would get ready to accompany Henrietta to rescue her painting and put any thought of marriage from his mind.

Dropping her shoulders and straightening her back, Henrietta glanced in the small mirror on the dressing table before she left her room. She had taken meticulous care over her appearance this morning, feeling as though a pristine appearance was a layer of protection, a shield or disguise to cover what she was really feeling.

Underneath the stiffness was heartbreak. There was no other word for it. She might have told herself she wouldn't fall in love with Milton, but she had. Some time in the last week attraction had evolved into love and now it hurt to think they would not be together.

Downstairs Milton was waiting for her. Esther, the lady's maid Caroline had sent up to London with them, had arrived from Heydon's town house and dipped a little curtsy in Henrietta's direction. She was well wrapped up in a thick coat, but still her cheeks were rosy from the cold temperatures outside.

'Are you ready?' Milton was pulling on his gloves in the hall before taking his coat from the butler and slipping into it.

'Yes, but you really don't have to come with me.'

He waved off her protestation with a dismissive hand and offered her his arm. Even though she was wearing gloves she felt a tiny hum of energy pass through her skin as she placed her hand in the crook of his elbow.

'It looks a lovely morning. Shall we walk or would you prefer I try to hail a carriage?'

Henrietta grimaced, remembering the accident from

the night before and the man who had followed them afterwards. She didn't particularly want to be back in a confined carriage, but she felt a little nervous at the prospect of walking about with the footpad still at large. Inadvertently she swayed in a little closer to Milton, glad of his size and the demonstration the night before of his quick reflexes.

'Let's walk. It will only take half an hour. We will need to hail a carriage on the way back anyway—it'll be too far to carry the painting.'

With Esther following a few feet behind they began to walk through the streets. It was relatively early so most of the *ton* would still be at home, but there were plenty of merchants and shopkeepers and servants hurrying about the streets, the cold meaning no one was stopping to talk for very long, all eager to be back by a warm fire.

It was a bright, fresh day, their breaths forming little clouds in front of them and the pavements still a little icy. It didn't look as though the snow that had caused so much disruption in Kent had been anywhere as thick or deep here. There were no residual little mounds piled in corners and even the streets didn't have that muddy, post-snow look.

'Tell me how you came to start painting in a studio,' Milton said after they had been walking for a few minutes. 'You said something about a friend encouraging you?'

'I saw an advertisement for lessons, with an artist who used the studios. His target audience was not someone like me, but I enquired all the same. After a lot of persuasion he agreed to teach me a few things once a week at the studios. He wanted to do it at my house, but I knew my mother would never agree.' It had been the first truly rebellious thing she'd ever done and it had felt wonderful. After, she'd started to enjoy the secrecy, the feeling she got when she sneaked off to indulge in a little painting.

'The artist was…a young man?' She'd never heard jealousy in his voice before, but she wondered if there was just a hint of it now.

'Not particularly. Probably early thirties. It was hard to tell, his lifestyle was what you imagine an artist's to be—he was the perfect stereotype. He drank too much and made love to all his models. It was terribly thrilling for a sheltered debutante like me.'

'Did he…?' Milton coughed and cleared his throat.

'Did he take advantage of me?' She laughed. 'Good Lord, no. He made a few half-hearted attempts to touch me a little inappropriately when I was painting—I think he worried that *that* might be what I was really there for. Once we'd got the issue straightened out he was very gentlemanly towards me.'

'A gentlemanly artist,' Milton mused.

'Are you jealous?'

'Yes.'

She looked at him incredulously and he held his free hand out in a placating gesture.

'I know, I know. I can't help it. I find most of my feelings I don't actually have any control over. I feel jealous of the intimacy you shared with this man, even if it wasn't a physical intimacy.'

She thought back to the hours they had spent together, with the artist leaning over her, directing her brushstrokes with fierce criticism or enthusiastic praise.

'It was intimate,' she mused.

'Stop it, you're doing it on purpose.'

With a quick sideways glance she saw he was only half joking. He was feeling uncomfortable at the idea of her being close to another man. A sudden swell of anger nearly consumed her—if he felt so strongly then surely he shouldn't be putting up all these barriers for them to be happy together.

The rage subsided almost as quickly as it had come and she forced herself to examine the pavement for a couple of seconds before continuing.

'I carried on with my lessons for about six months, but they were expensive and, although Alexander was a good artist, he wasn't the best teacher. For a few weeks I didn't paint, but it was like I had a huge hole in my soul that nothing else could replace.' She remembered the knot in her stomach the first time she had walked up to the little house the old woman hired out rooms in for the artists to use. 'I went back to the little studio and asked the woman who owned the space if I could use it on a weekly basis to come and paint.'

'Did she supply everything?'

Henrietta nodded. 'All the materials, the space. If you wanted, she would even source models for you, but I didn't want to paint staged scenes, I wanted to paint real life.'

'And she stored your paintings when you were finished?'

'Again for a fee, but once I had sold one or two it was easier to pay for things. I was nearly out of all the pin money I'd saved over the years before I sold my first painting.'

'How did you sell it?'

'One of the other artists saw it and he said he thought he knew a man who would like it. He arranged a viewing and the man just assumed it was my friend's painting, not a mere woman's. He paid quite well for it.'

'Does it bother you, not being able to sell them under your own name?'

Henrietta shrugged and then nodded. It did bother her. She would love to be able to stand up and tell the world what she did, to claim her paintings as her own, but if she did she doubted they would sell as well. There was an awful preconception that women couldn't create serious art. They were good for needlework and watercolours, but it was men who painted the masterpieces. It infuriated her.

They were walking familiar streets now, following the route she followed from home to the little house where she painted.

At least the walk had allowed her to clear her head a little. She needed to be strong, to put all thoughts of the previous night from her mind and focus on anything but the man beside her. It would be easier when they got back to Kent with Caroline and little Harry to distract her. And if it wasn't, if she couldn't stand the heaviness in her heart every time she looked at Milton...well, then she would go and stay with some other friends. She had plenty who would be happy to have her for a few weeks, who often extended invitations. Many people were heading out of London soon to return to their estates for the Christmas celebrations. There were easily four friends she could write to and she would be confident they would be eager for her visit.

'You look like you're planning something.'

'Just thinking of where I'll go after staying with Caroline and Heydon for a while.'

'You don't think you'll return home?'

In her mind she had been putting off thinking about the longer term. She didn't want to return home, but as an unmarried woman there weren't that many options open. Often in her imaginings she saw herself in a little cottage in the country, free to paint whatever she wanted whenever she wanted. It was an unlikely outcome, at least while her parents were still alive. As it was she was dependent on them financially, them or Caroline.

'No, not at the moment. Perhaps one day. I have a few friends I could stay with.'

'But you'll stay with Caroline for most of the time.'

She didn't meet his eye. Perhaps when they got back to Kent she would be able to forget everything that had happened, but she doubted it.

They were only a street away from the little studio now and Henrietta was about to pick up her pace when Milton stopped, spinning her round to face him. Behind them Esther nearly barrelled into them at the abrupt halt and Henrietta let out a low cry of surprise.

'You don't have to leave on my account,' he said firmly.

'I'm not.'

'But it is what you're thinking about, going to stay with someone else because I will be at Hailsham Hall.'

She was about to deny it again when she was overcome with a weariness that seeped through her whole body. Raising her chin, she met his eye.

'Yes. I don't think I can go back to pretending there is nothing between us. I don't think I can spend long hours in your company and act like I don't notice every time you move, every time you smile. It will be too difficult. Too painful.'

'I never wanted that, Henrietta.'

'I know. You never wanted any of it. I pushed you last night and I have to deal with the consequences.' She was aware they shouldn't be having this conversation in the middle of the street, but all the pent-up emotion was bubbling up and she didn't feel able to control it.

'I wanted it,' he said, his voice low. 'Never think I didn't want it.'

'But you could control yourself.'

He fell silent at that and she took a deep steadying breath and made to continue onwards. Milton reached out and caught her arm, his fingers sliding down the material of her sleeve until he was holding her hand.

'I...care for you, Henrietta. More than I've cared for anyone in a long time. I've tried not to, but despite that I care all the same.'

Taking a step in closer, she saw the light glinting off the green of his eyes, saw the truth in his words.

'That just makes it even worse,' she whispered. 'I care for you. No...' she paused, shaking her head '... I love you. I love you so much it feels as though there is always a heavy hand around my heart, squeezing it tight. I love you and you care for me, but still you will not even consider us being together.'

'You know why that is, Henrietta.'

'I know. And I'm not trying to force you to do something you don't believe in, something you don't want. But I need to tell you how I feel.'

'I don't know—' He was cut off by a cry from across the street and Henrietta turned sharply to see her mother almost leaping from a carriage before it had rolled to a stop.

'Henrietta Harvey,' she shrilled. 'What on earth are you doing?'

Self-consciously Henrietta took a couple of little steps back so she wasn't standing so close to Milton, although the damage was obviously already done.

'Need I remind you both you are standing in the middle of a public street,' her mother trilled, 'where anyone and everyone can see what you're doing.'

Henrietta looked down to where Milton was still holding her hand and quickly pulled it away.

'Mrs Harvey,' Milton murmured, inclining his head in greeting, although only a fraction.

'What were you thinking? Holding hands. Standing so close together. It's not proper.' She eyed them, her eyes resting on Milton.

Henrietta knew her mother well enough to know exactly what she was thinking. Slowly the cloud lifted from her mother's face as she realised it wasn't quite the disaster she had initially feared. Milton wasn't a scoundrel or wastrel, he was an earl and well known for being an honourable man.

'Don't,' Henrietta groaned as her mother opened her mouth to speak.

'I assume you two are engaged.'

'No,' Henrietta said quickly before Milton could say

anything. The last thing she wanted was a forced engagement, forced by her mother's meddling. 'We are not. And we will not be getting engaged.'

'Don't take that tone with me, young lady. You may well have to. I doubt I'm the only person who has seen you acting so inappropriately.' Mrs Harvey turned to Milton. 'I assume you will do the honourable thing by my daughter.'

'That is between me and her, madam.' Henrietta had never heard him so stiff and formal before, not even in the first few days they'd spent in Kent together.

Mrs Harvey reached out to grab Henrietta by the arm, but she stepped away, moving closer to Milton. His presence was reassuring, not that she thought she needed his protection against her mother.

'What are you doing here, Mother?'

'Exactly what I told you I would do, Henrietta. I'm going to this seedy little studio of yours and I will find any of these paintings you're so fond of.'

'And then what?'

'If you come home, then nothing.'

'You're actually threatening me?'

Henrietta saw the flash of normality in her mother's eyes and then the slightly feverish look returned.

'For your own good, Henrietta. Although if you marry Lord Hauxton I don't suppose anyone will care if you paint or roam the streets of London unchaperoned.'

'No one is getting married.' Henrietta looked between her mother and Milton and made a decision. Mrs Anderson, the woman who owned the house where Henrietta painted and where her painting was being stored now, would have no scruples in handing over the picture to Mrs Harvey, especially if money was offered. The only thing for it was to get there first and use Milton to dazzle Mrs Anderson with his title and air of superiority. Then Henrietta could slip in, claim her painting and take it to safety.

'Let's go,' she murmured to Milton. He seemed to understand what she was suggesting from just those few little words and together they turned and hurried down the street, leaving Henrietta's mother stunned behind them.

Thumping on the door, Henrietta looked nervously behind her. Her mother was just rounding the corner of the street, too dignified to break out into a run and having to settle for a hurried walk instead. It meant they were inside before she reached the front door and Henrietta saw Milton close the door firmly behind them, placing his boot in front of it to stop it from being opened.

'Miss Harvey. What is happening?' Mrs Anderson was a small woman, always dressed in black, in perpetual mourning for a husband she had lost almost half a century ago. She straightened a little as she took in Milton's fine clothes and upright bearing.

'I am Lord Hauxton, it is a pleasure to make your acquaintance.' There was charm in his voice and the hint of a smile on his lips and for the first time in all the years Henrietta had known the older woman she saw her thaw a little. 'We're here to pick up Miss Harvey's painting. The one you've been so kindly storing for her the last few months.'

There was a gentle knock on the door and Henrietta had to hide a disbelieving shake of her head.

'Henrietta darling, let me in,' the faint call came. She

knew her mother wouldn't raise her voice, she wouldn't want to make a scene.

'Who is that?'

'My mother. She gets a little confused. She's fine to wait outside. If we could just have the painting?'

Mrs Anderson looked dubiously at the door and for a long moment Henrietta held her breath, but then the older woman started to move up the stairs, emerging a minute later with the painting in a cheap wooden frame. It was covered with a cloth, but when she handed it over to Henrietta the cloth fell to the side, exposing the painting underneath. Milton inhaled sharply, taking the frame from her and casting his eyes over the picture.

Henrietta found she was holding her breath. His opinion mattered to her and she felt as though she wanted him to approve more than anyone else.

'Henrietta,' he said, drawing out her name, 'This isn't just good. This is incredible.'

It was a picture of a mother and her two young children sitting at an old wooden table. The mother's bowl stood empty, the food given to the children who looked thin and half-starved. There was an expression of love in the mother's eyes, but also a hint of desperation.

'Are they real people?'

She nodded. She'd come across them on the edge of the slums of St Giles. The door to their house had been open and Henrietta had seen the scene inside, the one that she had ended up painting.

'I saw them just like that on a walk about London. I went back many times to see them so I got the details right.' Each time she'd taken food, clothes, anything to help the struggling family. She'd needed to tread care-

fully. The mother had been a proud woman, used to
fending for herself and suspicious of kindness, but over
the months Henrietta had managed to win her trust.
When the painting was finished she had taken them
some money and helped them find nicer rooms in a better area and, probably more importantly, she had helped
the mother find some reliable work. She still dropped
in on them every few weeks, taking a basket of food
and sitting helping to peel potatoes at the old wooden
table from her picture.

'It's haunting.'

'You owe me for storage,' Mrs Anderson said, breaking the moment.

Before Henrietta could protest he whipped out a few
coins and pressed them into the widow's hand. Carefully he adjusted his grip on the painting and then
moved his foot from the door, opening it suddenly and
leading Henrietta outside.

'You have it,' Mrs Harvey said, her face pale.

'Have you seen it, Mrs Harvey?'

Henrietta saw the momentary confusion in her mother's eyes.

'Seen it?'

'Yes. Have you seen it? This painting you so badly
want to destroy.'

He held it up in front of him, forcing Mrs Harvey
to look at it. She took a sharp breath and for an instant
Henrietta thought she was going to turn away, but instead her mother studied the painting as if she were a
celebrated critic.

'True talent is rare, Mrs Harvey, but your daughter

has it. If there was any fairness in the world, this would be hanging in a gallery.'

Henrietta watched as her mother continued to look at the painting. It was as if she were mesmerised by it, unable to tear her eyes away.

'What do you think, Mama?'

She waited, hoping for a kind word, but steeling herself for further criticism.

'It's good,' Mrs Harvey said eventually. 'It's very good.'

'Your daughter wasn't coming here to paint to disobey you, or to risk her reputation. She was coming because she *had* to. With a talent like this, of course she had to.'

'It's true, Mama. I never wanted to be involved in a scandal. I just wanted to paint. It's part of me, a big part of me. When I don't paint it is as if there is a chunk of me missing, as if I'm denying who I really am.'

Still her mother remained silent, although Henrietta thought she saw a slight softening of her expression and maybe even the hint of tears in her eyes.

Then suddenly it was as if the older woman crumpled before her, her shoulders sagging and her head dropping so her chin almost touched her chest.

'Henrietta, I…' Her words trailed off and she looked pleadingly at her daughter. 'How could I have been so stupid?'

Henrietta felt a lump forming in her throat and saw her mother transforming back into the woman she knew and loved. Without hesitating she threw herself into her arms and felt the familiar warmth of her embrace.

'I was just so shocked. I couldn't believe you had been sneaking off all those years and I hadn't noticed.'

'I was very careful, Mama.'

'And coming somewhere like this, unchaperoned. I imagined all sorts could have happened to you.'

'But it didn't. I was very safe, very careful.'

'And your reputation, I got so fixated on your reputation.'

'Well, it is important,' Henrietta conceded.

'It's just not...normal.' Mrs Harvey waved a hand in a conciliatory fashion. 'None of this is normal.'

'It is extraordinary,' Milton murmured. He stood back, quietly letting her and her mother enjoy their reconciliation. She felt another swell of emotion towards him and quickly dampened it down. He hadn't responded with an answering declaration of love when she'd told him she loved him. She needed to stop dreaming, stop hoping for something that wouldn't ever be.

'I knew I'd gone too far. Can you believe I came to Kent meaning to apologise, meaning to ask you to come home, but I spent the whole journey mulling over what could have happened if someone had seen you and it was as though it were someone else in the room with me.'

'I know I've put you in an awkward position by my behaviour,' Henrietta said, allowing her mother to reach out and take her hand, squeezing softly.

'Come home, darling. At least for tonight. Come home and have lunch and let's forget everything that has happened. Can you forgive me, Henrietta? Even after I did that terrible thing to your painting?'

She knew it would take a while to forget how her

mother had reacted, but the apology was a good first step. Perhaps in a few weeks they would be able to work through everything that had been said and Henrietta's deception and find some way back to the easier relationship they'd shared before.

'Of course.'

'Lord Hauxton, I would like to hang my daughter's picture somewhere very visible in our house. Would you mind terribly carrying it to my carriage?'

'Of course.'

'You must come for lunch, too.'

'I wouldn't want to impose on such a tender family reunion.'

'I insist. It would appear you and Henrietta have become…close this past week.'

Milton's face remained expressionless and unreadable.

'Unfortunately I have a prior engagement—another time, perhaps.'

He led the way to the waiting carriage, giving his hand to Mrs Harvey and then passing the painting up to her. Henrietta paused in front of him, wondering if this was going to be it, if this was going to be the last time she saw him for weeks. It felt anticlimactic.

'Perhaps you might join me for a stroll around the park this afternoon?'

Henrietta felt a weight lifting and reminded herself it was only a walk. Probably he wanted the opportunity to make sure she really understood the previous night would never be repeated, and that she understood that, although he might care for her, he didn't return the love she felt for him.

She nodded, not trusting herself to speak.

'I shall call for you around three o'clock.'

'I will be ready.'

The pressure of his hand on hers increased for a second and then was gone so quickly she wasn't sure if she had imagined it.

As the carriage door closed she looked out, but Milton had already turned away and was walking briskly down the street.

## Chapter Twenty

'You're distant, Henrietta darling, what is on your mind?'

Her mother was sitting in her normal spot in the drawing room and Henrietta had just been thinking it was as if she had never been away. Lunch had been just her, her mother and her father, and it felt like a thousand lunches they'd had before. Her father had barely noticed she'd been away and after the meal had retired to his study—he certainly hadn't been aware that her absence had been unplanned. She supposed one day she would have to tell her father about her paintings, but she and her mother agreed that it was best she decided what she wanted from her future first. Her mother had twittered around nervously for a while, but now she seemed happy Henrietta wasn't about to flee again, she had settled.

'Nothing really, Mama.'

'Nonsense. A mother always knows. It's Lord Hauxton, isn't it?'

'Why do you say that?'

'He's a handsome man. And a rich one. Good title, good family...' she paused '...and he has kind eyes.'

'He is kind.'

'You've fallen for him.'

Henrietta began to shake her head, but realised it was futile denying it. Her mother was self-centred and didn't always notice what was going on around her, but she could sometimes be very perceptive when it came to emotions.

'He would be a very good match for you.'

'He's not a match for me.'

'Why ever not? He clearly cares for you. No man traipses round London for a girl he doesn't hold in high regard.'

'He does care for me.'

'Well, then. You just need to drop a few hints, let him know you are interested in marriage and then I don't doubt a proposal will follow.'

'He doesn't want to marry again.'

'Of course he does. Every man wants a wife warming his bed and looking after his home.'

'He doesn't.' Henrietta shook her head. Everything was so definite in her mother's world, she had no time for possibilities and maybes.

'What's wrong with him?'

'Nothing is wrong with him, Mama. He just doesn't want to marry again.'

'His wife died a long time ago. Surely he's not still in mourning for her. There's devotion and then there's obsession.'

Henrietta felt her temper begin to rise as it often did with these sorts of conversations with her mother. She took a couple of deep breaths and picked up the book she had placed down beside her on the dainty wooden table.

'It's not natural, that's all I'm saying.' Mrs Harvey shook her head, but Henrietta knew that wouldn't be the last word on the matter. Suddenly she wished she was back down at Hailsham Hall with Caroline. There she could sit in silence if she so wished and she didn't have to put up with her mother's pestering.

*Uncharitable*, she scolded herself, but she stood all the same, deciding she would leave before she said something she couldn't take back.

'I think I will go and change before Lord Hauxton comes to call.'

'Good idea. Wear the dark pink dress, the one with the lace trim. It brings out your colouring perfectly. And take your cloak with the fur trim rather than that plain coat you insist on wearing.'

Henrietta clenched her teeth, but refrained from answering, instead striding from the room. She would wear something other than the dark pink dress, anything else just to assert her independence even a little, although the cloak with the fur trim was wonderfully warm and comfortable so she might deign to wear that over her plain coat.

It was only half an hour until Milton came to call for her. Half an hour during which she would have to try her very hardest not to go mad with nerves.

She didn't know what to say to him when he did arrive. Before they'd been interrupted she'd just declared her love for him. There wasn't an easy way to pick up that conversation.

She walked through the small hallway, having to skirt around one of their footmen who was busy hanging her picture at the foot of the stairs. Henrietta paused for a moment to look it over, still not quite able to believe it was going to be hanging here at home.

Slowly she got changed, turning this way and that as her maid adjusted the material of the dark blue dress. At five to three she made her way back downstairs, hoping to be ready for Milton when he arrived so she could just slip out without the need for him to have to come in and answer her mother's pointed questions about his intentions and his plans for the future.

Thomas had arrived ten minutes early, but rather than knock on the door and be ushered inside he had decided to do a few laps around the surrounding streets. He had hoped it might clear his head, but instead he'd spent all his time remembering how Henrietta had looked at him when she had told him she loved him.

It was impossible. All these years he'd been looking for someone like Henrietta, someone to share a life with, someone to love.

'It's only you stopping yourself,' he muttered, causing a young man walking in the opposite direction to give him a strange look and pick up his pace.

It was the truth—nothing else was stopping him from sweeping Henrietta up into his arms and declaring his undying love for her. If he asked her to marry him, he knew she would say yes. He knew they would live a happy life together.

It was so tempting. He wanted to be happy, he wanted to feel alive again and that was exactly how Henrietta made him feel.

* * *

At three o'clock exactly he knocked on the door to the Harveys' town house, surprised when Henrietta herself threw open the door and rushed outside, shouting out a farewell to her mother over her shoulder.

'Is everything well?'

Henrietta grimaced. 'I've been back home with her for four hours and already I feel as though I could murder her.' She sighed, seeming to take a moment to compose herself. 'I wanted to escape before she could drag you inside.'

'Thank you.'

'I did it for me as much as you.'

'All the same…' He glanced at her out of the corner of his eye. As she had rushed out of the door she had instinctively taken his arm and now they walked side by side, occasionally brushing up against one another. 'Did you sort everything out between you?'

Henrietta shrugged. 'She apologised, which is quite unusual for my mother. I don't know if I can ever forgive her for shredding my painting, but I can try. I did find myself wishing I was back at Hailsham Hall, though, I find it much more pleasant a place to stay.'

For an instant Thomas had a memory of the first few days they'd spent together at Hailsham Hall, snowed in and bumping into each other at every turn. He would give all the money he owned to go back to that for even just a couple of days.

They walked in silence for a few minutes until they reached the gates of Hyde Park. It was quiet out, the skies still grey and overcast and the air cold. When the wind blew it was biting and dropped the temperatures even further. It meant the park was almost deserted with just a few couples walking arm in arm in the distance.

'We have the whole place to ourselves,' Henrietta said quietly.

Thomas didn't know how to start. He needed to clear the air between them, but to do that he had to know what he wanted. In his heart he wanted Henrietta, he wanted to make her his wife as quickly as possible and spend the rest of his life making her happy. His head still protested, telling him he couldn't guarantee he wouldn't lose her, and if he did it would destroy him.

'Henrietta, we need to talk.'

She turned to him, her eyes wide with just a tiny hint of hope in them. He felt like a cad to even be considering dashing it. Even as he opened his mouth to speak he didn't know what words would come out.

'I love you,' he said, surprising himself with his candour. He'd suspected as much for the last few days, but had been too scared to admit it. There had been that heady feeling whenever Henrietta was close, that sense that he couldn't concentrate on anything but her. When she wasn't there he yearned for her company and when she was he couldn't take his eyes off her.

'You love me?'

'I do.'

'I love you,' she said, her expression completely serious.

'I know.'

'Where do we go from here?'

Thomas closed his eyes for a second, trying to focus his thoughts. As it was there was just a jumble inside his head, worry after worry mixed with hope and love.

Normally he was a decisive man, but he felt at war with himself and unable to make a decision.

They were walking down the main path leading to the Serpentine, a wide and open walkway normally crowded with couples taking the air, but today they were the only ones, probably due to the already darkening skies. Thomas felt the first drop of rain on his face and looked dubiously at the clouds. It hadn't been the best idea to come out for a stroll in this weather, but inside they had to be chaperoned, out here they could talk without anyone overhearing.

'I love you and you love me,' he said slowly, trying to ignore the flare of hope in Henrietta's eyes. He wanted so badly to make her happy, to take her hand and ask her to marry him. Surely if they both wanted it so much it couldn't be wrong.

Henrietta nodded vigorously.

'You can't live your life worrying about something that may never happen,' she said.

'Yet I do.'

They were almost down at the Serpentine now and the rain was getting a little heavier, big fat droplets bouncing off the path.

'We should find somewhere to shelter.'

There weren't any manmade structures nearby as they looked around, but a dense little copse of trees was off the path to their left and would give them some shelter at least. Quickly they picked up their pace as the rain began to fall heavier, the droplets icy as they hit their skin.

Thomas was just about to pull Henrietta off the path when there was a sudden loud thump in front of them, followed by the frightened whinny of a horse. The stampede of hooves came so rapidly that neither he nor Henrietta had time to react. He was standing on Henrietta's left and as such had just stepped off the path, but she was still at the very edge as the horse came charging towards them. It felt as though he were moving through treacle, he couldn't get his limbs to obey fast enough. In his mind he was screaming to pull Henrietta to one side, to get her out of harm's way, but before he could even grasp hold of her the horse was upon them.

Thomas couldn't look away. He was convinced Henrietta was going to be trampled by the riderless horse, but his eyes remained focused on her.

The horse swerved at the last minute, catching her on the shoulder and throwing her backwards into the mud, but somehow she didn't end up underneath its hooves.

'Are you hurt?' a man asked, hurrying up, eyeing the horse that was already thirty feet away.

Henrietta shook her head and the man offered a quick apology and then sprinted off after the errant animal.

Thomas felt his whole body begin to shake as he reached down and helped Henrietta up. She was holding her shoulder and gingerly allowed him to examine it for any damage.

'You'll likely have a nasty bruise,' he proclaimed after satisfying himself she could move it in all directions without any limitations. 'But I don't think you've done any more damage.' His voice sounded thick and foreign to his ears and he felt a swell of nausea deep in his belly.

'What happened?' Henrietta asked, her face pale

with shock, although every second a little more colour was returning to her features.

'Something must have spooked the horse and thrown the rider,' he said as they both looked out into the distance. The man was still running after the animal, which had slowed to a trot now it had distanced itself from whatever had scared it.

The rain was coming down heavily now and Henrietta shivered as he led her under the shelter of the trees. He felt the heaviness in his legs as he walked, as if his whole body was reacting to the decision he had to make. Once he'd told Henrietta he wasn't a superstitious man, but he would be a fool to ignore the signs. Just as he was about to invite Henrietta in to share his life she had almost been trampled by a horse. If that wasn't a sign from up above he didn't know what was.

'Have my coat.' Before she could protest he slipped it off and whipped it round her shoulders. It dwarfed her, but at least it afforded her some extra protection from the rain.

'I'll get it all muddy.' She grimaced as she indicated her lower half that was entirely caked in mud from her fall.

'It doesn't matter.'

He reached out, pulling the coat more firmly around her shoulders, his hand lingering for a minute until her eyes came up to meet his.

'You're going to say we can't be together,' she said so quietly her voice was barely audible over the patter of the rain.

'We can't.'

'Because of that stupid horse?'

'I can't lose you, Henrietta.'

'But you will be losing me if you push me away. We won't ever see each other again, won't ever talk again, won't ever touch again.' She reached out and took his hand, holding it in both of hers.

'I know it will be painful, but better to go our separate ways now, before every aspect of our lives are intertwined. If I lost you, then...'

'You're not going to. I'm young, I'm healthy. I don't plan on doing anything risky.'

'I can't, Henrietta, I just can't.'

He couldn't watch as her face crumpled and the tears began to flow. Slowly she dropped his hand and started to back away and then without another word she turned and fled.

'Henrietta,' he shouted after her.

It felt as though he had been shot through the heart. He couldn't breathe, could hardly stand. He gripped hold of a tree, steadying himself until his vision had cleared a little and his breathing returned to normal.

'What have I done?' he muttered to himself. Still he wasn't sure if he'd made the right decision, but he knew he would have a whole lifetime to regret it.

## Chapter Twenty-One

'Come on, Bertie,' Henrietta said, catching hold of the big dog and expertly fastening his lead to his collar. In the past couple weeks she had spent a lot of time with the dog, using him as an excuse to get out of the house and be alone. She knew she was moping, knew she had smiled only a handful of times since returning to Hailsham Hall, but she couldn't help it, she felt miserable and heartbroken.

After Milton had pushed her away she had run back home and locked herself in her room for two weeks. She knew Milton had tried to call on her—each time she'd sent down the reply that she wasn't up to visitors. After four attempts he'd stayed away and started writing her notes instead.

In her pain she had burned them before reading a single one. She didn't need to hear again how they couldn't be together, how he loved her, but they could never marry. Two weeks she'd lasted in London, barely coming out of her room and just picking at the food her mother had sent up to her.

The idea to come back to Kent had been Caroline's. Her mother must have written, for ten days after she had last seen Milton a letter arrived from her cousin, urging her to come back to the countryside. She talked of long, bracing walks and cosy afternoons by the fire as well as the distraction of Harry. Henrietta had been tempted, but felt paralysed and lethargic, so it had taken a few more days for her to realise she was just wallowing in her misery in London and she must plan her escape to Kent.

'I'll come with you,' Caroline said, hurrying out of the dining room where she had been finishing her breakfast. Yesterday she had told Henrietta that most of her nausea had passed and she was slowly trying to get back into a little bit of a normal routine.

'Caroline, it's freezing—shouldn't you stay in the warm?'

'Hush, stop fussing, you'll start to sound like my husband.'

'It looks as though it may snow again.'

'It's hardly going to settle in the time we're out for a walk.' Caroline grimaced. 'Although I do hope it doesn't snow, otherwise we might be forced to cancel our Christmas Ball.'

Henrietta smiled. For the past few days the preparations for the Christmas Ball had taken over the house. Freshly cut seasonal vegetation was hung in the corners of the ballroom and circled the banisters of the stairs. From the kitchen came a barrage of delicious smells that took Henrietta back to the Christmases of her childhood. The ball was tomorrow night and lots of people would be arriving tomorrow in preparation, with quite a number travelling from London. If it snowed, many of them probably wouldn't even leave the city. The guests travelling more locally from the village and surrounding area had a better chance of making it, but only if there was no heavy snow.

Waiting while a footman fetched Caroline's coat, Bertie was almost pulling her out the door by the time they were ready to leave.

'Slow down.' Henrietta laughed.

'It's good to hear you laugh.'

'Have I really been that miserable?'

'Understandably.'

Henrietta shook her head. 'Not understandably. I was always adamant that I would never let a man control me, that I would always be independent and make my own decisions.'

'You didn't let Milton control you.'

'I let him control my heart.'

Caroline was silent for a moment. It was the silence Henrietta knew well—it meant her cousin was thinking of the right way to phrase something that Henrietta might object to.

'We can't control who we fall in love with, Henrietta. There was *nothing* you could have done differently. If Milton was the man you were destined to love, then there was nothing in the world that could have stopped you from loving him.'

'It's just so unfair. All this time I've pushed gentlemen away, I've fiercely guarded my independence. The one time I've actually wanted something and it couldn't happen.'

'What will you do now?'

Henrietta was distracted for a moment by Bertie's barking and pulling on the lead. He must have caught the scent of something. He was so keen to dash off he almost pulled Henrietta off her feet.

'Let him run,' Caroline said, trying to suppress a laugh. 'If we can't catch him, I'll send James out to hunt him down.'

'If only the country could see their favourite Duke running around after that dog.'

'It's good to stay humble.'

Squeezing her arm, Caroline reminded Henrietta of the question she'd just asked.

'I don't know. I suppose I'll have to go back home at some point.' She bent down and unfastened the lead, letting Bertie dart off after whatever trail he wanted to follow. 'Do you know what I would really like to do?'

'What?'

'Travel. I'd like to pack up my paintbrushes and a few canvases and go off and see the world, stopping wherever took my fancy to indulge in a bit of painting.'

'You may be limited as to where you can go on your own, but that doesn't mean you can't travel a little, Henrietta. You could see a bit of this country, travel to Scotland or Wales even. I'm sure there would be something to catch your interest somewhere on your journey.'

It was a sensible suggestion. A woman on her own just didn't travel to Italy or India. Scotland didn't seem far enough, though, she wanted distance, to run away, to be able to walk down a street and be completely confident she wouldn't bump into anyone she knew.

'You will heal with time,' Caroline said quietly. 'The heart is a wonderful thing.'

'Don't say I'll find someone else. I don't want anyone else.'

She just wanted Milton. Even now it was impossible to stroll through the grounds of Hailsham Hall without the memories of the time they'd spent there together assailing her. The wall by the gates where he'd helped her over on their trip to fetch the doctor, the frozen lake where they'd shared their first kiss, the spot in the garden where Bertie had tangled their legs together and they'd tumbled into an embrace. All the memories were bright and vivid and a little painful, but she didn't want them to fade, they meant too much to her.

'Are you sure he won't change his mind?' In the first few days after she'd returned to Kent Caroline had allowed her to keep her silence, but slowly Henrietta had started opening up about what had happened with Milton. It was impossible to keep something so important from her cousin.

'Quite sure. I told him I loved him, I told him twice.'

'But he said he loved you, too.'

'Yes, but then he said we couldn't be together.'

'Stupid, blind fool,' Caroline burst out in an uncharacteristic fit of anger.

'It's my own fault. He always told me he didn't want to marry again, that he *wouldn't* marry again. I knew his feelings on the matter before we...' She trailed off, desperately trying to find some way to cover her slip. Caroline did not know about the night she'd spent with Milton when they'd returned to London.

'Before you...?'

The blood rushed to her cheeks and she mumbled

something incomprehensible, hoping Caroline would lose interest and move on. She should have known better.

'Before you what, Henrietta Harvey?'

'It doesn't matter.'

'You didn't spend the night with him?'

'It doesn't matter,' she repeated.

'Of course it matters. What if you're with child?'

Henrietta snorted. 'Even I know that's unlikely.'

'Unlikely, but not impossible.'

Caroline paused and Henrietta could feel her cousin's eyes studying her face.

'Do you remember all those years I was in love with James, when he saw me as nothing more than his best friend?'

'How could I forget? What's your point?'

'Things have a funny way of working out in the end.'

Henrietta stayed silent. Her cousin might have got her happy ending, but there were many, many more in this world who did not.

'Let's talk of something else.'

'Very well. What are you painting?'

Three days ago Henrietta had picked up a paintbrush for the first time since her mother had destroyed one of her paintings. She'd been overcome by a sort of fervour, a need to paint that just had to be satisfied. It had been after she'd spent a few hours wandering around the estate with just Bertie for company.

'You know the fields that border your land to the east?'

'The ones with sheep in them?'

'Yes. I was walking up that way with Bertie and I saw the old shepherd tending his flock. He had a boy of no more than four or five with him, learning what to do. They were great-grandfather and great-grandson, at least sixty years between them. It was a stark image, one I wasn't able to get out of my mind.'

'You're painting the shepherd and his great-grandson?'

Henrietta nodded. It was slightly different from what she had chosen to paint in London, but she knew herself well enough now to know that once an image got stuck in her brain the only way to exorcise it was to paint it.

'I asked him if he would mind and he said he'd be pleased to be painted. I'm going to go up there again tomorrow morning to sketch some of the details, some of the little features I can't remember.'

'I'm sure it will be as wonderful as all your others.'

Henrietta shrugged. It was a different setting, different light, but it felt good to be holding a paintbrush again, to start bringing a canvas to life. When she had first picked up a paintbrush again she'd felt a lightness to her as if all her problems were floating away and only she and the canvas in front of her mattered.

'We'd better catch that dog of yours before we all freeze,' Henrietta said as she cast her eyes over the horizon trying to make out the quick movement that signified Bertie's location.

Caroline raised her fingers to her lips and whistled, seemingly enjoying Henrietta's astonished look.

'When did you learn to do that?'

'James has been teaching me. When he does it Bertie comes running.'

'And when you do it?'

'He completely ignores me like he always has. Even

when he only saw James intermittently he always preferred him to me.'

'Bertie,' Henrietta shouted. Still the dog ignored them.

'Let's start walking back. Hopefully when he sees we're returning to the house he'll follow.'

They strolled slowly back, huddled together, but enjoying the crisp air.

'Maybe Milton will come for the ball,' Caroline said as they reached the steps.

Henrietta turned in horror to her cousin. She almost let out a string of curse words, but was saved from the out-of-character outburst by Bertie rushing up past them and barrelling through the door as one of the footmen opened it.

'You don't think he really would.'

'Perhaps not, but would it really be so awful? It would give you chance to see if there was any hope.'

'There is no hope, none whatsoever. I've accepted that, Caroline. I just need to move on now. And seeing Milton isn't going to help that.'

'You may be right,' Caroline said slowly. 'I doubt he'll make the journey anyway.'

Henrietta grimaced. The last thing she needed was Milton turning up and bringing all the heartache to the surface once again.

## Chapter Twenty-Two

Thomas raised his head from his pillow long enough to work out where the loud noise was coming from and then promptly collapsed back down. He'd imbibed far too much alcohol the night before, as he had on the previous three nights, and now he was paying for it. His head was spinning and thumping and his mouth felt dry and as if he'd swallowed a mouthful of sand.

Thankfully one of the servants answered the front door and the knocking ceased. A few minutes of silence followed and Thomas had almost dozed off before the knocking resumed, only this time somehow closer.

'What?' he mumbled, knowing his voice was nowhere near loud enough to reach the door.

Thirty seconds passed and he was hopeful whoever it was had just gone away when the door opened and his butler stepped into the room.

'Excuse the intrusion, my lord, Mr West is downstairs and is rather insistent on seeing you.'

'Mr West?' he mumbled, his mouth feeling so dry his words came out as a throaty croak.

'I believe he is a friend of yours, my lord.' As if he could have forgotten his friend. Thomas couldn't help but smile at his butler's polite tone that vied with the slightly disbelieving look as he took in Thomas's dishevelled form.

'He's downstairs?'

'He came to call yesterday evening, but unfortunately you weren't in.'

For a moment he considered telling Richardson to inform West he was indisposed, unwell, perhaps, but he knew it was futile. West was tenacious when he wanted to be and he would no doubt track Thomas down at some point. He hadn't seen his friend for a few weeks, not since before he'd set off to Kent, before Henrietta had been anything more than…

With a groan he sat up, having to hold on to the edge of the bed to steady himself while it took a moment for the world to catch up with him.

'Inform Mr West I will be a few minutes, then send in Towriss.' Today he would need the help of his valet if he were to face his friend looking at least passably presentable.

Fifteen minutes later he was washed and dressed, but there hadn't been time for a shave so he still felt more unkempt than he would like as he navigated the stairs and made his way to the drawing room. Still his head was thumping and spinning, but the cold water he'd splashed on his face had helped a little. At least now he could walk straight.

'You look like you've spent the night in a ditch,' West said as Thomas entered the room. He was grinning, looking as if he were glad for once he wasn't the one who had overindulged and was now paying the price.

West had initially been Heydon's friend, with both of them being at school at the same time as Thomas's eldest brother William. After the fire, West and Heydon had rallied round, providing practical support for Thomas in his new role as Earl and over the years a mutual respect had blossomed into a friendship.

'Nice to see you, too,' Thomas murmured.

'Heydon sent me,' West said without any preamble. 'I received a letter in which he all but ordered me to come and visit you.' He didn't seem put out by the order and just smiled. 'It looks like I was just in time. You're not enough of a seasoned drinker to keep punishing yourself like this.'

Thomas regarded his friend, wondering how much Heydon had told him in the letter, how much between them they had worked out.

'I understand there is a young woman,' West continued, not minding that Thomas was for the most part keeping silent.

'There was.'

'What happened?' West's voice was quieter now, with a hint of concern.

Thomas sighed, wondering where to start. He didn't want to recount the time he'd spent in Kent, the happiness he'd felt. The way he had started to feel alive again after a long time of nothing but numbness. He'd smiled more in those few days, laughed more in those few days, than he had in the past year.

'Do you know Miss Harvey?'

'Lady Heydon's cousin, of course. Nice girl.'

'She was at Hailsham Hall, we both arrived while Heydon and Caroline were held up by the snow in Hampshire.'

'Ah, illicit love in the countryside.' He sounded flippant, but underneath the light tone Thomas could see the real concern in his expression.

Thomas closed his eyes as he remembered the first night when she'd slipped in to bed beside him and then all the moments that came after.

'I fell for her,' he summed up.

'I don't know her well, but from the little contact I have had she seems a pleasant young woman. Respectable, from a good family, pretty, accomplished. If you've fallen for her, what's the problem? It's not like she's some farm labourer's daughter.'

'I can't marry again.'

West regarded him for a long moment as if trying to decide what to say next. 'If ever a man were meant to be a husband, Milton, it is you. Me, I struggle with marriage, struggle with the idea of being with just one woman for the rest of my life, struggle with how to navigate a relationship that is meant to span forty years…' he shook his head '…but you, you thrived in your marriage to Emily. Why on earth would you think you can't marry again? Are you still mourning her?'

'No.' It was the truth. A part of his heart would always belong to his first wife, but he didn't still mourn her.

'What, then?'

Thomas closed his eyes and gripped the arm of the chair he was sitting in. 'I've lost a lot of people in my life. My parents, my brothers, all my comrades during the war. Then Emily and our child, and more recently Jemima. Each loss has ripped a hole in my heart and I don't think I can stand to lose anyone else.'

There was a long moment of silence and when he looked up West was shaking his head.

'Never think I don't appreciate your loss, Milton. You've lost more than most people do in a lifetime and I can't pretend to know how that must feel...' He paused before continuing, 'But I think you're wrong. What are you planning to do for the next forty years? Shut yourself off from the rest of the world, go through life not caring about anyone else? You will love people and you will likely lose some of them.'

'You don't understand...'

'No, I don't. I don't think I can.'

Thomas closed his eyes. He wanted to be with Henrietta so much, wanted to take her in his arms and never let go. When he closed his eyes he always saw her, images of her as his wife, surrounded by their beautiful children. Painful images, images he wanted so much to be true. Thinking of her moving on with her life, doing things without him, made him want to shout out in frustration, to run to her and beg her to include him.

'Are you happy?'

'No.'

'Would Miss Harvey make you happy?'

'Yes, but...' He trailed off. He was miserable. Ever since they'd parted ways in Hyde Park he'd been miserable. Each day had been a drag, he'd found it hard to summon up the energy to get out of bed and start his day, something that he hadn't ever encountered in himself before. He'd made the decision to not be with Henrietta to protect himself from heartbreak, but here he was sitting alone with a broken heart anyway.

Closing his eyes, he saw again the expression on Henrietta's face when she'd realised he wasn't going to give her the happy ending she had hoped for. It had been an awful moment, as painful as some of the other awful things that had happened in his life. And this one had been all his doing.

'What if I lose her?' he murmured. 'What if I marry her and then I lose her?'

West stood and clapped him on the shoulder. 'You're a strong man, Milton, stronger than anyone else I know. You would get through it just like you have everything else life has thrown at you, but you're thinking about this all wrong.' He started to move towards the door, seeming to sense his friend needed some time alone to think. 'Perhaps you'll have five years together or perhaps fifty. Who can know? But wouldn't you rather five years of happiness to fifty of misery?'

Thomas barely heard West leave, his mind was too preoccupied with thoughts of Henrietta. Five years of happiness, that sounded wonderful. And what if it was actually fifty? Standing up suddenly, he started pacing the room. He'd just made the worst mistake of his life. He'd pushed Henrietta away, the woman he could have been happy with, and all because he was too afraid he might love her and lose her.

'You already love her,' he said to himself. 'And you've just lost her.'

Thomas couldn't believe how obtuse he'd been, pushing her away to try to protect himself when he was already head over heels in love with her.

'You're a fool, a blind fool.'

He needed to get her back, needed to do everything to try to make this right. She might not have him, it would be a miracle if she would after everything he'd put her through, but he had to try.

She was back down in Kent, that much he knew. After he had written to tell Heydon and Caroline he would be staying in London rather than returning to Kent as was the plan, Caroline had written him a mildly worded reply that had hinted at so much more, telling him Henrietta was there and that she expected he would want to make whatever foolish thing he'd done to upset her right. Thomas gave a grim smile. He would do anything he could to make it up to Henrietta, he just hoped she would find it in herself to forgive him.

## Chapter Twenty-Three

Twisting to check her back in the mirror, Henrietta gave a nod of satisfaction to Esther, the young maid who had helped her get ready. At least she looked festive, with a beautiful maroon dress with golden flowers embroidered up one side, silky and luxurious, the swathes of material cascading over her body. Her hair was pinned up with tiny pearl pins added to the back. Her cheeks were rosy from the warmth and the wine she'd had with dinner and her skin was clear and fresh from all the time she'd been spending outside recently.

On the outside she looked ready for the ball, but on the inside she was crying. Henrietta knew she had to make the effort for Caroline. So much work and planning went into the annual Christmas ball she couldn't ruin even a tiny portion of it by crying off and hiding in her room. No matter how much she wanted to.

'Henrietta darling,' Caroline said as she knocked on the door, not waiting for a reply before she entered. Caroline was radiant, her blonde hair perfectly complemented by the midnight-blue gown she was wearing, a gown that had been cut to skim over the slowly growing bump and hide it from all but the most observant of people. 'You look beautiful. You'll be the toast of the ball.'

Summoning a smile, she handed Caroline the heart pendant necklace Henrietta had chosen to go with this dress and waited while her cousin fastened it around her neck.

'Perfect. Are you ready? The first guests from the area should be arriving soon, but if you would rather wait to come down until a little later I don't mind.' Some people from London had arrived earlier in the day, the ones who were staying overnight after the ball. They were already congregating in the drawing room and Henrietta could hear the swell of conversation and laughter from downstairs.

It was a tempting offer, but Henrietta forced a smile on to her lips and shook her head. 'I'll come and greet the guests with you.'

'Wonderful, I was hoping you would. I find it so tiring and James can never remember anyone's name.'

Together they walked arm in arm down the stairs, pausing only when Heydon came striding down behind them. He murmured an apology to Henrietta and swept his wife into his arms, kissing her as if he hadn't seen her for a year.

'You look ravishing tonight, Cara,' he said. Henrietta noted how his eyes couldn't stop flickering over his wife's body and the glow of pleasure that came to Caroline's cheeks at his words. They really were the perfect couple, completely in love even a few years after they'd married.

'You look rather handsome, too.'

'Thank you, good to know I can still seduce my wife.'

'James,' Caroline admonished him half-heartedly.

'Sorry, Henrietta.' He didn't sound sorry, but seeing her cousin and Heydon together made her smile the first genuine smile she had all evening.

She waved a hand, rolled her eyes and carried on down the stairs without them. 'Catch me up when you've stopped being so sickeningly in love,' she called over her shoulder.

The house looked beautiful. All along the drive outside the servants had set candles in little jars to light the way. There was already the start of a frost and the candlelight glinted off the silvery grass giving it a magical look. There were more candles on the steps leading up to the front door and inside the hallway. Henrietta had spent the last couple of days directing the household on where to hang the sprigs of holly and mistletoe, tied together with red ribbons and fastened with large bows.

Pausing by the front door, Henrietta took a deep breath to steady herself. Tonight was going to be hard. These past few weeks she had felt despondent and melancholy, preferring her own company to anyone else's. This evening she had made a promise to herself that she would at least appear as if she were enjoying herself, then tomorrow she could go back to eschewing any social events.

'Are we all ready?' Caroline asked as she extracted herself from her husband. 'Could you ask the quartet to start playing? I think I can see a carriage approaching.'

The next hour was a whirlwind of introductions and small talk. Henrietta knew some of the guests, mainly the ones who had ventured from London as well as a couple she remembered from previous balls at Hailsham Hall. Everyone was in good cheer, eager to enjoy the festive season, but also to make a good impression on their hosts. Henrietta sometimes forgot that Heydon was a duke and, as such, one of the most wealthy and influential men in England. To her he was just Caroline's husband, a man she loved dearly for how happy he made Caroline.

'I think that must be most people,' Caroline said during a lull about an hour in. 'Gosh, that's exhausting. I always forget how much work it is to host one of these things.'

'Do you need anything?' Henrietta asked, studying her cousin carefully.

'No, darling, I'm just fine.'

'You look a little pale,' Heydon said, leaning in closer. 'Henrietta, would you mind greeting anyone else who arrives, I'm going to take Cara for a glass of water and a few minutes' rest.'

'Of course.' Henrietta ushered them away, silencing Caroline's protests with a stern look.

Over the next ten minutes a few more people arrived, hurrying in out of the cold into the warmth. Most people had headed through to the ballroom or the drawing room where games of cards were set up, so Henrietta was now alone in the hall, with Perkins, the elderly butler, coming and going as he took coats and organised the servants. She slumped a little, massaging her cheeks which ached from smiling so much. In a minute she would go and join the guests in the ballroom. She would dance and socialise and smile at all the right people, but for a moment she just wanted a minute alone.

'There's another carriage approaching, Miss Harvey,' Perkins said, indicating the dark shape at the end of the drive. She turned back to the door and peered out, stepping forward slightly and catching an icy blast of air.

For some reason she held her breath even before she could see the crest on the side of the carriage or the fine horses pulling it. Even when it was a few hundred feet away and just a moving shape in the darkness somehow she knew. It was him.

'Are you unwell, Miss Harvey?' There was a note of concern in Perkins's voice and she was aware of him stepping closer. Henrietta realised she had slumped against the doorway and quickly straightened herself up.

'Yes, thank you, Perkins, just fatigued for a moment.'

'Did you want me to get you a drink?'

She hesitated. Part of her wanted to run away and not face Milton, but she knew she would have to at some point. Perhaps it would be easier to greet him now and then she could hide for the rest of the evening.

'Yes, please, Perkins. A lemonade would be wonderful and refreshing.'

'Very well, Miss Harvey. I will be just a moment.'

She was left alone, watching the carriage slow and halt outside the front door. It seemed like an eternity before the door of the carriage opened and the figure of a man emerged. Henrietta felt every muscle in her body tense, but still it was not enough to save her knees almost buckling as Milton looked up and their eyes met.

Despite her determination to meet him head-on and get the awkward moment over and done with, she took a step back and then another. She felt the tears spring to her eyes and a lump begin forming in her throat.

'I can't do this,' she whispered, then turned and fled.

As he opened the door of the carriage and stepped out Thomas looked up. He felt time slow for a moment as standing there in the doorway, silhouetted by the light of the house behind her, was Henrietta. She was alone and unmoving, although there was no way she hadn't seen him. Her eyes were fixed on his and even at this distance he could see the glint of the tears.

He paused for only a moment, but it was enough. In that time Henrietta had turned and darted into the house, disappearing down the hallway until he lost sight of her.

'Damn,' he muttered under his breath. Now he would have to search the crowded ball for her and perhaps still not find her. Henrietta was much more familiar with Hailsham Hall than he was, she would know all the best spots to keep hidden.

'Good evening, Lord Hauxton,' Perkins said as he emerged from the door down to the kitchens, holding a glass of lemonade. He looked around in confusion.

'Is that for Miss Harvey?' Thomas asked, shrugging off his coat and handing it to the butler.

'Yes.'

'I'll take it to her.'

With a frown of confusion Perkins handed over the glass of lemonade. Thomas walked towards the music and the hum of voices coming from the ballroom, wondering if Henrietta would choose to hide herself among the crowds or if she would find a quiet part of the house to seek sanctuary in.

'Milton.' It was Caroline's voice, surprised and filled with joy. He spun and saw her on her husband's arm. Heydon embraced him, clapping him on the back, and Caroline kissed him on the cheek. 'I'm so glad you're here,' she said, smiling up at him. 'I assume you realise you've made the worst mistake of your life and you're coming to put it right.'

'Yes.'

'Good. Then I would be happy to help you.'

'Do you think…?' Thomas said and then trailed off. He wasn't sure if he wanted to hear the answer. Caroline knew Henrietta better than anyone else and if she said she didn't think Henrietta would forgive him he wasn't sure he could bear it.

'She loves you,' Caroline said simply. 'I'm hopeful that will be enough.'

Thomas nodded, feeling the tightness in his chest he had experienced the whole journey from London.

'Did you speak to her?'

'No, she saw me get out of my carriage and disappeared inside.'

'We'll check upstairs,' Heydon said, clapping his friend on the back. 'You start in the ballroom. We'll meet you in there if we can't find her and divide up the rest of the house.'

'Thank you.'

He watched as Heydon and Caroline disappeared upstairs, discussing quietly which rooms they would need to check. Taking a deep, steadying breath, Thomas headed for the ballroom, placing the lemonade down on one of the little tables in the hall—it would likely get spilled in the bustle of the ballroom before he could find Henrietta.

There was a crush of people inside, the swell of voices much louder in here than in the hallway. The string quartet were playing a waltz and a dozen couples were on the dance floor, twirling and stepping in time to the music. Thomas edged along the periphery of the ballroom, all the time his eyes flicking over the occupants trying to see if Henrietta was hiding among them.

'Lord Hauxton, it's been such a long time, how lovely to see you again,' a middle-aged woman said, pushing her way through the crowds. 'Have you been introduced to my daughters?'

'Delighted,' he said quickly, bowing over both their hands before stepping back. 'I'm sorry, there's someone I need to see.' He strode away, trying his hardest not to make eye contact with anyone, but still desperately searching for a glimpse of Henrietta. He hadn't even managed to see what colour dress she was wearing where she had been silhouetted in the doorway.

For five minutes he walked through the ballroom, drawing room and morning room, all the places where the guests had congregated, but there was no sign of Henrietta. Reluctantly he headed back to the ballroom, hoping Heydon and Caroline had been luckier with their search upstairs.

'Did you find her?' He'd waited by the door to the ballroom from the hall for Caroline and Heydon, watching hopefully for some sign of Henrietta entering behind them, but he could tell by their faces they had drawn a blank.

'Where else would she go?' Heydon asked, turning to his wife.

Caroline frowned, taking a minute to think. 'Perhaps the library, or, if she really wanted to avoid you, downstairs in the servants' quarters. All the servants adore her and would happily tuck her away somewhere if she asked.'

'Don't worry,' Heydon said, his eyes studying Thomas's face. 'Even if you can't find her while the ball is in progress you'll find her later tonight or at the very latest tomorrow.'

Thomas didn't know how to explain that he felt he couldn't wait for tomorrow. He needed to find her now, to take her in his arms and beg her forgiveness. To tell her he had been a fool, he'd been blind. He needed to know if she could forgive him or if he would be blaming himself for his future unhappiness for years to come.

'I'll try the library.' He summoned a smile for his hosts. 'You get back to your guests. You're right, I'll find her eventually.'

'Good luck,' Heydon said.

'Don't mess this up.' Caroline squeezed his arm.

Quickly, before anyone else could accost him, he headed out of the ballroom and into the darker parts of the house. Heydon and Caroline had clearly marked out where their guests were welcome by lighting the rooms with hundreds of candles, but the private rooms they'd left dark. As he made his way towards the library he found himself relieved to be stepping away from the crowds. It would be easier to talk to Henrietta if they were alone, easier to make her remember how she'd felt about him before he had gone and ruined everything.

Inside the library it was completely dark and as he closed the door behind him the noise from the ballroom quietened. He let his eyes adjust to the darkness for a minute, then looked around the room. For some reason he'd thought this the most likely place Henrietta would head to, she'd always seemed most comfortable in here, but perhaps she knew he would think that.

Just as he was about to leave the library he glimpsed movement on the terrace outside. It was too far from the ballroom to be likely to be any of the guests from there. Watching for a moment, he couldn't see any more, so quietly he walked towards the glass doors that opened out on to the terrace.

She was standing with her back to him, looking out over the gardens. He paused for just a second, then pushed down on the handle and stepped out on to the terrace.

Henrietta spun round and her eyes met his. He saw her take a deep breath in, her hands clutching at the balustrade behind her. She was wearing a deep maroon-coloured dress with gold flowers embroidered down one side. It had a large skirt and low neckline and for an instant all words left him as he marvelled at how beautiful she looked.

'Henrietta,' he said, stepping out.

'Milton.'

He walked over to her, feeling the bite of cold in the air and quickly shrugging off his jacket and holding it out to Henrietta. She hesitated, but she must have been frozen to the bone, for it was only a couple of seconds before she took it from him and laid it across her shoulders.

'What are you doing here?'

'I needed to see you.'

She shook her head. 'I don't think I can do this.'

'Please, Henrietta, I've got something I need to say to you.'

He hated the flat expression on her face, as if he had sucked all the love and warmth from her.

'I don't know what else you can have to say to me, Milton.'

He took a step closer and then another, reaching out for her hand. Her fingers were freezing and he couldn't help but start to massage them between his.

'Come inside, Henrietta, you're freezing.'

She glanced at the door behind him as if deciding whether to be stubborn and remain outside or retreat into the warmth of the library.

'Come on.' He pulled her gently by the hand, back through the door. 'Sit and I'll see if I can get the fire started.'

The logs were already piled in the grate, set ready for the next day. It took a while, but after a few minutes he managed to get a spark from the tinderbox and light a taper and then slowly coax the fire to life. Once he was satisfied it wouldn't die out he stood, then instead of sitting opposite Henrietta he crossed first to the door and turned the lock.

'No one will disturb us now.' Although most guests wouldn't leave the ballroom or the card tables, there was always the chance a couple might slip into a quiet bit of the house for an illicit dalliance. The last thing he wanted was that sort of interruption.

Now he sat opposite her, pulling his armchair close

so their knees were almost touching. He would have preferred to be able to hold her hand, to touch her in some way, but Henrietta had wrapped her arms protectively across her chest and she didn't look as though she would appreciate him trying to coax her to move.

'Why are you here, Milton?'

'Ever since you left London, ever since that moment in Hyde Park, I haven't been able to stop thinking about you. I've been completely and utterly miserable, Henrietta.' He paused, trying to gauge how she was taking his words, but unable to tell as her expression remained stony. 'I love you, I love you so much being apart has been torture.'

'But you said…'

'I was a fool, a complete and utter fool. I pushed you away to protect myself from losing you in the future, but I should have realised that I was just making that a reality now.'

'What made you change your mind?'

'I was in London, completely miserable, and I realised it was all my own doing. You'd offered me your heart, you'd offered me a future of happiness, and I'd pushed you away.' He studied her face, hoping to see some flicker of a smile, some acknowledgement that she still felt the same way about him. 'I'm sorry,' he said quietly. 'I was a stubborn fool. I should have listened to you.'

'You hurt me.'

'I know and I hate myself for it.'

'So now you're saying you do want us to be together. Even if it means you could lose me in the future.'

'Yes. If we get five years together, or even just five

months, that would be better than not being with you at all, Henrietta. I can see that now.'

She looked down for a long moment and when she raised her head again there were tears falling down her cheeks.

'I don't know...'

'Please, Henrietta. A few weeks ago you told me you loved me—is there any of that love left in your heart?'

It felt like an eternity before she spoke, even though it could only have been a few seconds.

'Of course I still love you, but you broke my heart when you pushed me away.'

'Let me spend the rest of our lives making it up to you. I promise I will show you how much I love you each and every day.'

He could see she was softening towards him, see her leaning forward slightly as if her body couldn't help but forgive him, even if her mind was lagging behind.

'Marry me, Henrietta, marry me and with you by my side I will never be so foolish again.' This made her smile as he hoped it would.

'You mean it?'

'Of course I mean it. I want you to be my wife.'

Slowly she nodded and he felt the weight that had been resting on his heart begin to lift. She was going to forgive him and she was going to be his wife.

'I love you, Henrietta,' he said as he looped is arms around her waist and pulled her from the armchair on to his lap. She let out a little squeal of surprise, but when she was settled on top of him she looked up and smiled, resting her head on his shoulder.

'I love you, too,' she whispered.

He kissed her long and hard, his hands running across her body as he reminded himself of her curves and the softness of her skin.

'We should marry in haste,' he murmured as he pulled away to plant a kiss on her neck just below her earlobe.

'Why?'

'Because I don't want to be apart from you again.'

'There will be gossip.'

'I can't seem to make myself care.'

Henrietta looked at him and grinned. 'Me neither.'

He kissed her again, this time not stopping until they were both breathless.

'Two weeks,' he murmured in her ear. 'Two weeks and I promise you'll be my wife.'

'Two weeks?'

'I know the Archbishop of Canterbury very well, he's an old family friend. He'll be happy to grant us a special licence. Then you'll be my wife.'

Wriggling backwards so she could see his face, Henrietta looked at him solemnly for a moment. 'And you're sure this is what you want?'

'Completely sure.'

'Good. Two weeks it is.'

# *Epilogue*

'**A**re you nervous?'

Thomas's voice made her jump as she was jolted from her thoughts.

'Exceedingly.'

'You've nothing to be nervous about. It's perfect.'

Henrietta looked around the room critically. On the wall hung twelve paintings, all individual, but linked by their theme and style. They were the pictures she had painted on their extended honeymoon, each depicting a scene from the countries they'd travelled through. There was the beggar in the streets of Paris, the children playing in the ruins of the Colosseum in Rome, the men haggling over spices in a market in Egypt.

'What if no one shows?' She bit her lip. 'What if everyone comes and they all hate my paintings?'

'Not possible, my love. They may not be to everyone's taste, some people have no appreciation of a masterpiece, but no one can deny your talent.' He looped an arm around her waist and pulled her in closer to him. 'You're good—no, more than that, you're brilliant and this exhibition will show that to the world.'

Henrietta nodded, her eyes flitting from one painting to the next. Thomas had been the one to encourage her to find a gallery to exhibit her paintings. He'd written letters and organised a space and spread the word, allowing Henrietta to put the finishing touches to her pictures and organise the little details like selecting the right frames to properly showcase them.

'Thank you,' she murmured, raising up on her tiptoes to kiss him on the cheek.

'It truly is my pleasure.' Thomas kissed her and, even though they'd been married two years, it still felt like it did when they had first met. She still got butterflies in her stomach when he entered the room and felt every rational thought fly from her head when he touched her.

'Henrietta darling, it looks amazing.' Caroline hurried through the door with Heydon a step or two behind her. 'You're so clever.'

'Do you like it?'

'Of course, it's perfect.' Caroline kissed her on the cheek and Heydon followed suit before they both greeted Thomas warmly. 'Take me for a walk around the room and tell me about them, pretend I'm one of the guests wanting to know all about your inspiration.'

Henrietta linked her arm through Caroline's and they began a slow stroll around the room.

'Have you told him yet?' Caroline asked as soon as they were out of earshot of the men.

Henrietta shook her head.

'You'll have to soon, you'll start showing in a few weeks.'

'I know. I just don't want him to worry too much about me.'

'It's only natural.'

'I know.'

Henrietta fell quiet, resting her hand on her lower abdomen. She had suspected she was pregnant for a few months now and had visited a doctor last week who'd confirmed she was almost four months along.

'You two look as though you're up to mischief,' Thomas said as he came over.

Caroline nudged her in the ribs. 'Now is as good a time as any.' Quietly her cousin slipped away, going to look at the paintings on the other side of the room.

Over the past two years Thomas had slowly let go of some of his concerns about losing Henrietta. She was young and healthy and made sure she didn't do anything too risky and as such Thomas's worry over losing her had lessened. However, she knew once she told him she was pregnant it would bring back all the memories of how he had lost his first wife. They both desperately wanted children, but for him it was hard to decide if that desire was worth the risk of Henrietta having to go through childbirth.

'I have something to tell you.'

He turned curious eyes towards her.

She took a deep breath and then blurted it out. 'I'm pregnant.' Warily she watched his expression, but there was no hesitation to the joy that blossomed across his face. He picked her up and spun her round and then they came together, his lips finding hers.

'You're happy?' Henrietta asked as they broke apart.

'Of course I'm happy.'

'I was concerned you might be overly worried.'

'Not overly worried,' he said, kissing her lightly

again, 'but a little, of course.' He smiled at her. 'I'm sure you'll sail through this like you have everything else. You're my warrior, my strength.'

Henrietta felt the relief seeping through her body. Now they would be able to plan and prepare and get excited together.

'Now, one minute and those doors will open and your adoring public will enter. Are you ready?'

'No.'

He kissed her one final time, then led her over to the doors, standing a little to one side so she could be the centre of attention. Henrietta gripped hold of his hand and pulled him to stand directly beside her.

'Together,' she whispered as the doors began to swing open.

'For ever, my darling.'

\* \* \* \* \*